The Case of the
Imaginary Detective

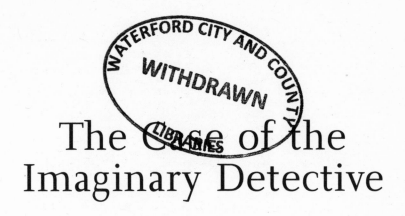

The Case of the Imaginary Detective

Karen Joy Fowler

VIKING
an imprint of
PENGUIN BOOKS

VIKING

Published by the Penguin Group
Penguin Books Ltd, 80 Strand, London WC2R ORL, England
Penguin Group (USA) Inc., 375 Hudson Street, New York, New York 10014, USA
Penguin Group (Canada), 90 Eglinton Avenue East, Suite 700, Toronto, Ontario, Canada M4P 2Y3
(a division of Pearson Penguin Canada Inc.)
Penguin Ireland, 25 St Stephen's Green, Dublin 2, Ireland (a division of Penguin Books Ltd)
Penguin Group (Australia), 250 Camberwell Road,
Camberwell, Victoria 3124, Australia (a division of Pearson Australia Group Pty Ltd)
Penguin Books India Pvt Ltd, 11 Community Centre,
Panchsheel Park, New Delhi – 110 017, India
Penguin Group (NZ), 67 Apollo Drive, Rosedale, North Shore 0632, New Zealand
(a division of Pearson New Zealand Ltd)
Penguin Books (South Africa) (Pty) Ltd, 24 Sturdee Avenue, Rosebank, Johannesburg 2196, South Africa

Penguin Books Ltd, Registered Offices: 80 Strand, London WC2R ORL, England

www.penguin.com

First published in the United States of America as *Wit's End* by G. P. Putnam's Sons,
a member of Penguin Group (USA) 2008
First published in Great Britain by Viking 2008
1

Copyright © Karen Joy Fowler, 2008

The moral right of the author has been asserted

Printed in Great Britain by Clays Ltd, St Ives plc

A CIP catalogue record for this book is available from the British Library

ISBN 978-0-670-91775-4

www.greenpenguin.co.uk

Mixed Sources
Product group from well-managed
forests and other controlled sources
www.fsc.org Cert no. SA-COC-1592
© 1996 Forest Stewardship Council

Penguin Books is committed to a sustainable future
for our business, our readers and our planet.
The book in your hands is made from paper
certified by the Forest Stewardship Council.

To Mike Burke:

mathematician, cook, teacher, backpacker, brother

It seems only fair that I live with the people I've killed.

—*A. B. Early, interview with* Ms. Magazine, *June 1983*

The Case of the
Imaginary Detective

Part One

Chapter One

(1)

Miss Time was seated with her feet on the floor and her head on the table. Her neck and back were stiff, but stiffness was her natural condition; perhaps nothing should be made of this. The kitchen curtains were pulled. There were two glasses on the counter. One was empty, the other half so. A wine bottle (red) was beside the glasses; the cork was in the sink.

A tiny clutch purse had fallen to the floor beside Miss Time's leg. Among the contents spilling out were a lipstick, keys, and a pair of reading glasses. Someone had written something on the tablecloth, using a faint red ink, or maybe the wine. It might have been a phone number back from the days when phone numbers began with an exchange. A D and an A were clearly legible.

Davenport 7, 3, and then maybe a 5 or maybe a 2. Those numbers had spread and the rest were fat and indistinct.

The purse was the size of an aspirin, the lipstick slightly larger than a grain of rice, the kitchen floor about as big as a sheet of typing paper. Poor murdered Miss Time was only three inches tall. And the whole tableau was on the bedside table under the reading light, where Rima would see it first thing every morning and last thing every night.

"I'll have Tilda move that tomorrow," Addison told her. "I guess you don't need it in your bedroom. I'm so used to it I don't even stop and think anymore how it looks to someone else."

Rima already knew about the dollhouses. Of course she did; they were as famous as Addison was. This was the way Addison outlined her mysteries, spending the first few months of each book making a meticulous replica of the murder scene, right down to its tiny clues and tiny gore. "If I can just get the murder scene right," she told *Ms. Magazine* ("A. B. Early Thinks Small," an interview Rima kept for many years in her sock drawer and reread often), "well, then the book practically writes itself."

The interview was accompanied by a picture of Addison making minute adjustments to a pin-size bread knife. She'd aged since then, though not much. In her middle sixties now, she was too thin, but she'd always been too thin, all bone and sharp angles, as if she'd been made from coat hangers. Deep-set eyes and Eleanor Roosevelt's teeth.

"I got my first dollhouse when I was four," she'd said, first in an interview with *Ellery Queen,* October 1985, and then in many interviews after. "And a few years later a little man and woman to live in it. Mr. and Mrs. Brown.

"I hated the Browns the second I laid eyes on them. I loved the little furniture. The little people made my skin crawl.

"I didn't want *anyone* to live in it. I wanted it to be *my* house. Or maybe fairies, you know, that you wouldn't ever see, but you'd pour milk into the thimble-teacups and when you came back later the milk would be gone.

"So I rigged a noose from a rubber band and hanged Mr. Brown from the banister. Mother always said that was her first clue about me. He had a name, she always said, as if it wouldn't have been shocking at all if only I hadn't known his name.

"But there was something so creepy about little Mr. Brown. He wore a hat you couldn't take off."

All A. B. Early's books begin with a death. This one starts here, with Miss Time's plastic head on the table in the kitchen on the nightstand in the guest room of the old Victorian house on the cliff over Twin Lakes State Beach in Santa Cruz, California.

The house was called Wit's End. It was a bed-and-breakfast (though with a different name) when Addison bought it, and before that it had been the final home of some woman who'd survived the Donner Party. Rima heard her father say that once to her mother, she was five at the time, and for months she'd anguished over this deadly party the Donners had given. Was it the punch? She became frightened of birthdays, a fear that had never completely gone away.

Rima slept at Wit's End before she saw it. She'd arrived late, even later if you were on Ohio time, and Addison had taken one look and brought her straight up to the guest room—her room now, Addison said, for as long as she liked, Rima was her god-daughter, after all. Which was kind of Addison, because even though Rima was her goddaughter, they didn't know each other well and might not like each other. Rima would have said the odds of that were high. She felt that Addison was trying to make her welcome, and that the operative word there was "trying."

The guest room was on the third floor. It was a beautiful room with ivory walls, dove-colored wainscoting, dark sloping ceilings, a fireplace, a private bath, quilts that smelled like cedar, and candles that smelled like apples. In the bed-and-breakfast days, people paid two hundred fifty dollars a night to sleep in this room. There was no corpse on the nightstand then.

Rima had only two suitcases to unpack, but she was tired enough to leave them till morning. Even so, it took her a long time to fall asleep, and maybe this was because of Miss Time.

But maybe it was Berkeley and Stanford, Addison's matched set of long-haired miniature dachshunds. "They don't know you yet," Addison said. "You should probably hook the door." So the dogs spent the night in the hallway, egging each other on, clicking back and forth on the wood with their claws, and occasionally hurling their little bodies against the guest-room door to see if the hook still held.

Or maybe it was the invocation of Rima's father. "You know I was very fond of your father," Addison had said, which Rima did know, because her father had always said so, though her mother used to say that Addison had a mighty funny way of showing it.

Rima had heard once, or maybe read, that when someone important to you dies, they come back in a dream to say good-bye. She was still waiting for the dream about her mother, and her mother had been dead almost fifteen years. (Aneurysm.) Her little brother, Oliver, had died four years ago. (Car crash.) Probably her father (leukemia) was caught in the queue.

The stairs creaked. The window blinds rattled whenever the heat came on. Rima could hear the clock on the landing at the hour and the half-hour, and the tick, tick, tick of the dogs' nails. The pillow was too fat unless she slept on her side, and she had a pinch in her neck from the ghastly plane seat, a clamp in her chest from everything else. There was another incessant sound, a sort of sobbing heartbeat.

After several hours of not sleeping she got up, went to the window, and opened the blinds. As soon as she saw the ocean, she realized it was the ocean she'd been hearing. It was a cloudless, moon-soaked night. There were lights in the distance—a single green one on the top of a very small lighthouse, a white cluster at the yacht harbor, and farther off, a line of lights where the wharf was. To the right of the wharf, less lit, more ghostly, she could just make out the high curves of a roller coaster, a second roller coaster, a Ferris wheel, brightly colored, but all distant and small, like something for Miss Time.

Rima recognized these things though she'd never seen them before; she had stepped into one of Addison's books. And even as she looked right at them—the yachts, the wharf, the boardwalk— they remained make-believe, the night too bright, the ocean too black, the lighthouse too small.

In fact, wasn't *everything* too small? A mocked-up, scaled-down representation of the real thing? Rima made a little mental list:

the tiny lighthouse

the tiny boardwalk, no bigger than the pane of glass in the window

Addison's tiny dogs and their tiny teeth

Addison's tiny dollhouses and their tiny deaths

And Rima was fine with that, relieved—in fact, eager to be little herself, to do and have and feel little things. A little room of her own. A little job for Addison. Someone else's little life that she could just slide inside until all her emotions had shrunk enough to be manageable.

The night Rima arrived at Wit's End she was twenty-nine years old. The list of things she'd lost over those years was long and deep. Her father used to say that when they decided to get rid of Jimmy Hoffa they should just have handed him to her. Among the missing: countless watches, rings, sunglasses, socks, and pens. The keys to the house, the post office box, the car. The car. A book report on Wilkie Collins's *The Moonstone* plus the library's copy of the book plus her library card. Her mother's dangly turquoise earrings, the phone number of a guy she met playing pool and really, really did want to see again. One passport, one winter coat, four cell phones. One long-term boyfriend. One basically functional family.

The boyfriend left when a lump in Rima's breast turned out to be benign. "I just can't go through this," he said, and when she repeated that there was nothing to go through, that she didn't have cancer or anything else, he said, "But when I thought you might, I saw that I just couldn't go through it."

"You'll always have me," Oliver used to say whenever a boyfriend went missing, but this time he wasn't there to say it. Rima still had her father then, but they both knew about the leukemia and no one was making any promises no one would have believed even if they had.

Rima pulled the quilt from the bed, wrapped herself in it, and sat in a chair at the window. A bright road of moonlight lay on the water. She imagined herself walking it, the warp and dazzle beneath her shoes. She began to dream. It wasn't a big dream, not like her father's last good-bye, but Maxwell Lane was in it and she'd never dreamt of him before. She supposed it made sense that he'd show up here; she supposed, in fact, it's just what you'd expect. Rima remembered that Addison had once called this The House That Maxwell Bought, before she learned that the original name, the name the Donner Party survivor had used, was Wit's End.

In Rima's dream, Maxwell Lane was walking beside her into Ice City. He put his arm around her shoulder. "Don't be so hard on yourself," he said. "Everyone misplaces stuff," which, of all the things someone could say to you, in or out of a dream, has got to be one of the nicest.

In Ice City, Maxwell Lane is Rima's father's archnemesis.

(2)

There is no Ice City. There is no Maxwell Lane. It was one of the peculiarities of Addison's profession that she, though quite famous in her own right, was considerably less famous than the detective she'd made up. She'd never been in a movie, for one thing, and he'd been in eight, plus three television series, none of which lasted more than a season, but still, there'd been three of them. And a television season was a lot longer back in those days; it lasted most of the year.

Rima had her own colorful history with fictional characters. Her father had been more fictional than you might guess. A character in Addison's seventh book was named after him—Edward Charles Wilson Lanisell—though the name he went by was Bim; even on Rima's birth certificate he was listed as Bim Lanisell. Addison had used every one of these names, and one of her father's verbal tics as well—a habit he had of starting a conversation with "Okay, then." There could be no mistake about Addison's intentions.

Addison and Rima's father were old pals, unless they were something more. Rima's father was a writer too; for many years, he wrote a newspaper column that appeared in the Cleveland *Plain Dealer.* Once, when their finances had taken a tumble, he went on local TV, shilling for a tire company in a silly voice and a silly tie. He was famous enough. But nowhere near as famous as the made-up man of the same name who killed his wife with her own cat and almost got away with it.

In Rima's case, the character came first and she later. Rima was named after the heroine of *Green Mansions,* and she'd liked her name until some kids at school figured out that you could do dirty things with it if you worked phonetically. Her brother Oliver, who heard some of them, said she should have a name all of her own anyway, and offered her four choices he'd made simply by rearranging the letters she already had. She could be Irma, he said, or Mari or Mira or Rami, and he took it in turns to call her all four, each for a week, so she could test them out. Rima liked Rami best, but she couldn't get people to switch over. Oliver liked Irma—the Irm part made him laugh—and he called her Irma until the day he died, though no one else did, which was so Oliver, that intimacy of a private name. Of all the people who'd died, Oliver was the one she missed the most.

The *Green Mansions* Rima was the last survivor of a doomed people, a fact that, in retrospect, her parents might have paid more attention to.

Even Oliver was an orphan's name.

(3)

But the names were only the beginning, and arguably the least of it. Sometime when Rima wasn't watching, sometime after her mother died and she was kept busy being both motherless and adolescent, Rima's father's writing changed. Bim Lanisell had been a political journalist. When he became a columnist, his work turned personal. He was struggling to learn how to be a father and a mother both, he wrote, and he was sharing his struggle with the entire population of Cleveland, Ohio. And its environs. A few international subscribers.

Rima found this out one day after he'd been actively soliciting confidences. She remembered it later with outrage, how she'd offered up her biggest secret so that he could feel like a good parent. She'd told him about a boy she liked in her world history class; she told him that this boy didn't know she was alive. She asked her father how to get a boy to notice her, even though she knew this wasn't a problem he could help with. It was all about him, this generous pretending that it was all about her.

The whole conversation was the topic of his next column, a musing on how you didn't really grow up until you watched your children grow up. He stopped short of discussing the boy, but not his daughter's—he actually used these words—budding sexuality. The next day when Rima went to school, there was no one there who didn't know she was alive.

Rima was particularly incensed at how well her father had come off in his own column. Not stammering and useless, the way he had actually been, but awash in midwestern profundities. Every woman in Cleveland was in love with him—the number of women who wished to date him was directly inverse to the number of boys who wished to date Rima, if negative numbers could be applied, and Rima felt they could. And he wasn't even completely real. (But when has that ever stopped a woman in love?)

Rima herself loved the useless, real father so much more than the wise, revised one. "I was very fond of your father," Addison said when she called to insist that Rima come stay with her, and of course it was Addison who'd added the third Bim Lanisell, the entirely fictional one.

And why, Rima's mother had asked Rima's father from time to time, make you a wife-killer? And, once or twice, why the sort of wife who would be (though wasn't) played by Kathy Bates in the movie version?

The entirely fictional Bim had actually killed three people, but the wife was the only one Rima's mother ever seemed to talk about. Granted it was the murder with the most panache, the murder Addison had clearly put her heart into. Surely this was the murder in the original dollhouse.

Rima had her own questions for Addison. If Addison thought it was fun going through the Shaker Heights public schools with a famous murderer for a father, she could think again. Addison might technically be Rima's godmother, but it was a decision long regretted, at least by the women in the family. Addison had never really risen to the role anyway.

None of Rima's friends had thought that going to Santa Cruz was a good idea. It seemed like a dangerous place, they'd told Rima, and they didn't know the half of it. They didn't know about sharks, or the undertow. They didn't know that at the same time the sea cliffs were eroding, the ocean was rising—at least two millimeters, maybe more, every year. They didn't know there was a disease you could catch from sea-lion urine that no doctor knew anything about, and if you were infected, you'd be sent to a veterinarian, who wouldn't know much about it either. They didn't know that the mountains were dotted with meth labs or that Highway 17, the route in from San Jose, was one of the deadliest stretches of road in the whole gigantic state, and was commonly referred to as Blood Alley, at least until the highway dividers went in. They didn't know that a clown stalked the downtown like something from a Fellini film.

What they knew was earthquakes and vampires. Some of them had been watching the World Series with their families all those years before, when the Loma Prieta quake hit. They remembered how the television went black, and then came on again briefly to show the stadium rocking, and then went black for good. They remembered that Santa Cruz had been near the epicenter, though what they really remembered was the collapsed freeway in Oakland and the car that went off the Bay Bridge. Anyway, it was all California, wasn't it? California had earthquakes.

All of them had seen the movie *The Lost Boys*. When they pictured the boardwalk, they pictured it infested with vampires. Of course, they didn't suppose it was really infested with vampires; they thought that "Murder Capital of the World" stuff was just made up for the movie, not based on an actual, dreadful period in the seventies when Santa Cruz had been home to two serial killers and one mass murderer. They didn't know how hard (and unsuccessfully) the city had tried to be known as Surf City instead.

They just said that Santa Cruz seemed to have a sort of dark energy. And then they dropped the subject, having cleared their consciences by speaking up. Honestly, they were relieved to have Rima going. They loved her, and they hoped she'd come back, and it wasn't her fault that she was in a dark space, but she was kind of bringing everyone down.

So when I tell you that she woke up on that first morning at Wit's End with the sun floating over the house like a big, bright pie and a sense of peace in her heart just because of what Maxwell Lane had said in her dream, you will understand how unexpected, inappropriate, and downright miraculous that feeling was.

Chapter Two

(1)

That first morning Rima was slow to get up. Getting up would mean getting started, as company or hired help or goddaughter or whatever it was she was going to be here. Getting up would very likely involve chatting; her good mood was too baseless to survive a chat. Better to stay in bed, watch an odd medallion of light slide slowly down the wall, smell the cedar on the quilt, listen to the sound the ocean made, like a distant washing machine. Better to note, as if from that same distant place, that she had taken comfort from her father's archnemesis and shelter from her mother's. If her parents found that objectionable, then they should have stuck around to prevent it.

In fact Wit's End was empty, as Rima would have known if she'd gone down to the kitchen, read the note Addison had left on the counter for her.

It was an opportunity lost. Rima would have liked having the whole house to herself, would have explored a bit, maybe seen if she could find the dollhouse for *Ice City,* the book in which her murderous cat-wielding father starred. Sometime last night she'd wondered whether Addison would mind if she moved that one into her bedroom in place of *The Murder of Miss Time,* and then she'd wondered what was wrong with her that she would even think such a thing.

Rima," the unread note said. "The dogs are being walked, I'm working in the studio, and Tilda has gone out. Help yourself to breakfast. Eggs and tomatoes in the fridge. Bread in the breadbox. See you at lunch. A"

Here is the long version:

1. Berkeley and Stanford were down on the beach, ecstatic and leashless, chasing gulls the size of beach balls and getting sand on their bellies, between their toes, inside their ears. They would quarrel over a dead fish, have to be forcibly separated, and come home in disgrace. Addison referred to each and all of their frequent fights as The Big Game.

2. Addison was out in her studio, and no one knew what she was doing anymore. She hadn't finished a book in three years, and two had passed since anyone who knew her well had asked how the new one was coming.

The studio had been added after Addison bought the house. She called it her outback, though it was really to the side of the main building. You walked on a paved pathway to get there, through a Spanish courtyard, past a trellis of roses, a clay birdbath, and a sticky, sweet-smelling fig tree.

The studio was a modern room with wireless broadband. Addison had a Norwegian recliner for napping, a desk, and a craft table. The ocean-side wall was made of five glass doors, each of which slid inside the next like a telescope, so that in good weather the room could be opened to the sea. A mobile of murder weapons, made by a reader in New Hampshire, hung from the ceiling, and when the breeze came off the ocean, the dangling knives and blunt objects struck against one another with a soft sound like wind chimes.

And who knew what else? No one was allowed in during the dollhouse phase of a book, which meant that no one but Addison had been inside the studio for three years now, with the exception of one much-loved computer technician, Ved Yamagata, who also worked for the university. Ved kept Addison's gear upgraded, and his silence apparently could and had been bought, though on the subject of Japanese *manga* he was chatty enough.

You would have had to scramble up the rocks at the cliff base and then scale the face just to look inside, which you could hardly then claim to have done by accident. Even so, Addison closed the shutters whenever she left.

For some writers three years isn't a long time to work on a book. For Addison it was unprecedented. Perhaps there was no new one, her friends said to one another, but only when she wasn't around. Why should there be? How many books could one woman write?

Addison was a national treasure. She didn't have to write

another word to collect lifetime achievement awards for the rest of her life. The reviews of her last two books had been chilly. They mentioned the earlier work with the sort of conventional courtesies people adopted when speaking of the dead; no one wanted to be in the room with Addison when she read them. There was no shame in knowing when to quit.

Still, Addison went to her studio, without fail or interruption, from eight every morning until lunchtime, so usually this was when Tilda vacuumed up the sand and dog hair, but today

3. Tilda was over in Soquel attending her twelve-step meeting at the Land of Medicine Buddha. Since the weather was so good— no season warmer and sunnier in Santa Cruz than the glorious fall—she would stay after and do the forty-minute hike through the sequoias up to the red-gold temple. Two acolytes worked full-time painting the temple. Like housekeeping, this was a job acknowledged to be endless, red and gold paint until the heat death of the universe. Tilda might or might not be home for lunch, depending on what they were serving at the Land of Medicine Buddha.

Tilda was a tall, athletic woman in her mid-forties. Her hair was shiny, dark, and short; there was a tattoo of a snake, coiled, head down, around her left biceps. She took yoga at the Santa Cruz veterans center, where her headstand was rock steady. She was Addison's housekeeper unless she was something more, had lived with Addison for nearly three years. Sometime before that she'd been homeless, and while she was fond of Addison, her real love was Wit's End. She loved the house the way a captain loves a ship. She listened for plumbing problems, sniffed for bad wiring, kept the wood oiled, the glass polished.

Her affection did not extend to the dollhouses. They were nests of constant dust, requiring constant dusting. Before the earthquake, Addison had told her, there'd been four more, but they'd been crushed when some bookcases fell. Tilda tried to remember this whenever she was thinking that there were way too many. Not only did they all have to be dusted, but they all had to be dusted so as not to disturb the crime scene. She had to use toothpicks on some parts.

Tilda hadn't been living in Santa Cruz at the time of the quake, but she was retroactively proud of how little damage Wit's End had taken. Such a good house! One crack in one bedroom wall, some china and four dollhouses lost. When the cliff beneath gave way, as all Santa Cruz cliffs eventually would, Tilda pictured Wit's End sliding into the ocean, floating on the water like an ark.

This, then, was the household: Tilda on the first floor, with a bedroom off the kitchen and a private door out to the garden. Addison on the second floor, with the large master suite, an even larger library, and a small room for watching television. And Rima on the third floor, with two bedrooms besides hers, which Addison sometimes offered to artists she knew but which were empty at the moment.

"You'll have the whole floor to yourself," Addison had promised Rima when she suggested the visit, so when Rima did finally get out of bed, she felt free to check out that part of the house.

She saw immediately that the other two bedrooms were smaller than hers and that they shared a bath. One had a view of the ocean, the other of the lake (though no one in Cleveland would have called that a lake—it was a pond in a good mood, or a puddle in a bad), but only Rima's windows overlooked it all, and the boardwalk too. Addison was being so good to her!

Something else was pleasing Rima; she felt this long before she was able to tease out what it was. It had to do with the woman who'd lived here once, the woman who'd survived the Donner Party, and it had to do with the rooms, with the house. Finally Rima got to it—that later in her life, the woman had had so many people around her she needed a big place like this in which to keep them all. Who doesn't like a happy ending? Even Addison wrote one occasionally.

The bedrooms were all similarly decorated—brass bedsteads, shadow quilts, glassed-in bookcases (sometimes containing Addison's own books), pile rugs, and murders. On various shelves and tabletops, Rima quickly found: *Our Better Angels* (young woman stabbed in the backseat of a blue convertible); *Absolution Way* (old woman drowned in her bathtub); and *It Happened to Somebody Else* (old man beaten to death with the Annu–Baltic volume of *Encyclopaedia Britannica*).

There was no sign of the dogs. This puzzled Rima until she looked out a window and saw them climbing the stone stairs up from the beach. Tall stairs, short legs, they hopped from step to step like Slinkys, only upward and all tired out. A man with a bandanna over his head and a woman with red hair were holding their leashes. By the time Rima got downstairs, all four were in the kitchen, finishing off what seemed to have been a breakfast of poached eggs and toast. The dogs looked up from their bowls briefly when Rima came in, and then back down, as if now that she was actually in reach, the prospect of ripping her open with their bare teeth had become tedious to them. The kitchen smelled of melted butter, dead fish, and exhausted dog.

The couple looked to be about college age. (Were college age, as it turned out. Junior and senior at UC Santa Cruz.) The young woman was talking. "So she goes, 'Excuse me. Your hair is touching me.' And I say I'm sorry, because I always say I'm sorry, it's like a reflex, you know, I just can't help myself, sometimes I say I'm sorry for saying I'm sorry. So I push my hair down and five minutes later she's tapping me on the shoulder, going, 'Your hair is touching me again,' like she's really losing patience with me now. I can't hear the music, I'm so busy trying to figure out how to make my hair stop doing that. And it's not like I have big hair."

"Maybe you have rude hair," said the young man. He was reading the paper, mopping up the last of his egg with the last of his toast. It was possible that he himself had no hair, though with the bandanna it was hard to be sure. "Maybe you're a rude-head."

"So funny." The young woman looked at Rima. "Do I have big hair?"

"No," said Rima. It was very red, though. Except for the short bits right around her face, which were pink, it was very red, but not red like red hair, red like strawberry Jell-O. The woman was wearing camouflage pants, which seemed pointless with such unstealthy hair, unless the only thing she didn't want looked at was her legs, because then the hair was diversionary. But no one would have said big.

"See?" the young woman told the young man. And then, "You must be Rima. I'm Scorch. I walk the dogs in the morning and pick up the mail. This is Cody. He thinks he's my boyfriend.

Addison said you were to help yourself to breakfast. She left you a note. She's out in the studio and can't be disturbed, on pain of death. Do you want a piece of toast? We made one too many. How do you know Addison?"

"She's my godmother."

Scorch took a moment to process this. "I don't have a god-mother." Her tone was aggrieved, as if everyone had a godmother but her. "My family doesn't go in for that."

"Water's hot if you want some tea." Cody didn't look up from the paper.

"I'm sorry," Scorch said. "I should have said. Water's on the stove and the tea is over there." She pointed to the window above the sink, where several canisters were wedged on the sill between the potted ferns and ivy. Rima went to look.

Someone in the household had a powerful faith in tea. There were fruit teas, green teas, black teas; cleansing teas, fortifying teas; teas that sweetened your thoughts, improved your rest; teas for longevity, teas for celebration, teas for contemplation.

Wisdom, fortune, health, or happiness? What kind of a monster would make a person choose only one? Rima went back to the table and took the spare piece of toast instead.

One of the dogs came to sit beside her. It was Berkeley, the female, though Rima didn't know it; she couldn't tell them apart yet. Berkeley looked up at her with brown, brown eyes, sighing in a smitten sort of way. She hardly seemed to notice the toast, just the shadow of a blink when it moved to and from Rima's mouth.

But when Scorch began to gather her things—backpack, coat, car keys—Berkeley lost interest in Rima. She joined Stanford at the door, tail wagging hopelessly. Scorch knelt to say good-bye, and the dogs collapsed like deflated balloons. Rima wouldn't have thought they could get smaller. "Don't look at me like that," Scorch told them. "I'm sorry. I'll be back soon."

And then to Rima—"Tell Addison that Maxwell Lane got a letter. Just junk. He can get a credit card or something. It's on the table in the entry with the rest of the mail."

"He's in the ether again," Cody said. "They're rerunning the television show. The eighties one. With the moustache."

Scorch coughed suddenly. It was a painful sound. "My throat is killing me." She wiped one hand across her eyes. "I think I'm getting a cold."

"We're all going to die of the bird flu," Cody said. He folded up the paper with a shake and a snap. "I got to get to class."

(2)

The breakfast table was in an alcove overlooking the courtyard. Fig leaves pressed like hands against the windowpanes; sunlight rippled on the table, softening the butter in its wake. There was a hutch built into one corner with china on the top shelves and a dollhouse on the bottom: *Spook Juice*—man in a tux, brained in the atrium with an unopened bottle of Brut Impérial Champagne. Rima thought she remembered that the fact that it was unopened had been a major clue. Or maybe that had been another book, an Agatha Christie or an Elizabeth George.

The china was painted with poppies, a replication of the pattern once used in the dining car on the Santa Fe Railway. Rima knew this about the dishes, and she wondered how. There were many things Rima inexplicably knew, the residue, presumably, of lost conversations, books, classes, television shows, crossword puzzles. Like her mother before her, Rima was a devotee of the *Nation* crossword puzzle, and as a result, she had a surprising store of slang circa World War II, much of it British.

She looked at the paper Cody had left, a thin magazine-style weekly called *Good Times,* which said fifty-one people had been arrested on Halloween, two for stabbings, and an unspecified number for public urination. The paper said this was a vast improvement over last year.

Rima made herself another piece of toast and considered the possibility that she was going to die of bird flu. She couldn't make herself think so. But everyone else probably would, Rima could easily picture that.

Next she thought about Maxwell Lane's letter. She should go get it, apply for that credit card. Buy something. That's what Oliver would have done. (Don't start thinking about Oliver.) Oliver would have done that, just to see what happened next.

She was still in the kitchen when Addison arrived, hungry for lunch after a hard morning of whatever it was she'd been up to. Rima considered escaping to her room, but it would have been rude. Sooner or later she and Addison were going to have to get to know each other. Sooner or later they would have a couple of drinks together and Rima would find herself feeling oddly comfortable, or maybe drunk, and against all her better instincts, she would suddenly say, "Okay, then. What was it exactly that went on between you and my father?" Even though, right now, drinking nothing but orange juice, Rima truly believed it was all so long ago, who cared?

This regrettable conversation could occur only after an initial extended period of politeness. So Rima stayed put, getting on with the politeness part, and Addison fixed herself a lunch, slicing, salting, and eating tomatoes while making a sandwich with many tomatoes in it, because this was California and the use of the word "autumn" here was no more accurate than the use of the word "lake." Eventually Rima remembered to mention Maxwell's letter.

Addison told her that Maxwell Lane got a surprising amount of mail. He was on any number of charitable lists, and not a single nonprofit had ever been discouraged by the fact that he never responded. It was an inspiring testament, Addison often noted (though not on this occasion), to the tenacity of the world's do-gooders.

In addition to charitable requests, there were the political. Maxwell seemed to have been identified as both a leftist and a white supremacist. You could understand the latter, but it was a sad misreading, or else the white supremacists didn't read her at all, which was the explanation Addison preferred. White supremacists, she was fond of saying, were the living refutations of their own theories. In point of fact, Addison had a lot of readers of whom she did not approve. Most of them, if you really want to know.

Anyway, Maxwell received special introductory offers from *The Skeptic* and *Mother Jones,* but also from *White Hope, White Heart* and some group called the New Thules. One unsolicited newsletter kept him updated on the schemes of the mongrel races, another tracked Big Pharm, Big Oil, and Big Brother.

Only very rarely did he get a personal letter. Sometimes these contained proposals more suited to a younger man. At least that was Addison's opinion. A silence followed this statement, broken only by the sound of the knife on the cutting board.

Rima would have liked to hear more about those proposals, but not if Addison was going to make her ask. "How old is Maxwell?" she asked instead.

Rima genuinely wanted to know the answer. Addison had been careless with her details; greater minds than Rima's had struggled to put together a coherent timeline that worked over the many books, and failed. It simply couldn't be done, not with any math yet invented.

"Eight years older than I am. Seventy-two."

This Rima seriously doubted. She didn't suppose even Addison believed it. Fictional characters don't age at the same rate as the rest of us. Some don't age at all. Rima's father, to give just one example: Rima's father was dead, but the murderer with his name was fleeing east in a green Rambler station wagon on Interstate 80 and always would be.

And then there was the man in Rima's dream. There was no proposal he would have been too old for. Rima felt the ghost of his dream hand on her dream shoulder.

So how about this math instead? Addison was twenty-eight when she published her first Maxwell Lane book. Ergo, instead of being eight years older than Addison, Maxwell must be twenty-eight years younger. Strange to think that back when Addison first met Rima's father, Maxwell Lane didn't even exist.

Twenty-eight years younger than Addison was a perfectly plausible and entirely suitable age. Mid-thirties. His whole life ahead of him. Rima had a peculiar sense of satisfaction. She'd just given

Maxwell Lane an additional thirty-six years in which to solve all sorts of crimes, and she'd done it with only simple arithmetic.

Addison finished making her sandwich and came to sit with Rima. Addison's hair was flattened on one side, as if she'd been sleeping on it. She looked more fragile by daylight, her elbows sharp enough to shatter on contact. Countless interviews had remarked on the paradox that the author of such chilly books could be this pale, frail woman with the friendly smile. Rima wondered briefly if "friendly smile" was magazine code for big teeth. Not that Addison didn't have a lovely smile. Probably. Rima had hardly seen it so far, but it was probably very nice.

"I've had the same postman for almost twenty years," Addison said. "Kenny. Sullivan. Kenny Sullivan." She took a bite of sandwich.

When Rima looked next, there was a little tomato on her cheek, and a seed and a smear of skin the color of blood in the deep crease beside her mouth. Funny what a difference one tiny bloody smear made on an otherwise friendly face.

Rima's mother had thought there was something vampiric about the mere act of writing murder mysteries; Rima heard her say so once at a dinner party. How it had come up, she didn't remember. In a gesture of daughterly solidarity, she decided not to tell Addison about the tomato skin.

Anyway, Addison had a napkin; it might well get taken care of without anyone's saying a word.

And anyway again, only Rima was there to see. She wasn't making a decision as much as removing herself from the outcome. Leaving things to fate.

When Rima began to listen again, Addison was still talking about Kenny Sullivan. Kenny Sullivan was a famous postman,

Addison was saying, because he had once delivered the mail to a bank right smack in the middle of a robbery. He hadn't even noticed that the tellers were all facedown on the floor, just walked in, put the mail on the counter, walked out again. He'd always been the sort of postman who lived mostly in his own head. He'd been on *Letterman* after.

But reliable, certainly, neither sleet nor snow nor armed robbery, et cetera, and Kenny could be counted on to bring any mail for Maxwell straight to Wit's End no matter how it was addressed. When there was a substitute postman, Maxwell's mail might go to a rug shop on Cooper Street that was owned by a widow from Portugal. She had Addison's number; she would give Addison a call, so no harm done. The widow's rugs were beautiful. There were two of them in the living room.

"We need to tell Kenny that you're staying here now," Addison said, just as calmly as if she weren't a really famous person with bits of tomato all over her face. "Is your mail being forwarded?"

There had been some discussion of Rima's handling light secretarial work for Addison—keeping her calendar, answering her phone. It would have been nice, therefore, to demonstrate a bit of organizational competence. "I didn't think to do that," Rima said.

"Who writes letters today?" Addison shook her head, embarrassed to have brought it up. She herself was guilty as anyone! It was all e-mail now. She wiped her eyes with her napkin. Her eyes were nowhere near the tomato skin. "I pity social historians." Addison wiped her hands. "A hundred years from now, we'll know more about daily life in 1806 than in 2006." She wiped her chin.

"What about novels?" Rima asked.

"Unreliable. No one in novels watches TV," Addison said. "Would you be interested in Maxwell's old letters? I think I have some up in the attic."

Rima heard boots on the brick walkway outside the kitchen door. Addison heard them too, because she was saying she'd have Tilda get the letters down for Rima at the very same moment that Rima was telling Addison there was tomato on her face, pointing to her own cheek—key in the keyhole—her own mouth—doorknob turning—so when Tilda came in, stamping her feet and saying what a beautiful day it was, she'd seen an osprey at the Land of Medicine Buddha (surely not, Addison said, maybe a hawk, maybe a redtail, when even Rima knew that an osprey looks absolutely nothing like a red-tailed hawk) and first thought there was a mouse in its talons, but later seen it was a ragged old tennis shoe, Addison's face was perfectly clean.

What happened next was that they all went up to the *Our Better Angels* bedroom on the third floor, where Addison made Tilda pull some stairs out of the ceiling. The stairs didn't come easily—Tilda had to wrap the rope around her hands and hang from it with her feet braced and the coiled snake swelling on her biceps. They didn't come quietly—wood ground against wood, hinges squealed and popped. The noise brought Berkeley and Stanford racing in from wherever they'd been, both of them barking frantically.

"There was a mouse in the attic once," Addison said. She raised her voice to be heard over the dogs; she was shouting. "Maybe four, five years ago. Ever since, it's their favorite place in the world. Better let them go first. You'll trip over them if you don't."

Tilda returned to the osprey and the tennis shoe, a sighting she thought had all the earmarks of portent. "What could it mean?" she shouted. It was one thing to get a message from the universe. It was entirely another to successfully decode it.

The steps landed and the dogs swarmed up them. The barking rose in pitch and excitement. "Static on the radio," Addison said. She was too focused on the probable misidentification of the bird to think deeply about the tennis shoe.

Chapter Three

(1)

The attic was a disappointment to Rima. It wasn't a romantic attic with rocking horses, birdcages, and bridal veils. It wasn't a spooky attic with taxidermy, dress dummies, and bridal veils. Mostly it was filled with boxes, some of which contained Addison's published books and had never even been opened. There were first editions, foreign editions, large print, book club, hardcover, trade paper, and mass market.

Light sifted in through two screened vents, just enough for Rima to make out the general terrain. Addison had brought a flashlight. She flicked it on, and gave it to Tilda, who began to move through the stacks, tipping the top boxes to the side so she could read the labels of those beneath. Dust rose and spun in the beam of light. The dogs were quieter now, snuffling in an efficient, disciplined fashion. They wormed their way under a heap of old dining room chairs, making them rock briefly.

As Rima's eyes adjusted, she found more to interest her. She almost stepped on a lamp with a sphinx for a base. It had no shade, no bulb, and no place to plug into. The sphinx's nose was chipped, and Rima couldn't decide whether it was supposed to be that way, eroded and faux ancient, or whether someone more recent had broken it. What Rima didn't know was that the lamp was actually a trophy for a literary award called the Riddle Prize. As such, it had a complicated iconography involving the sphinx and a light going on. Addison had won any number of awards over the years, including this one in 1979 for *Average Mean.* She preferred trophies that could be eaten, but there weren't so many of those.

A couple of posters were draped over one of the tallest stacks of boxes. The one on top was of Harrison Ford, rugged in a blue work shirt, a book by his knee. Rima couldn't see well enough to determine its title. She tried to guess what Harrison Ford might read, but really had no idea. In any case, he wasn't reading it. She slid him aside to look at the poster underneath. This turned out to be Addison, the mobile of murder weapons dangling over her head with a balloon crayoned around them like a thought in a comic strip. She was reading *Gaudy Night,* which Rima knew only because she'd seen this poster before. It announced the American Library Association's Celebrity READ series and had hung in Rima's college library during her freshman year. Eventually it was replaced by Antonio Banderas holding *Don Quixote,* and it was hard not to see this as an improvement, even if Addison was your godmother, at least when it suited your purposes to say so.

Most arresting by far was a row of plastic Santas, each about four feet tall, and strangely numerous. Rima counted eight of them, all lined up against one wall as if they were about to be shot.

The dogs had given up the mouse hunt. Rima thought they were playing together until it became clear something less palatable was going on. Addison leaned over to brush the top one (Berkeley) aside and pick the bottom one (Stanford) up. "They're brother and sister," she told Rima. "Fixed, of course. No consequences. Beyond the sheer horror of it."

Stanford shuffled in Addison's arms until his muzzle was on her shoulder. He stared morosely at Rima from under the fringe of Addison's hair. "Do you think he's gaining weight again?" Addison asked Tilda.

"Last time we were in, Dr. Sanchez said he was down a pound," Tilda said. "Celebrations all around."

"Dachshunds love to eat," Addison told Rima. "Never happier than when you're feeding them. But their backs can't handle the weight. We have to be cold and cruel." Rima remembered the breakfast of eggs and toast she'd witnessed. Some of us were colder and crueler than others.

Tilda moved along the front of the attic. The stacks were higher here, so Rima joined her, taking the flashlight and letting Tilda wrestle the bigger boxes with both hands. Rima could smell the morning hike on her. Not sweat so much as trees and dirt and underneath all that an almond-scented soap.

Tilda read the labels aloud as Rima illuminated them. " 'Reviews and Interviews, 1982–85.' 'Maps and Floor Plans.' '1962 Gubernatorial Race.' 'False Starts.' 'Correspondence slash Letters to the Editor'?"

"Mine, not Maxwell's," Addison said. "Unless otherwise specified."

The dust was beginning to get to Rima. She sneezed and the ball of light jumped. "Bless you," said Addison.

The attic was beginning to get to Rima. The boxes seemed to her sad remnants of things much larger, a book, a cause, a life. Santa Claus. Here is what we can keep, Rima thought. Here is all that remains. And what did it accomplish, this hanging on to leftovers? If you make a lamp shaped like a sphinx, is the real sphinx made larger or smaller by that? If a bird takes a shoe, is it more than a shoe or less?

" 'Palo Alto,' " said Tilda. " 'Interviews, 1990–92.' 'Photos slash Ventura.' 'Receipts, 1974–84.' Christmas cards . . . Datebook 1989."

She realigned the boxes and moved to the next stack. The box on the top here was small—a shoe box with one crushed corner, the lid bound on with twine. When Rima shone the light on the label, she saw the single word "Bim."

Tilda did not read this aloud. She took the flashlight back from Rima, since the stacks had narrowed and now there wasn't room for them both. It was possible the label meant nothing to Tilda. Rima couldn't see her face, just the black, unblinking eyes of the snake tattoo.

The label was probably about the character Bim and not her father anyway. Or maybe she'd misread it. It could have been Bin. Or Ben. BIM. Bank of Inner Mongolia. Bureau of Interstellar Management.

"I had a phone call from Martin." Tilda's head was down. She straightened and turned to Rima, dust and dog hair swimming in the flashlight beam between them. "My son," she said. "Not that I was much of a mother, his dad raised him. Did a great job, he's a great kid. Well. Not really a kid anymore. Twenty-six."

Oliver would have been twenty-six if he'd lived. Rima felt an instant dislike for Martin, who got to be twenty-six years old and probably didn't even appreciate it. It was such an unfair feeling that having it made her sneeze again. "Bless you," Addison said, which Rima didn't deserve; it only added to the guilt.

"He's coming over Friday after work. Okay if I give him a bedroom? I hate him to be on the Seventeen after dark."

"Martin's always welcome." Addison glanced at Rima.

Here is what the glance meant: Don't worry. No way will Martin stay the night. Here's what Rima thought it meant: I know I said you'd have the whole floor to yourself, and now I'm sorry I said so.

" 'Letters slash Maxwell'?" Tilda asked.

"Bingo," Addison said.

The box was large enough that Tilda needed two hands to pick it up. She handed the flashlight to Addison. The light bounced about the attic, hitting the sphinx lamp, the dining room chairs, Rima's shoes. It swept the Santas, brushed over the shoe box with the crushed corner, turned a dachshund's (Berkeley's) eyes to mirrors.

"You'll like Martin," Tilda told Rima, and from the darkness behind Tilda's shoulder, Addison gave Rima another look, hard and right at her.

This look meant: Martin's a conniving little snot. Here's what Rima thought it meant: I know I said you'd have the whole floor to yourself, and now I'm sorry I said so.

(2)

There were more letters in the box than Rima would have expected, and they were jumbled together, some in envelopes, some not, some typewritten, some by hand, and none in any order that Rima could discern. She wondered if Maxwell had answered any of them; she wished she'd thought to ask. Though honestly, she wasn't as interested in the letters as Addison had assumed; it had simply seemed rude to say so. She would rather have brought down the box with her father's name on it.

Since her father's death, she'd lacked the concentration for books. The letters were short and undemanding, and just enough like reading to substitute for reading. She read a few that night before she went to sleep.

The first was on three-ringed binder paper, in a faded blue ink. There was no envelope.

1410 King St.
Jackson Hole, Wyoming
July 7, 1981

Dear Maxwell,

I think you would like me if you knew me, we have a lot in common. We were both raised by our fathers and we both had lonely childhoods. A lonely childhood is hard to get over, isn't it? When I was a little kid all I wanted was to grow up as fast as I could and go somewhere else and now all I want is to go back, have a "do-over" in a different place with a different family. You can get past a bad childhood, is what I think now, you can have a "good life," but you'll never stop wanting a good childhood and you can't have one later, there's no way.

You and me, we're both real quiet. My wife is always after me to talk more. She says, cat got your tongue and penny for your thoughts, until I tell her, baby, you don't even want to know.

I don't solve mysteries, but I've done okay for myself. I own a gas station and bait shop that I got all on my own, nobody helped me with that, and now I'm saving for a boat. I get to live all year round in a place lots of people come for vacation. It's all about saving your money and having a plan. Anyway, I just wanted you to know there is someone out there who "gets you."

Sincerely yours,
Bob Cronin

Ps. I read a lot of books when I was a kid, because it was a good escape, not because anyone ever encouraged me. I used to think the characters in them were real people. I know you're not real, but you seem real to me. I think my life would be a good book and maybe even encourage other kids like me to make something of themselves. B.C.

In pencil on wide-ruled paper:

In the most boring house
On the most boring street
In the most boring town
In the world.

Dear Mr. Lane:

I am ten years old and I can't check your books out at the library, because they're in the adult section. The adults where I live care a whole lot about what kids shouldn't read. If there was ever a real murder here, they would just die! But surprise! I read you anyway, because I have my ways. What do you think about kids who are allowed to watch you on tv, but not allowed to read your books? I know a family like that!

Respectfully yours,
Amanda Chan

In black ink, Eaton stationery:

March 17, 1985

Dear Max,

I know you're not ready to hear this yet, but you're better off without her. She was never good enough for you and I'm not the only one who thinks so. You know what would make you feel better? Hair of the dog and fish in the sea. You tell A.B. Early that it's past time you had a new girlfriend. You tell her that there are readers out there who care about you and want you to be happy. I mean, it's really up to her, isn't it? The rest of us, we can spend ten years thinking we have this great marriage and aren't we the lucky one, didn't we just do everything right? And then it turns out we don't have a friend in the world our husband didn't try to screw at some barbecue or back-to-school night, and no one said a word about it to us so we were the only one in town who didn't know. Real life is no story; it's just what happens. But you can be happy any time Ms. Early chooses. So it's annoying when she doesn't and I won't keep reading your books forever if you're always going to be so mopey. If I were in charge, I'd start with your mouth and keep you guessing about what's coming next.

You need me, but you don't need to know my name . . .

Rima supposed this fell into the category of inappropriate proposals. She hoped they wouldn't all be so vague.

The effort required to read the handwritten letters was getting to her, so she fished through the box for something typed. And found, on an onionskin paper so thin some of the periods were holes, the final page of a longer letter. The first thing she saw was her father's name.

someone else with motive and opportunity. So here it is—I just don't believe Bim Lanisell would kill anyone. He always seemed like a pretty straight-up Joe to me. Think you got it wrong this time.

Bet if you put poison on a cat's claws for real, the cat would lick it right off, no matter how bad it tastes. Cats are very aware of their bodies. I know whereof I speak. I have twenty-two of them.

Of course, all this assumes Ice City is a mystery novel. Can we be sure of that? Not clear from the cover. In a horror novel the cat could have acted alone. There is a larger world than you allow, Mr. Lane, and the truth you end up with

often depends on where you are when you start. I knew your
father about as well as anyone knew him. Not highly
thought of today, but that much he had right.

                                        VTY,

                                Constance Wellington

PS. Joking about the cat, of course.

Rima felt a friendly connection to this woman who thought her
father had been falsely accused. She stirred through the letters,
looking for the first page, but it didn't surface and her hands
became unpleasantly dusty. She put the box on the floor and went
to wash up and get ready for bed.

She thought that she'd look again for the first page tomorrow
and maybe reread *Ice City* too, see if a case could be made for
someone's wanting to kill the cat. Of course, that still wouldn't
explain the other deaths, but murdering two people is not as bad
as murdering three. And only the one with the cat was premedi-
tated. Only the wife's death was Murder 1.

Rereading seemed like something she could manage. It wasn't
the same as reading, not when you'd read a book as often as Rima
had read *Ice City*. You didn't need to concentrate so much when
you already knew a book backward and forward.

It would be hard on Maxwell if she found out he'd been wrong
all those years. He was already angsty enough. He was filled with
angst. But her own loyalties had to lie with Bim; anyone would
understand that.

Chapter Four

(1)

Ice City, prologue

A girl came to the house today claiming to be a reporter. She had dirty-blond hair and a sharp chin. She said she was doing a history of Camp Forever for the local-color section of the paper. People are interested in communes again, she said. It's because of that mass suicide in Guyana.

Then she took me quickly to the end of things, the events of 1963, the deaths, starting with my father's. Who can blame her? What reporter doesn't hope that every story will have blackmail, sex, and murder in it?

I wondered for a moment if her interest was personal. I thought she might be Kathleen's daughter. She had something of the look of that demented elf, Kathleen.

I made her a cup of coffee she didn't drink. I showed her

a photograph of my father when he was a far younger man than I am now, and another of Brother Isaiah, a publicity shot with the sun lighting him up. I asked her, if there was a way she could live forever, would she? She didn't answer.

"Tell me about Maxwell Lane," she said instead. "You were the one who hired him, right?"

There was no way she could have known that.

I used to get asked about Mr. Lane a lot. I had my answers back then, scripted them out and stuck to them. In my whole life, I never told anyone that I was the one who brought Maxwell Lane to Camp Forever.

I've worked hard over the years to forget that simple fact. I told her she had it wrong, and then I showed her the door. Now I'm alone with the cold coffee and the smell of lavender perfume and cigarettes. Now there is nothing I can do that stops me remembering.

(2)

The next day it rained. Not a driving rain, but a steady drip, just loud enough for Rima to hear over the ocean when she woke up. She couldn't remember her dreams, only that they'd been bad, and instead of feeling relieved the way most people get to do, waking from bad dreams, she was in a bad mood. Her real life was what it was—lonely, abandoned, all the wrong people around her. Nothing to be done about that. But there was no reason her dreams couldn't still have been good. She decided to stay in bed until she was so hungry she couldn't stand it anymore.

The clock in the hallway chimed the quarter-hour, the half, the three-quarters. She heard the dogs once, barking their way down the stairs. Later, deep in the house, there was the muffled sound of a phone ringing. The clack of eco-friendly clogs in the hall. Three soft knocks on Rima's door.

The knocking was Tilda, brisk but apologetic. The phone had been Scorch. She had a terrible cold, or maybe the flu, there was something really nasty going around at school, and given the weather, she didn't think she could walk the dogs. She was really sorry about it. The thing was that Cody couldn't walk the dogs either, because he had an exam this morning, and Addison, of course, couldn't be asked; she was already working. And Tilda had a dental appointment—living on the street was hard on your teeth—to which she was already late, and if she was much later she'd lose the appointment entirely but still have to pay for it and not be able to get another for weeks.

The dogs would hate being out in the rain, but the only way to convince them of this was to take them. So would Rima mind too terribly? There was a rain hat she could use, hanging by the kitchen door, and plastic bags on the counter. "Just let them run around for a few minutes," Tilda said, "and they'll be cold and want to come back inside."

Rima thought that it was early in her relationship with the dogs for such responsibilities. Why, it seemed only yesterday they'd been hurling themselves against the bedroom door like little furry battering rams. What if they ran away? Plus this was a lot more active than the morning she'd planned.

But there was no way to say no. Rima got up heavily, dressed, and went down to the kitchen, where Tilda was already gone but the dogs were waiting, leashed and dragging their leads, shivering with the excitement of it all.

An Asian woman with a large white dog was coming up the stairs to the beach as Rima and the dachshunds went down. The woman spoke and the white dog halted to let the little dogs go by. The woman spoke again. In labored English, as Rima passed, she was explaining that she would be gone all afternoon, but that there would be another walk before dinner. It made Rima wonder. She was, after all, talking to a dog. Why not use a language in which she was fluent to do so?

Rain dripped from Rima's hat, soaking the shoulders of her jacket. The sea was the dull color of iron. The Monterey Peninsula was hidden behind a wall of cloud; the seam between sky and water blurred as if it had been penciled in and then badly erased. At the shallow edge of the water, sandpipers drilled for whatever it was sandpipers ate. A pelican flew across the waves so low the tips of its enormous wings dipped into the water like oars. Rima knelt down and let the dogs loose.

She turned and took her first daytime look at Wit's End from the outside. It was painted in white and Nantucket blue. Shingles like fish scales covered one wall, and a row of gold shells was pressed into the roofline along the eaves. A round cupola with a whale weathervane. Rima found the window to her own room, the blinds halfway down. Below, off the second floor, was a porch looking out to the ocean. If the weather was warm, Rima thought, if it were Rima's house, she would sleep on that porch sometimes.

There were only two other people on the beach—a woman in a green hooded sweater, hood up, and a man in an orange slicker who turned out to be Animal Control. There was a leash-free beach up the coast, he told Rima, more in sorrow than in anger, but this was not it. He wrote out two tickets, one for each dog. As the rain hit the paper, the ink spread. There was no way Rima would be able to read them.

Rima had a number of reasonable points to make.

She was from Cleveland and hadn't known about the leash laws. [The beach was posted. All she had to do was read the signs.]

Who were they bothering? The beach was practically deserted. [The law was pretty straightforward on this matter. There weren't a lot of clauses.]

She was staying in the house just there on the bluff behind her. She would probably have to drive to the leash-free beach, whereas this one was just down a flight of stairs. [Most of the people who used the dog beach had to drive to it. Did she know how expensive beachfront property here was? You would never buy a beach house on a ranger's salary, that was for sure. What was the address again?]

The dogs belonged to the famous writer A. B. Early. Had he heard of A. B. Early? [He had not. But he recognized the dogs. Last time they were on the beach, he'd let them off with a warning. Evidently, this had not had the desired effect.]

Had he heard of Maxwell Lane? A. B. Early wrote the Maxwell Lane books. [No shit. He had just watched that Maxwell Lane show on television last night. That was an hour of his life he'd never get back again.]

He handed her the limp tickets and left. By this time the dachshunds were back on their leashes, a development that startled and displeased them. The whole time Rima had been talking, they'd been circling her legs in some anxious, angry Maypole dance.

Soon she'd be unable to take a step. She leaned down to untangle them.

The woman in the hooded sweater came over. "Cool dogs," she said. Her hood was sequined with drops of water, her nose red and chafed as if she'd been blowing it often. Rima put her age somewhere between forty and sixty. "Bummer about the tickets. Sometimes they crack down. Let me help." She took the leashes out of Rima's hands, separated them, then passed Stanford's back and kept Berkeley's.

"It's okay," Rima said, holding out her hand, but the woman merely smiled, led the way up the stairs. She continued through the gate, up the walk, under the fig tree. She stood back while Rima opened the door, and then, instead of handing Berkeley over, she pushed past Rima into the house.

"Hey," said Rima. "Hey!" She dropped Stanford's leash and ran after her.

The woman was standing in the center of the kitchen, turning slowly, checking out the cabinets, the posters, the plants. She gave Berkeley's leash back to Rima. "Cool teas," she said. Then she left the way she'd come, with Rima standing at the door to make sure she descended the stairs, then throwing the lock behind her.

(3)

Rima consoled herself that the woman had been inside for only a few minutes and unobserved for even less time. There was further consolation in having proved she'd been right all along, that walking the dogs was more than she could handle. She went upstairs to take her wet clothes off and go back to bed, where she belonged.

When she heard Tilda return, she went downstairs again. It was lunchtime now; Addison as well as Tilda was in the kitchen. The teapot was whistling, the windows sealed with steam. Tilda was cooking sausages. The radio was on—John Fogerty's "Walking in a Hurricane." It was a cozy, fragrant, melodic scene. Rima wished she could leave it that way.

"Look at this." Addison handed Rima the front page of the *San Jose Mercury News*. The headline Rima read, "Sea Lion Attacks Swimmers in SF Aquatic Park," was not, in fact, the right headline. The headline Addison meant her to see was further down the page. "For Sale: Holy City (It Was Neither)."

Rima didn't know why she was being alerted to the sea-lion attacks. (Except who isn't interested in animal attacks?) Sometimes she could hear sea lions barking from her room. Obviously Santa Cruz had a lot of them.

She would have been even more puzzled by the Holy City story. If she'd read it, she would have found out that the asking price for Holy City was eleven million dollars. The property was one hundred forty acres in size, and the owners were three men in their eighties. Between the 1920s and the 1960s, Holy City had been home to a cult run by a man named William Riker. The *Mercury* described William Riker as a necktie salesman turned cult leader, noting that he'd run for governor four times but never been elected; been charged with bigamy, fraud, tax evasion, sedition, and murder but never been convicted. He'd died in 1969.

In the 1930s the cult had numbered three hundred or so, but this dropped precipitously when Highway 17 became the standard route to the beach. In the sixties, the property had passed briefly into the hands of an unnamed Hollywood musical director, who'd next sold it to a group of investors; and then, in 1968, the current owners had purchased it with the proviso that the eight surviving cultists not only be allowed to stay but also be paid either a thousand dollars a year for eight years or the equivalent in food, clothing, and shelter.

In the 1970s, hippies squatted in the abandoned buildings until they were evicted. The only going concern now was an art glass business. Riker's old farmhouse was one of the few buildings still standing, but the property boasted creeks, waterfalls, cliffs, and valleys as well as ten potential parcels for development. The owners would prefer to see it preserved as a park rather than go to housing.

All this was in the newspaper article. But Rima was intent on confession, and so the misunderstanding neither knew was a misunderstanding wasn't straightened out. Instead Rima described the morning's intrusion but briefly, without the added drama of detail.

What did she look like? Addison asked. Did she have red hair? Was she wearing an ankh necklace? There was a female fan who haunted the beach below, and once they'd caught her going through the garbage. Rima couldn't tell whether Addison was upset or not, or if so, how much. She wasn't looking at Rima, and some people didn't look at you when they were angry, but Rima didn't know if Addison was that sort. The radio station in the background identified itself as KPIG.

"Of course, anyone can buy an ankh," Tilda said. "That doesn't mean anything."

"She had a hood on," Rima said. "I didn't see a necklace. Or her hair. She was only here a minute. Only here in the kitchen."

"You shouldn't let strangers in the house," Tilda said, as if this were something Rima needed to be told. The dogs, unusually for a mealtime, had made themselves scarce. Where were those tiny teeth when you needed them? Why was Rima the only one taking the fall?

Suddenly she remembered the tickets. The last memory she had of them was on the beach, the ink smearing in the rain. She hoped they were upstairs. She should go get them. Oliver was a great believer in delivering great wads of bad news all at once—his reasoning was that it was more thoughtful not to upset your mother repeatedly when you could do it all in a single go. Sometimes their mother would find out something he hadn't told her, and he would explain that he'd been saving it until he had more.

Rima rose, intending to go up to her room, check the pockets of her jacket and pants, see if she could produce the actual tickets. But Tilda seized her arm as she passed, swung her to face the corner.

Tilda's finger pointed into the tiny glassed-in atrium of the *Spook Juice* dollhouse. The murder weapon, the Brut Impérial Champagne bottle, lay under the ferns, cork intact, everything just as it should be. But the tuxedoed corpse was gone.

Chapter Five

(1)

The missing corpse had a name. He was, he had been, Thomas Grand, undercover agent specializing in domestic terrorism, back before Waco, before Oklahoma City, before the Unabomber, back when middle-class white people hardly knew there was such a thing. Tilda and Addison discussed the advisability of calling the police.

Tilda was against it. There'd been two murders of homeless people during the time she'd been on the street, and the police hadn't solved either of them. All they'd done, as far as she could see, was make comments about the homeless, comments she could describe only as gratuitous. Tilda had no faith in the police.

Rima considered telling Tilda that only sixty percent of all reported murders are ever resolved (as distinct from solved, so Rima wasn't even sure what the statistic meant), but since she didn't know how she knew that and maybe it wasn't even true, she kept her mouth shut. Was sixty percent a lot or way too little? It apparently beat the success rate in other cases—rapes, muggings, thefts—all hollow.

Addison was also against making the call. This seemed to her the sort of story that would immediately make it into the paper and onto the Internet, where it would live forever. And not on some little site no one ever visited either; Addison could picture this in the day's AOL headlines. If they were willing to post "Airline apologizes to passenger. He couldn't hold it any longer," then obviously there was nothing too low. Addison had lived much of her adult life faintly convinced that a large segment of the reading public and the entire news industry would be really happy if she died in some bizarre and puzzling way. She said that she'd put a watch on eBay, and proposed that they all start locking the doors even when someone was home.

They were interrupted by Kenny Sullivan, postman of myth and legend. Addison stepped out onto the walkway to tell him all about it, and Rima heard him promising to spread the word to the neighbors, with utmost discretion, of course. Possibly someone else had seen something.

Then the women sat together, eating the sausages, drinking the tea, and listening to the radio. Addison and Tilda assured Rima many times that none of it was her fault. They repeated this once too often; it lost its credibility.

Rima was amazed. A crime had been committed in the home of a world-famous mystery writer, and as far as she could see, nothing was going to be done to solve it. It occurred to her that she herself was the most likely suspect. A troubled young woman, new to the household, with an unlikely story, and offering only the vaguest description of the perpetrator.

"The best way to clear yourself," said Maxwell Lane, "is to find the one who's guilty," and if Rima were a world-famous mystery writer, then surely she would know how to go about doing that. If she were Addison, she would at the very least search Rima's room. Really, the only thing that could be said in Rima's favor was that she was too obvious.

(2)

Even minus Thomas Grand, Wit's End had no shortage of tiny corpses. Over the next few days Rima found: *The Box-Top Murders,* poison in the breakfast cereal; *One of Us,* rattler in the medicine chest; and *The Widow Reed,* weed whacker in the hedges. *The Widow Reed* was a particularly grisly dollhouse, bits of tiny gore on the leaves in the garden and on the flagstones of the walkway. Rima was ashamed to remember that this had been one of her favorites among Addison's books; she hadn't pictured the body quite so chewed. Addison had the *Widow Reed* dollhouse in the formal dining room.

What Rima didn't find: the dollhouse for *Ice City;* the tickets she'd been given for the leashless dogs; the first page of the onionskin letter.

She *had* managed to find another onionskin letter that appeared to be from the same woman:

21200 Old Santa Cruz Hwy
Holy City, California 95026
May 4, 1983

Dear Maxwell Lane:

Expect you got my letter of April 20th even though you didn't respond. I meant no insult, hope none was taken. Expect you are just real busy with your crime solving. Me, I feed the cats (did I mention I have twenty-two of them?), let the ones outside in, put the ones inside out, repeat, repeat, repeat until the sun goes down. Drop by anytime, is what I tell people. Here I'll be.

Looked at the book again, by the way, since I wrote. It just doesn't seem like your others. Not in a bad way, but it unsettles me. Like maybe my copy is missing a chapter.

Of course, I'm no detective. Probably you got it right, after all. You read people real well, and no one's ever accused me of the same. Would I be here if I did? I've always liked you, but you probably aren't impressed by that. You've always been too hard on yourself. You couldn't have known what would happen.

I might write you again. Don't worry about answering. You're probably real busy.

VTY,

Constance Wellington

And a postcard, handwritten and signed with the same name in the same hand. The script was New Palmer. Rima had no idea how she knew that. The postmark was July 6, 1976:

Regarding my letter of July 2, you know how cats sometimes engage in heroic battles with imaginary enemies? Am persuaded I've done the same. Please disregard.

The picture was of a musical group identified in a cursive made of ropes and lassos as the Watsonville Cowboy Wranglers.

As for the *Ice City* dollhouse, there was still the whole second floor in which to look, and Addison's studio. But Rima decided to shortcut the process and asked Tilda outright if she knew where it was. "I can't ever keep straight which one goes with which book," Tilda told her. "They're all just dust to me."

"There would probably be a cat," Rima said, which didn't help; Tilda claimed there were lots with cats, even though Rima had yet to find a single one. Tilda didn't appear to like the dollhouses or want to talk about them, so Rima didn't press her.

She wouldn't have asked Addison, though she couldn't have said why. Rima had expected that she and Addison would talk about Rima's father. It had seemed inevitable, in light of his recent death, that Addison would reminisce. Rima had steeled herself for this. Now that it wasn't happening, she longed for it. When she ate with Addison, there were lots of silences between them. They might have been awkward silences, or they might have been companionable. How did you tell the difference?

Addison's main mode of conversation was to tell stories. She was, as you would expect, quite good at it, but there was a polish, a sense of practice that, no matter how intimate the content, kept Addison behind glass. Tilda told stories too, and she was terrible.

She always left out some crucial piece and had to go back and add it later. "Did I say he was blind?" "Did I tell you they were identical twins?" "Did I say they were on horseback?"

Rima was surprisingly comfortable at Wit's End. She loved her room. She loved looking at the ocean. The night before, among the ticking clock, the rattling shade, the pulse of waves, and a distant train, she'd imagined she heard someone walking in the attic above her bed, somewhere in the vicinity of the Bim shoe box, and even this noise was comforting, as if someone—Maxwell Lane, maybe, or maybe the woman from the Donner Party—was watching over her. She'd fallen asleep imagining those circling footsteps. If Wit's End was haunted, it was haunted by her own people. Her tribe. Survivors.

Assuming she was surviving. Sometimes it seemed too close to call. Addison had told a story over lunch, a story Rima already knew. There'd been a time in her life when she did her best to find and read every interview Addison gave, and this story had appeared in those interviews often. It was the Mystery of A. B. Early.

When Addison told it, the story wasn't explicitly directed at Rima; in fact, it came up with regard to Tilda's son, Martin, and how Tilda had been absent for so much of his life. But something in the way Addison looked at Rima, just quickly and sideways when she finished, made Rima suspect she was the target audience.

(3)

The story started with Addison's mother, a little robin of a woman with sentimental ideas about children and their delightful imaginations. Addison recounted the triumph of a dinner party at which she'd told her mother's guests that she thought that every time a child made a wish and blew out the birthday candles, those same candles relit in heaven as stars. That the stars were the birthday candles of every child who'd ever lived, which is why you could wish on them too. She was six at the time. Her mother had been so enchanted that Addison was often called on to repeat the performance; she was all of twelve before it was finally retired.

Even at six Addison had known that she was pretending to be more childlike than she was and that the stars were nothing of the sort. A child's imagination is such a beautiful place, her mother used to say, but it was also, in her opinion, a public place. What are you thinking, little Miss Sunny Day? she persisted in asking Addison. Why that face? Why that tone? Why so quiet? No secrets allowed.

This put Addison in a difficult position. Her mother wished her to be thinking of fairies and dewdrops, but she was already the knives-and-curses type. You can tell me anything, her mother used to say, and then respond to anything she was told with disappointment or alarm. So Addison was compelled into a life of deceit and charade, which is what always happens whenever honesty is forced upon someone.

And yet this same mother had a secret so big. When Addison was in high school, she came home one evening after a planning session for the Model UN—her team had been assigned Sweden—to an awkward dinner at which she was told that her father wished to get married. And not to her mother. In fact, he couldn't marry her mother, because they were brother and sister.

Apparently (it took some time for Addison to piece this

together; she was in shock, and no one there managed a linear narrative), apparently, he'd come to live with her mother to help out during the pregnancy, and since they shared a last name and there was a baby on the way, people had made certain assumptions, which he was too gallant to contradict. But now he'd fallen in love with a court stenographer he'd met at the library, in the travel and adventure section, and he felt the years he'd already given to his sister's reputation were maybe sufficient. "Nothing will change with us," he'd assured Addison. "You'll always be my girl." The dinner was corned beef, which was Addison's favorite.

"So who's my father?" Addison asked her mother later that evening, when she'd stopped crying.

"Lot's wife," her mother answered, which seemed unlikely. But was her way of warning Addison not to dredge up old news.

And then there was a small wedding, in which Addison was carefully made important, and the couple left on a honeymoon cruise, and everyone, the neighbors, the milkman, Addison's mother's bridge group, but especially Addison's mother, behaved as if they'd never thought he was anything but Addison's uncle. It was an amazing thing to watch. They'd all wheeled in unison like a school of fish.

Addison counted the corned-beef dinner as the first day of her writing career. In her interviews, this was the point of the story. This was the day that her obligation to her mother was canceled and she was free to begin to think up the dreadful books she would someday write. It took her many more years to do so, but from this day on she never pretended again that her imagination was a frolic through the dewdrops. She gave up the Model UN, and the piano too.

In telling the story to Rima and Tilda, her point was a different one. Sometimes something happens to you, she said, and there's no way to be the person you were before. You won't ever be that person again; that person's gone. There's a little freedom in every loss, no matter how unwelcome and unhappy that freedom may be.

You have to think of it like a reincarnation. One life ends.

Another begins.

Chapter Six

(1)

There was a bonfire on the beach, and near it, three kids, two male (one black, one white) and one female (white). The boys were reenacting something—a scene from a movie or a video game, something maybe with swords, but also kung fu. The black kid wore a long coat that flapped around his legs. The boys moved in slow motion through an intricate set of maneuvers with much stopping, restarting, and arguing, while the girl watched them both, and Rima watched all three from her bedroom window above.

It was just past sunset, and Rima thought these kids should be getting home. She thought that if she were a vampire, these were just the kids she'd be looking for. She thought they were probably just about the same age as the ones she used to teach history to, back before Oliver died. The black kid in particular reminded her of Leroy Sheppard, who'd once told Rima that teaching black children about slavery was just one more way to keep them down. Planned and executed as such. Not that he was accusing Rima; he could see she was just a tool.

The sea was an indigo blue. Rima was becoming a connoisseur of Pacific colors—a pale, translucent blue near the shore at dawn, but a silvered blue farther out, and the color of sunrise reflected on the sheen of the sand; green waves on a sunny afternoon, though purple in the shade of the dredge, throwing white water into the air; indigo after the sun set and then black, but with lights playing over the surf in small, unexpected reds, greens, and yellows. There was a great deal to see, even at night.

And to hear too. It was Friday evening, and over the sound of the ocean, at reasonably regular intervals, Rima heard the screams of people on the roller coasters. It was a puzzlingly pleasant addition to the score. Except that Rima was just grabbing her coat and would miss it all.

It had been Addison's idea that Rima go out for an evening with Scorch and Cody. Addison was concerned that Rima was spending so much time in her room. Sixty-four years old herself, Addison had the impression that the age gap between Rima at twenty-nine and Scorch and Cody at twenty-one and twenty-two, respectively, was not great—an impression not shared by Rima, Scorch, or Cody.

Rima agreed to go, regretted agreeing, tried to renege, saying that she was still on Ohio time and couldn't make a late night of it (which was even true but caused a fuss, so that she regretted reneging), agreed again to go, though somewhat more resentfully. She would rather have stayed in, read some more of Maxwell's letters, a few pages of *Ice City,* sat and looked out the window, which someone should be doing, because there was always a chance the woman from the beach would reappear. Perhaps she'd be good enough to wear the same green sweater, so that Rima could recognize her.

Addison had given Scorch money for the cover charge and the first round of drinks. This was not quite paying Scorch to take Rima out, but it was just as well that Rima knew nothing about it.

What Addison didn't know was that Rima and Scorch were feeling awkward with each other. Rima had done an online search of obese dachshunds, with such distressing results—crippled legs, broken backs—that she'd forced herself to speak to Scorch about the poached-egg breakfast. Scorch had agreed instantly that of course she was in the wrong, of course it had to stop, and she was so very sorry and would never do it again and was really, really sorry, and would Rima please consider not telling Addison, which Rima had never planned to do, so on the surface everything was fine, only clearly Scorch was still uncomfortable, Rima was still uncomfortable, and the dogs were in shock. They hadn't yet figured out that Rima was to blame, but surely that was simply a matter of time.

While Rima was having this horrid conversation with Scorch, Tilda was moving Miss Time from Rima's nightstand to the first-floor bathroom. She put the tableau by the sink, since there was already a murder scene—*Chain Stitch,* man strangled with the unfinished sleeve of a hand-knitted sweater (and really, you'd think there'd be more hand-knitted-sweater murders)—on a shelf by the guest towels.

Rima hadn't asked for Miss Time to be moved, although she'd

not said not to move her either. What this meant to Rima was that Tilda could and would go into her room without invitation. It made the bedroom less of a sanctuary, but less of a sanctuary in a dusted, mopped, sheets-freshly-washed kind of way. Rima's feelings about the intrusion were mixed.

Meanwhile, the nightstand was surprisingly bare. Tilda had left a vase with dried flowers, but if you stopped and thought about it for even a moment, the flowers were deader than Miss Time had ever been.

Martin arrived while Rima was upstairs getting her coat. She met him on the stairs, she going down, he going up to leave his duffel in the *Our Better Angels* bedroom. He was taller than Oliver, but the same height as Rima, if she stood a step higher. "You must be the famous Rima," he said. "I'm Martin. Tilda's boy," and there was nothing in his tone to suggest this was sarcastic, though Rima felt that it must have been.

Martin was wearing a pair of expensive sunglasses on the top of his head. He took them off and his hair fell into his face—his mother's hair, dark brown and straight. Martin also had a postage-stamp patch of hair under his lower lip. There was a name for that, but it wasn't a moustache, it wasn't a beard, it wasn't a goatee, and Rima couldn't remember what it was called. She herself didn't pay more than twenty-five dollars for sunglasses as a matter of policy; she wondered that anyone would. In her experience expensive sunglasses seldom went home with the girl who'd brought them.

"I've invited myself along tonight. I'm just going to dump my stuff," Martin said, "and I'll be right down."

They went in Scorch's car, an old maroon Saturn. The backseat was littered with discarded clothes as if Scorch changed there often. There was a red bra printed with white hearts on the floor by Rima's foot, and a matching pair of panties on the back window ledge, flung there, perhaps, on some happier occasion, because on this one Scorch and Cody appeared to be having a fight. He turned on the CD player; she snapped it off. He lowered his window so the ends of his piratical bandanna fluttered in the wind. She promptly raised it.

The car curved between the ocean and the lake, which, Rima had recently learned, most people called the lagoon in spite of the beach's being Twin Lakes State Beach. The moon was behind them, round and white as bone. Martin pointed it out to Rima, framed in the back window above the heart-print underwear. "Wolf moon," he said. He howled and shook out his hair. "Damn, I'm in a good mood. Is everyone in a good mood?"

Silence in the car.

"Then you *get* in a good mood," he said. "I can't do this alone." He stretched his arm along the backseat so that his fingers were near Rima's neck. He drummed them briefly. "Addison's your godmother," he said.

"Yes," said Rima.

"Your fairy godmother," and Rima didn't know where Martin was going with that. It seemed to her there were multiple possibilities, none of them meant to be nice, even though he was smiling nicely at her. She decided not to respond.

They tried three parking lots before they found a place down by the river, and then had to walk several blocks through the downtown. They passed the Santa Cruz clown—a man in pink clown shoes, pink clown pants, and twirling a pink umbrella. His cheeks were painted with pink circles and he had an extremely unsettling smile on his face. No one but Rima appeared to notice him, though he would have been very eye-catching in Cleveland.

Everyone else was dressed as if it were cold out. Scorch and Martin found themselves in absolute, delightful agreement that it was crazy fucking cold. Scorch gave Martin her hand so he could see how cold *that* was, and Martin put her hand on his chest inside his jacket—it was so cold, he said, he was afraid fingers would be lost if drastic measures weren't taken—and then, partly because Cody was looking off to the side and saying nothing, Rima told them both to go to Ohio for a winter and cowboy up.

The bar was upstairs in a building with no sign on the street to suggest it. They passed through a lobby of faded gaud with gold-flecked red wallpaper, a dusty chandelier, and a wall of headshots—a bouquet of Miss Santa Cruzes from the 1930s, the 1940s, the Marilyn Monroe 1950s. Rima followed Scorch's shoes—metallic gold sneakers with green laces—up the stairs and into the heat of the crowded bar.

Scorch and Cody were greeted by name. They produced no IDs, and none was asked for, while Rima's and Martin's were examined with care. Before she was allowed inside, Rima was tested on her birth year, which fortunately she did know, and then they all got to stamp their own hands with a stamp of their own choosing, though the selection was limited to moody pigs. Scorch's pig was wistful, Rima's was angry. Martin's was lovelorn. Cody's was the same as Martin's, only on his hand it looked conspiratorial.

Over Rima's protests, Scorch insisted on paying the cover for everyone. The room was noisy enough to make talking difficult, and it smelled of hops, pot, and sweat. One seat at the bar was vacant. This was given to Rima while Cody went to see if there were any empty seats farther in. Having failed, he returned and bought Rima a glass of red wine, a Tanqueray Collins for Scorch, and something on tap for himself and Martin. He stood, leaning against the bar on one side of Rima. Martin and Scorch were on the other, Martin so close to Rima that her head was touching the green corduroy sleeve of his jacket.

There was live music—a band called Control Your Dog with a throaty female vocalist and a powerful bass—so the rest of the evening took place in shouts between songs. "If I've got it coming, give it to me," the vocalist sang. "Don't take me something something down to something you."

Final chord, sustained finish, and then Martin leaned across Rima to Cody. "You in the doghouse, man?"

"He knows what he did," Scorch said. There was loud laughter in another part of the bar. "You can all go fuck yourselves," someone was saying at a table to Rima's left, while the man on the other side of Cody said something about love, which he thought was either unconditional or wasn't, Rima couldn't hear enough to know. Later in the evening she would realize with surprise that he'd been talking about God.

"Just tell her you're sorry," Martin said. "You're better off being wrong than being right."

"Like an apology just fixes everything. Like it's some fucking delete button," and Scorch was still talking, but Rima couldn't hear any more of that either, Control Your Dog was revving up for another song. "Dorsal pie down on a quiet street," the vocalist sang, or maybe Rima had misheard the words.

(2)

Several songs and a drink later:

Martin was talking into Scorch's ear. Cody had joined the conversation on the other side of Rima, the one about unconditional love, but Rima couldn't hear it, so it probably was about something else by now. Someone at the table on the left was being told to fuck himself, but in an affectionate way.

When Martin saw that Rima was watching, the music fading, he raised his head and his voice. "It takes money to make money, is what I'm saying," he told her. "Fact of life. Sad fact of life. You've got to have some kind of stake to start with. Maybe it doesn't have to be money. Something. Take Addison. With a little initiative she wouldn't even have to write her own books anymore. She could get someone else to write them, share the profits, cash the checks. All because she's got the stake to begin with."

Scorch shook her head so that some of her hair landed on Martin's shoulder. In the bar light, her red hair was black and her pink hair silver. "She's very fussy about Maxwell Lane," Scorch said. "She'd never let anyone else have him," and then there was another song, a song in which someone Rima was never able to identify killed himself with car exhaust, which you would think would be a quiet song, but wasn't, and when it ended, Scorch picked the conversation right back up as if there'd been no interruption. "Like she's always going nuts about the fanfic. Especially the sex stuff."

It was the evening's first mention of sex, and it came in a shout and it came from a sexy young woman. Those men close enough to hear stopped their own conversations. The air thickened. "What sex stuff?" Rima asked.

"Oh my god!" Scorch said. As she'd drunk and danced and drunk some more, she'd been shedding clothes. There was a small pile of them now under Rima's stool, and Scorch was down to a backless tank top, her shoulders and the tops of her breasts sparkling. She was dressed for ice dancing, except for the shoes. "You haven't read it? Maxwell Lane sex fantasies. Written by fans and posted like all over the Internet. Tons of them. Very explicit, but sort of soft-focus too."

Rima had never heard of fanfic, but she could see how Maxwell would prompt fantasies. As a young man, he'd been an FBI informant and done some things that haunted him; betrayal and bad faith were his particular issues. There he was, all alone, so tortured by his past. Addison was practically begging for it.

"I hear it's all written by women," Martin said. "So I don't get why so much of it is man on man."

"I think it's often written by gay women," Scorch said.

"But see, that doesn't clarify things."

"A ton of it is Maxwell and Bim," Scorch said.

It was the evening's first mention of sex with Rima's father. Rima's glass was empty. She waved the bartender over, but it took too long, so when Martin wasn't looking, she helped herself to his beer, just until her own drink came.

Second set, three drinks down:

"Until the cat walks in," the vocalist sang, or maybe, "Only the fat wax on." Followed by, "You love you love you love you." Scorch was talking to Martin, fast, the way she usually talked, but with an excess of enunciation clearly aimed at Cody. "So he's taking this class in primate behavior," she said, "and suddenly we're all laid bare, you know, everything we do, he knows what it means. What it really means, not what *we* think we're doing, not what we *mean* to do, god no, it's all status and display or alliance or intimidation or accommodation. And I'm sorry, but it's fucking annoying, is what it is. So tonight, I'm getting dressed, and I ask him, Am I a high-status female? He's been going on about high-status females, so I ask, Am I one of those? Of course, it's not really, Am I a high-status female? so much as, Do you, my so-called boyfriend, do you see me as a high-status female?"

"Dude." Martin turned to Cody. "I'm surprised you could get that one wrong."

"I didn't," Cody said.

"That's what he says now. That he said yes. That he said definitely, definitely yes. But first he laughed. That was his very first answer, that was his real answer, spontaneous laughing."

Cody seemed to Rima to be the sort that, in a fight, outlasted rather than overwhelmed. "You're so far above me, baby," Cody said. "I can't even see you from where I am."

Scorch set her drink down and turned to Rima. "You want to go dance?"

"Alliance-building with a high-status female," Cody said. He put a hand over his mouth. "Whoa. That just slipped out."

"Rima?" Scorch's voice was hitting the high notes now. "Rima is a high-status female?"

"Look how she has the only seat," Martin said.

(3)

Two songs later, still drink three:

Rima had given Scorch her chair and taken the place next to Martin. He leaned into her. "You think Addison will leave you her money?" he asked.

Rima was so startled she spilled some of her wine onto her pants. She could feel the dampness spreading down her thigh, and sometime during the last set, she'd torn her cocktail napkin into tiny strips for no reason at all. Someone at the table on the left was being told to go fuck himself.

Martin reached across her to grab a napkin. There was the brush of corduroy on Rima's cheek, the smell of him, smoke and euca-lyptus and fabric softener, and his hand pressing on her leg, soak-ing up the wine. "My mother can get that out," he said. He spoke directly into her ear, his breath warm. "She has something for red wine stains, something for white. She's just a wiz at all your pill- and booze-related laundry disasters."

If Rima turned to him, her mouth would be an inch from his. "Why would Addison leave me anything?" she asked.

"Why is, who else does she have? You and my mother."

"Friends. Dogs. Causes. I hardly know her." Rima took another sip, slow this time and careful. Martin's hand had remained on her knee. She shook it off and he straightened up, grinning at her.

"So when did you start listening to me?" the vocalist sang. "Something, something, something me."

"I already have an inheritance," she told him. Control Your Dog was beginning another song, apparently a favorite; the opening lines were greeted with applause. Even with their heads so close together, Rima had to repeat herself twice. She had to shout it before he heard.

"You are so fucking lucky," Martin said.

Drink four or maybe five or maybe, in a better world, still the end of three:

The singer was getting hoarse, but in a good way. "Something something something," she sang, all raw emotion, all open wound. "Something, something." Rima's head was light, and her ears hurt from the loud music. Her throat hurt from all the shouting after talking to almost no one for weeks, or else she was catching Scorch's cold. The night continued in disconnected bursts. Apparently Cody had gone outside to get some air, though Rima hadn't noticed he was gone, and apparently someone he didn't know, someone who hadn't said a word, had shoved him and then taken a swing as he was going down. He hadn't been hit hard, but there'd been a fist with a ring on one finger. Cody's chin was bleeding just slightly. Scorch wiped it with a napkin and disinfected it with vodka and Red Bull.

"Why?" Rima asked. Apparently the question had already been answered, and surely with a longer explanation, because the only parts Scorch was willing to revisit made no sense.

"He's tall," she said. "Guys like to brag how they took a big guy down, and Cody's tall, but he doesn't weigh so much, so he's a big guy, but not a scary big guy. He gets hit a lot." She took the napkin off Cody's chin to look at the cut, then put the napkin back. "Of course, it could be racism."

Someone was surprised at the suggestion. It might have been Rima. She might have said so.

"He's black," Scorch said. "You mean to tell me you don't see that?"

"I see it." Rima felt oddly guilty, as if there would be something racist in not recognizing a black man when you saw one. She looked at Cody again. He had dark eyes, teeth so white that in the dark bar they were faintly green. His arms were wrapped around Scorch and there was a Chinese ideogram tattooed on the back of his left shoulder. He could have been a lot of things. Black wouldn't have been her first guess. Rima thought they needed to talk more about the fact that someone had, just out of the blue, hit him in the face, but now Scorch and Cody were kissing, open-mouthed, tongue to tongue, so that some of her sparkly body lotion had rubbed onto his face and hands, plus the next song was starting and there was just no way.

Not so much later:

Martin's voice, dipping into Rima's ear. "Has anyone ever told you you have cat's eyes?"

Rima turned and was surprised to find his eyes looking so directly into hers. "Okay, then," she said. "Martin. You have to stop flirting with me. I have a little brother your age," and the minute she said it, she remembered it wasn't true. She started to cry, and it was not the silent-tears-on-her-face sort of crying, but the great gulping, full-body, nose-running sort everyone was bound to notice.

Scorch had been lost in the music. Now she gave Martin a look designed to turn him to stone. "What did you say to her?" she asked, and if he was sharing that bit about the cat's eyes, Rima didn't hear it.

"Nothing," he said. "Jesus."

"Come on," Scorch told Rima, who took one step in her direction, the toe of her shoe hooking the sleeve of Scorch's discarded coat. Instead of catching herself, she panicked and capsized completely. She landed in the arms of some guy she didn't know, but later she thought she remembered that he'd tried to pick her up earlier in the evening.

Careening drunkenly into his lap was a classic mixed signal.

Chapter Seven

(1)

I n a good bar, toilets are second in importance only to the liquor itself, and there should be lots of them. This bar had just two, though there were more downstairs, or so Scorch shouted through the door on the many occasions over the next twenty minutes in which someone knocked. Rima was sitting on the toilet lid blowing her nose. Scorch stood at the sink, putting her hair into lots of small braids, pasting the unruly ends together with soap from the dispenser.

Rima was trying to explain about Oliver, how her dad's death had been horrible, of course, but expected and, by the time it came, something of a relief to both him and her. When she was younger, he'd traveled a great deal. In those days, he seemed less like family and more like the circus coming to town. After her mother died, he'd come home to stay and been a good father, an involved father, a dependable father. Even so, family to Rima would always be Oliver.

The night after her mother's death, Rima and Oliver had to stay with the Whitsons, neighbors across the street, because their father had been covering a trial in the Netherlands and couldn't get home any faster. Rima remembered how, when her father had arrived with his suitcases, his eyes red, his face unshaven, she and Oliver had been sitting at the Whitsons' breakfast table. "Are you staying for dinner?" Oliver had asked, meticulously polite, as if he didn't care about the answer at all. He'd been eleven years old then.

Mrs. Whitson hadn't let them sleep together—they were too old for that, she said—and she'd made Oliver stay in the TV room all by himself while Rima took Becky Whitson's bed, with Becky in a sleeping bag on the floor. Becky was four at the time, and she'd cried because Rima not only wouldn't play Chutes and Ladders with her the way she did when she babysat, but told her that she hated Chutes and Ladders, had always hated it, that she would never, ever play it again.

Which she never did, exactly, except that when Oliver was fourteen, he made a whole new board (but used the old spinner) for a game he called Shaker Heights High Chutes and Ladders. There was a chute for mean girls in the hall, one for a pimple on the end of your nose, one for a stupid question you asked in class that made everyone laugh. But most of the chutes involved your father's saying something sadly quotable about you in his newspaper column; there were so many of these that the game was all but impossible to win.

This was mere solidarity on Oliver's part. When he did appear

in their dad's column, he appeared as he was—high-spirited, generous, original. No doubt Rima also appeared as she was. Whose
fault was it that Rima as she was looked so much worse than Oliver
as he was? She missed her father desperately, but she didn't miss
the columns in which she'd starred, saying things she hadn't said,
or sometimes had, only they'd been horribly misunderstood or
else they were accurate but meant to be confidential. Now there
was only Rima, private citizen. Now only Rima lived to tell the tale.
If there could be said to be a bright spot anywhere, this was it.

The Shaker Heights High board was still in a closet in her
father's house, with the Sorry and Parcheesi and Trivial Pursuit.
Someday Rima would have to deal with all the things in all those
closets.

None of this was what she told Scorch. Instead, in the moments
between people's knocking on the door, she said that her father's
death, being what it was and pretty awful all by itself, had also
reminded her of Oliver's death—too painful to be comprehended
at the time and therefore still seeping in slowly, even though four
whole years had passed. "Everything was better with Oliver,"
Rima said, and she was crying again, because, unbelievable as it
sounded, the rest of Rima's life had to be lived in its lesser, no-
Oliver form. No one would ever call her Irma again unless she
made them. "The thing people don't understand about grief,"
Rima said, "is you don't just feel sad. You feel crazy." She was
choking on her own breath when she said this, so there was no
way she didn't sound as crazy as she felt.

Death was death, she went on, and reminded you of nothing so
much as death, though her father's had happened over time, with
time to think about it, while Oliver had been gone in a minute,

killed a mile from his house by a drunk driver, so that Rima had even heard the sirens and not known whom they were for.

Scorch leaned closer into the mirror, turning her head from side to side to see the braids she'd made out of soap and hair. "Wasn't the drunk driver Oliver?" she asked.

Rima felt as if, out of the blue, she'd been punched in the gut. This was not the way she liked to tell the story.

And just that quickly she was ready to go back to Wit's End and her solitary room on the floor she had been promised would be all hers, and was now sharing with Martin. She offered to get a cab, but everyone else was willing to call it a night too, especially Scorch, who had to be back at Addison's in a few hours to walk the dogs.

Cody had had only two beers, and those at the beginning of the evening. He had stopped drinking so that someone would be sober enough to drive home. Scorch told Rima this in a careful, expressionless voice, as if she had no point to make by it.

The road home was dark, no moon, no bonfires on the beach, just the green light from the little lighthouse floating over the black ocean, and a bright window in Rima's bedroom at Wit's End, where she must have forgotten to turn the light off.

It wasn't until Rima was getting out of the car that she thought to ask how it was that Scorch knew how Oliver had died.

"I read it on Addison's blog," Scorch said.

(2)

Rima could see Addison's wireless on her laptop in her bedroom, but no one had given her the key, and until someone did, she was stuck with her own server and the intolerable dial-up. She wouldn't have connected if she hadn't really needed to see Addison's blog and needed to see it now. She brushed her teeth, and when she came back the site had only just finished loading.

www.maxwellane.com/Earlydays
Halloween photos posted. To be honest, we forgot to take them on Halloween, so we had a quick reprise. Berkeley's the one dressed as a spider. Little Stanford is Spider-Man. That's our lovely houseguest Rima in the background, fallen asleep on the couch and dreaming, no doubt, of masked wiener dogs. As one so often does.

http://ScorchedEarth.livejournal
I like Rima, and I feel for her and all—I wouldn't want to lose my parents, even though they annoy me sometimes, but everyone I love annoys me sometimes, yes THIS MEANS YOU, but I'm sorry, I just don't get what makes her a high status female. She's got money I guess, but she didn't really do anything for it except stay alive longer than anyone else. Before that, she was a junior high history teacher, and maybe she

was really good at it, I could see that, but
would it be high status even if she was?

And I think she's in deep denial about her
brother who got drunk one night and drove his
car off the road and into a wall. How much worse
would it be if he'd killed someone else instead
of himself? I mean, I am sorry for her, really
really sorry, but I think it's important to
remember that it could have been worse. A kid in
my high school got drunk and he hit a car with
three other people in it and all of them died.

Tonight she got seriously wasted, and maybe
this was just something she needed to do or
maybe drinking problems run in the family. I
really hope not, because I do like her and I
hope it doesn't sound like I don't.

(Link to www.maxwellane.com/Earlydays where
there is a picture of Rima sleeping on the
couch.)

http://www.maximumlane.com/maxbim/fireandicecity.txt
"You don't have to be alone," Bim told Maxwell,
so softly he wasn't sure Maxwell heard him. But
when he moved his hands, slowly as if he
expected to be stopped at any moment, down
Maxwell's arms to his waist, undoing his belt,
unzipping his pants, slipping first one hand and
then the other inside, he found Maxwell's cock
expecting him. "You never have to be alone

again. Neither of us does. All you have to say
is yes.
   "Or if that's too much, just don't say no."

(3)

Rima dreamt that Maxwell Lane was kissing her. He was nothing
close to seventy-two years old. She felt his breath on her cheek,
his tongue moving nearer to her mouth. It was all so real she
opened her eyes to find that she was, in fact, not sleeping alone.

Pressed against her right thigh was a furry lump she assumed
was a dog, since a second dog was draped over her neck, thoroughly licking her face. Which made the dream an extremely
embarrassing one, especially when she recalled that this same
man had been reaching for her father's cock in some online sex
fantasy just the night before. Was that what inspired the dream?
Something to seriously not think about.

The room was warm, and the dog on Rima's neck was damp
with her own sweat. Rima moved her (him?) aside and saw that it
was Berkeley; Berkeley's fur, she had figured out, was slightly
darker and curlier than Stanford's. She put her other hand under
the covers and felt around until she found Stanford's little bony
rump.

It was a puzzle, the dogs' being here. She hadn't thought they
liked her all that much. Plus, it meant, it must mean, that she
had left her bedroom door open, which she never did, and
would she have, last night of all nights, with Martin just down
the hall?

Besides, it was a high bed. The dogs could never have gotten into it without help. Maybe one could have stood with its front paws on the bed frame while the other scaled its back in some unlikely dachshund Cirque de Soleil, but even then there would be only one dog in her bed, not two. So either she had reached down and helped them up while she slept or someone else had tiptoed in and planted them in her bed. The latter didn't seem likely, until you remembered that she was living with people who thought nothing of posting your picture on the Internet without your knowledge or permission and were therefore capable of anything. (To be fair, it was mainly a picture of dogs; Rima had been barely visible in the background. Out of focus and covered with a chenille throw. Still.)

If Rima had been hoisting dachshunds into her bed last night, what else might she have done all drunk and unaware? She had a taste in her mouth like stewed Band-Aids. Her head was heavy and far too large, and the sun in the room seemed at best unnecessary, at worst malicious. She had to pee, and she had the niggling sense that something bad had happened, which she thought at first was explained by the blogs, her Sleeping Beauty picture, and her father's appearance in flagrante delicto with Maxwell Lane, but then she remembered she'd had a breakdown over Oliver. Scorch had said something mean about him. When Rima remembered what she'd said, it wasn't mean so much as true, though really, what could be meaner than that?

Oliver had had a wild side, which Rima admired and encouraged. Loved. If Oliver had been along last night, he would have picked up the clown early in the evening and partied with the band after. Oliver always maintained that it was a sad night when you couldn't even manage to party with the band. Rima remembered something his high school counselor had told her. It would be better for Oliver in the long run, she'd said, if we weren't all so charmed by him.

Oliver would be alive today if he'd had a proper mother instead of Rima to raise him.

Something was happening downstairs, something only a dog could hear, and suddenly both dogs were awake and alert, places to go, people to see. Rima lifted them down, and they raced for the sure-enough wide-open door, the hall, the stairs, yapping hysterically. She got up to use the bathroom and noted that she was in the clothes she'd worn the night before. Only her shoes were missing. She hoped she hadn't left them at the bar.

She brushed her teeth, combed her hair, changed her clothes, and readied herself to face the breakfast table, but this proved to be a false start and she went back to bed instead. Maybe she could sleep some more, dream about Maxwell Lane again, but she didn't and she didn't.

The next time she got up, the morning was over. She looked under the bed for her shoes, which weren't there, but she found a piece of paper, which she pulled out and read.

November 3, 2006
130 East Cliff Drive
Santa Cruz, CA 95060

Dear Ms. Constance Wellington,
    A few days ago, while poking about in my attic, I came across your old letters. This is long, long overdue, but I

wanted you to know that you were right to believe in Bim Lanisell's innocence all those years ago. He was eventually completely cleared. In this case, you were the better detective and I am

humbly yours,
Maxwell Lane

What a busy evening Maxwell had had! Rima might have almost suspected the hidden presence of a twelve-step program in his life. Step nine: Unfinished business. But the handwriting was her own. What else had she done last night, all drunk and unaware? She had written a letter.

In fact, she remembered writing it now, how it had all been done in a burst of drunken merriment. It was deeply unsettling to remember that she'd been drunk and merry, however briefly. Surely that wasn't a good combination. Surely that wasn't a good look for her.

By the time she made it to the kitchen, Scorch had come and gone, the dogs had been to the beach and back. Addison and Tilda had eaten breakfast and also lunch. Martin's door was shut when Rima passed, so she thought he was still sleeping, but it turned out he'd already left. Tilda, who'd hoped for dinner with him the night before and breakfast with him this morning, who'd shopped with that in mind—lamb chops with crushed mint, mashed potatoes with garlic and cheddar, eggs with chorizo—was hiding her disappointment by telling Addison about an article she'd read at the dentist's. According to this article, dying has its own smell. Not death, not the finished product, but the process of dying. The article said that someone named Burton could be taken through a hospital ward and could pick out those patients who would die, considerably before their doctors made the call.

"Did I say that Burton was a dog?" Tilda asked. "A bluetick hound." This was the sort of information Tilda could be predicted to like—mystical, but faintly scientific, and with animals. *There is a larger world than you allow, Mr. Lane.*

Rima liked it less. Was there a household anywhere, she wondered, in which death and murder were discussed more often at meals than in this one? The *Spook Juice* dollhouse minus its corpse had been moved accusingly to the kitchen counter. Rima had to reach over it to put in her toast, which she did, then waited, while Addison and Tilda bickered amiably about whether a mystery writer would be more suited to solving a murder (Tilda's position) or committing one (Addison's), until the toast popped up behind the dollhouse roof like the morning sun.

She joined Addison and Tilda at the table. "This is why conservatives so love a good mystery book," Tilda was saying in an aggressive non sequitur. She was in the mood for a fight and didn't care with whom. "It's the bald-faced fantasy that the world is run by competent adults." She looked closely then at Rima, leapt up in a competent-adult way. "I have just the tea for you," she said. "A cleansing tea. A great morning-after tea."

It was a hit-and-run. Nothing insulted Addison as reliably as being called conservative. She had given countless speeches to countless gatherings of mystery writers and readers arguing this very point. Why, then, did people persist in making it? But she was too pleased to have Martin gone to rise to the bait. The shock to her was not that he had left so early, but that he had stayed the night in the first place. He'd never done that before, and she'd no idea he ever would. If asked, she would have described Martin as a tireless critic. Or a tiresome one. Martin's life was clotted with utterly predictable disappointments that took him completely by surprise.

Rima was staring into her teacup. Something Tilda had said reminded Rima of something else, and she was trying to chase it down, but the tea distracted her. She was not looking into the tidy sort of cup a tea bag produced. Bits of twig and bird nest were floating on an oily surface. This was serious tea, and Rima respected that, while feeling no desire to drink it. She raised her head again.

Addison was looking very businesslike this morning in a black sweatshirt from Powell's Books Portland and with her gray hair brushed straight back. "Did you young people have a nice time last night?" she asked.

"You can read all about it on Scorch's blog," Rima said. She meant this to be a bit rude. If Addison looked at Scorch's blog she'd know that Rima had seen the link to her own. But the minute the words were out, Rima worried that she'd sounded just as rude as she'd intended. She didn't want Addison to think she was ungrateful. She wasn't ready to be sent back to Ohio. "The band was good and loud. Control Your Dog," she added, hoping to soften things. Which was probably more bewildering than mitigating, but it didn't matter because Addison had stopped at the main point anyway.

"Scorch has a blog?" She turned to Tilda, who shrugged to

show her innocent ignorance. "Everyone turns out to be a writer," Addison said. "Why? Why must everyone write?"

"Control Your Dog was the name of the band," Rima said, as if someone had asked.

"Why can't they just read? There are so many very good books, already written. Written and published. I could recommend any number. Is she posting about me?"

"Me. She must have logged on the minute she got home."

"I won't hire someone if I know they're writing," Addison said. "I once had a handyman who sold pictures of my bedroom to the tabloids. What little privacy I have, I value."

"Who wouldn't?" said Rima.

"I'll have to speak to Scorch." Addison spread a spoonful of lime marmalade over a piece of wheat toast. The bed hadn't even been made when the pictures were taken, and she still remembered the accompanying headline. "Where Maxwell Lane Gets It On." It must have happened during that week or so when disco was king. She didn't remember this; she deduced it from the finger-snapping faux hipness of the headline.

"Would anyone know anything about Margo Dumas's sex life if she hadn't had that assistant who forwarded those e-mails?" Addison asked.

Margo Dumas wrote novels involving ancient Rome and time travel. Rima had read one once. Beyond the fact that Dumas liked to detail the oddly mixed sensations of buttoned-up modern career women ravished by ancient emperors and gladiators, Rima knew nothing of her sex life. Probably the question had been rhetorical.

The three women sat in silence. Addison was thinking about

Scorch's blog. Diaries used to be private things—that was the whole point. They came with those little keys so that *no one would read them.* When and why had they turned into performance art?

Tilda was thinking this was probably not the moment to tell Addison she was writing a memoir. Time enough for this confession after it was published. It was mostly about being on the street anyway. Addison would hardly be in the book at all. Though it would be nice if she blurbed it.

Rima took a sip of her tea, but it was still too hot and burned her tongue. The sun came into the room through the screen of fig leaves. The color of that rippling light gave Rima the sense of being trapped in amber, the three of them breathing more and more slowly as the air around them thickened. A hundred years from now they would be found in just these postures.

And then this end-of-the-world scenario was suddenly too comforting, so she re-created all three of them from their DNA—hangover, scalded tongue, hand with half-washed angry-pig stamp, and all—and forced them to live again.

(4)

In fact, Rima was pretty comfortable with sloth and torpor. It was Oliver who would have minded, Oliver who would have said it was time to get a message out. Which is why, when Kenny Sullivan arrived, Rima had the letter from Maxwell stamped, addressed, and ready to be taken. Rima never could deny Oliver anything if he really wanted it.

Of course the minute the letter was irretrievably gone, Rima

wished it back. It occurred to her belatedly that Oliver's judg-
ments were not a sound foundation for her own actions. He was,
after all, in a spectacular lapse of judgment, dead.

But the letter did not really trouble her. What were the odds
that Constance Wellington was still at the same address? What were
the odds that she was even alive? The letter would be coming back
on its own soon enough; Rima just had to make sure she was the
one it came back to. If only all lapses could be so inconsequential.

Take the lapse of her missing shoes. They had been found in
Martin's room. They had been found in Martin's room by Martin's
mother. Tilda had returned them to Rima's closet without a word,
but Rima's conscience was so entirely clear that she asked where
they'd been, and then things were beyond awkward.

Rima was quite certain that she hadn't slept with Martin, but
when she imagined saying this to Tilda it came out so unpersuasive that she didn't even try. And because she hadn't said it right
away, her denial became increasingly unconvincing until even
Rima herself would not have believed it. She felt that a certain
something—coldness? suspicion? disapproval?—a certain bad
something had entered her relationship with Tilda. The snake
tattoo, which had seemed merely earthy and elemental, now had
fangs.

Once the shoes had been found, she remembered taking them
off. Undoing the laces had proved difficult, and going to bed with
her shoes on unthinkable, so she'd asked Martin for help, only he
couldn't untie them either. He'd cut the laces with a little blue
Swiss Army knife he carried on his key chain. Would Rima remember that the knife was blue, but not remember that they'd had
sex? She thought not.

"Thus do I loose all Gordian knots," he'd said, which had surprised Rima; she wouldn't have pegged him as a reader. (Though when Rima's students had surprised her like that, it always turned out to be something they'd seen on an episode of *The Simpsons.*) She considered the further possibility that Martin might have also helped her into bed and heaped dachshunds on her after. She was quite moved by the picture; in fact, she felt very friendly toward Martin once she remembered enough to feel so. When he wasn't obsessing about money, he seemed like a nice-enough guy.

He'd already e-mailed her twice, offering to come down and take her out the next weekend. If the weather stayed good, they could go to the boardwalk, he'd said. They could go to something called the Mystery Spot and see a ball roll uphill. Or there was a haunted winery up in the mountains. Martin offered this last with considerable confidence. Rima could see he thought he had her measure, and her measure was a wine-tasting with ghosts. She'd said no just to prove she could. And because of Tilda. And because, what with her father, Oliver, and Maxwell Lane, she felt she had as many men in her life as she could reasonably manage.

Chapter Eight

(1)

Tuesday was Election Day. Rima, Tilda, and Addison stayed up late to see the Democrats take the House, Addison running back and forth the whole time, between the second-floor computer and the television, dachshunds at her heels. Among Addison's close friends, several blamed the absence of a new novel on the delayed shock of having seen the Supreme Court, with no pretense of legal standing, hand George Bush the presidency, and everything that had happened since. There was a list on the refrigerator of the five justices who'd done this, pinned into place with a magnet shaped like a fish, next to the five worst Bush recount outrages. And down from that, the name of every congressperson who'd voted for the Military Commissions Act and the end of democracy in this country. Recently, when Addison was asked when the new novel would be done, she answered that she wouldn't publish again until habeas corpus had been restored. Addison was an intensely political person. She kept lists.

Wednesday morning, in a post-election euphoria, she added an e-mail she'd received on her website to the hall of shame that was her refrigerator door.

"I have always been a fan of yours, but I just read what you wrote on the Huffington Post with all your snotty little remarks denigrating President Bush. So now I know you despise the present administration, and prefer people who are so sleazy and morally bankrupt as to submit to blow jobs in the oval office, raping women, committing adultery, lying under oath, and are so stupid as to ignore the threats to American safety such as the first attack on the World Trade Center.

"I'm sorry you felt it necessary to express your Bush hating aging hippie opinions. I know my comments will mean nothing to you. Liberals never change, but I thank you anyway for revealing yourself. I never have to read you again. I think Maxwell would be just as appalled as I am." It was signed "a fan no more."

"Who says the gracious art of letter-writing is dead?" Addison asked. She was in a magnanimous mood. "You'll see. Food will taste better, jokes will be funnier, even television, even television will be good. All because the Democrats have the power of the subpoena." If only Rima's father had lived to see it!

(If only Oliver had lived to see YouTube. If only Rima's mother had lived to see . . . But that death was so long past, Rima was hard-pressed to think of anything her mother *hadn't* missed.)

They were celebrating. Addison was taking Rima downtown for

a quick congratulatory stop at the bookstore (which was forty years old this month, and Addison remembered every single year. The Loma Prieta quake had leveled it, and Addison had been among the four hundred volunteers who carried the books out of the rubble, but that was a story for another time, or maybe it wasn't, nothing more tiresome than people's quake stories, but anyway, that old rising-from-the-ashes feeling was as powerful today as it had been back then) and then a sushi lunch. Tilda said she couldn't go, she had a thing. Rima was relieved to hear it. It was hard to share raw fish with someone who thought you were a corrupter of impressionable young men.

The scene on the street was joyful. A man on a recumbent bicycle pedaled past. He was shouting like the town crier. "The Ring-bearer has fulfilled his quest! Frodo has destroyed the Ring!"

Addison pointed out a man downtown who would, for a dollar, debate you on any subject you chose, taking whatever position you opposed. His look was eclectic—stained navy pea jacket, deerstalker cap, ski gloves, mirror shades. His nose was purple, his cheeks veined. But he was refusing to argue. "We're all on the same page today," he kept saying. "One day only. Out of business! Tomorrow we'll talk about how the Democrats' taking the House is not the same as the end of the Iraq War." Addison said she'd never before seen him refuse an argument. It was unprecedented.

An a cappella group by the flower stand was leading a singalong of "You're a Grand Old Flag." "Aren't there any Republicans in Santa Cruz?" Rima asked.

"Apparently. They write letters to the editor," Addison said. "And the local results weren't as invigorating as the national.

"But that'll be a cold comfort today. Today you'll recognize the Republicans by the expressions on their faces."

She was wrong about this. The pink clown was just walking by. His umbrella was printed with little ducks, and he was wrapped in a sparkly shawl. His smile was both beatific and scary, but this had nothing to do with the election. Rima had seen exactly the same smile the weekend before. He could easily be a Republican; no one would ever know.

And once again, Rima seemed to be the only one to see him. Perhaps he was a hallucination. A visitation. Her own private clown.

A woman came toward Rima. She had wild wiry red hair and was carrying a string bag with groceries in it—loose carrots, soup cans, dinner rolls. For a moment Rima thought she was the woman from the beach. The nose seemed right, and the red-rimmed eyes, but Rima's suspicions were roused mostly by the way she stared at Addison. Rima almost said something, but then she saw another woman who could have been the woman from the beach. This one had black hair, sticking up from her forehead in spikes. Obviously Rima had no idea what the woman from the beach had looked like, beyond the fact that she was white.

And there were many people staring at Addison. Rima had forgotten how famous Addison was. Now she remembered. A famous writer going into a bookstore in her own hometown was likely to be stared at.

People came out from the stacks and behind their counters to say hello. The quick stop-in stretched to half an hour, then forty minutes, as there were remainders to be found and signed, and these were immediately bought, so they had to be re-signed, but personalized. There was the election to be exulted over, the California results discussed (schizophrenic, they all agreed), and a great many new books to be pointed out and recommended. Plus Rima had to be introduced to everyone. "My goddaughter from Cleveland," Addison said.

Well, Ohio hadn't delivered the complete Democratic rout that had been predicted. Still—a clear winner in the "most improved" category. People in the bookstore were letting bygones be bygones.

By the time Addison finally made it to checkout, she was buying three novels and the selected letters of Martha Gellhorn. There was a small book, more like a pamphlet, faceup on her pile. The clerk, a young woman with two short ponytails on top of her head like teddy-bear ears, picked it up to scan it. Addison stopped her. "I have that one at home," she told Rima, and the clerk set it aside on the counter by Rima's arm.

Rima looked at the cover. *Holy City: Riker's Roadside Attraction in the Santa Cruz Mountains: A Nostalgic History,* by Betty Lewis. How weird! Rima hadn't even known there was a Holy City until a few days before. And now she'd sent a letter there. She'd had no idea it was a roadside attraction. And now she had no idea what kind of roadside attraction. She pictured a small storefront. A pinball machine. A curtained doorway with a sign to the side. "Fifty cents admission. See the Horrible Thing!" She picked the book up, flipped through it while Addison paid. The Horrible Thing turned out to be a white supremacist cult.

(2)

They walked a couple of blocks to the sushi restaurant and sat at the bar. Here again, Addison seemed to know everyone. A martini appeared without having been ordered. To the list of things her friends had failed to warn her about Santa Cruz, Rima added the fact that the sushi contained crushed nuts. Even more surprising was what a good idea that was. "How about that election," the sushi chef said. He looked more like a surfer than a sushi chef.

There was a ceramic cat on the bar, mostly white, with calico patches and a raised paw. *Maneki neko.* A good-luck charm to bring in customers. This one was Americanized, beckoning with the back of its paw outward instead of the front, which was traditional. Or so Rima had read somewhere or other.

"I'd be happy to tell you about Holy City," Addison said, "if there's anything particular you want to know." She was stirring her drink with the olive in a careless, fiddle-dee-dee way, as if she knew nothing about the letter Rima had sent. But why else would she keep bringing up Holy City? Kenny Sullivan, postman to the rich and famous, must have sung like a canary.

Rima opened her mouth to explain why she'd sent a letter to a woman she doubted was alive, and signed it with a fictional character's name. No one was more curious than she to hear what she would say. But Addison was still talking. "What did your dad tell you?"

Although Rima had been wanting Addison to talk about her father, she would have liked to choose the place and time. She needed to be braced for it; the question struck her like a slap. "I never heard of Holy City until that box of letters you gave me," she said. Her voice began shaky but leveled out. She was changing the subject, and doing it as quickly as she could. "With Constance Wellington's letters?"

"I don't remember," Addison started, and then she started over. "Cat lady? God, I haven't thought of her in years."

The great advantage of sitting at the sushi bar was in not being face-to-face. Rima could avoid looking at Addison without appearing to avoid it. She stared instead into the glass case of ice, salmon, eel, avocado. She looked up into the round white Buddha-beaming face of the calico cat. There was music in the background; the soundtrack for this conversation was the Red Hot Chili Peppers. Rima took another piece of seaweed, raw fish, and crushed nuts, but she was too tense to eat it. *What was it exactly that went on between you and my father?* she practiced. This was not the way she'd planned it; the way she'd planned it was drunk. But Addison was the one with the martini. Rima had only her green tea. This was not a level playing field.

"She was a real mystery buff. Not just mine. That woman read every mystery ever written, and she wrote everyone about them too. I remember once at a convention, there was a whole panel about her and her letters. Always so sure we were all getting it wrong.

"She was postmistress out there. We used to joke about how she must give herself a bulk discount on stamps.

"She might have been the last survivor of Holy City," Addison said. "I think she was. I picture it like something out of Flannery O'Connor. The post office long closed, cobwebs over the scales. Just her and her cats, living in a labyrinth made from piles of paperbacks."

"Still in her wedding dress," Rima offered. *What was it exactly, what was it exactly . . .*

"Something like that."

A sushi roll called Clouds and Rain arrived. Rima seemed to remember that Clouds and Rain was a traditional Japanese euphemism for sex. Or else Thunder and Rain. Or else it was Chinese. This Clouds and Rain was diced scallops in a spicy mayonnaise and not at all traditional.

"I actually met Ms. Wellington once," Addison said. "How ironic is that? I spend a whole evening with her, and she writes her letters to Maxwell as if I don't exist. Not that she should remember me. I wasn't a writer yet when we met. Though we talked for quite some time."

The sushi chef returned. He and Addison spoke briefly about the prospects for the Senate. A month ago it had seemed impossible. Now it all came down to Montana, where the vote was still being counted, and Virginia, where things looked awfully good. He asked about the dogs and heard about their Halloween costumes. He suggested that Rima must be really happy to be in California instead of Cleveland, but since he lived in California he said "real happy" instead of "really happy." He asked how she liked living by the ocean. "Not that you don't have water in Cleveland," he said. "I know you have lakes. Great lakes is what I hear."

Californians always thought they were all that. They had no idea how great a lake could be. Instead of saying so, Rima did him the courtesy of pretending not to get the joke. "I like the pelicans," she said. This severely understated the case. Rima loved the pelicans, loved watching their hard, slow wing beats, their unfathomable, indifferent, prehistoric silhouettes. She loved the way they surfed the air in front of the curl. Just this morning she had seen a flock of ten. Sometimes, on the rocks or the water, they were so large she mistook them for sea lions.

Rima ate another piece of sushi. She was just calming down, feeling that the conversation was under control again, that she could talk about pelicans. But she was also beginning to feel that it would maybe be okay to talk about her father, as long as she could initiate it, be the one asking the questions, not be ambushed again. *What was it exactly that went on . . .*

The sushi chef moved down the bar. Addison rolled her chopsticks in her fingers. "I met Constance Wellington on August 5, 1959," she said. "The same night I met your father."

(3)

In 1959, Addison had been seventeen years old, working part-time for the *Santa Cruz Sentinel.* Her beat, as you'd expect, was the obituaries. Bim Lanisell was twenty-three, working at the *San Jose Mercury News.*

They met at the annual meeting of a journalists' professional group called the Fill Your Hole Club. In 1959 this meeting took place in Holy City's Showhouse and Lecture Hall, which had been rented for the occasion as a lark. The journalists were a larkish bunch, and why not? Back in those days, there was no Internet, with bloggers checking every fact in every story. Journalists then didn't know how great they had it, making it up as they went along, not a care in the world.

Plus Father William Riker, the patriarch of Holy City, was always good for a few inches. He was on hand for this occasion in the role of gracious host. The keynote speaker, Bill Gould, inspired by the cult's aspiration to perfect governance, waxed lyrical about what a perfect world might look like to journalists. No deadlines. No assignments. At least a murder a day, all done in broad daylight on the other side of a saloon window, so the reporters could cover them without leaving their barstools.

An arsonist had been plaguing Holy City that summer. If he would only set a fire in the Showhouse and Lecture Hall that night, Bill Gould said, he could personally guarantee him the front page of several papers. That last joke had been an uncomfortable one. During the course of the evening, the remaining cultists all managed to wander into the banquet and check things out. It wasn't far-fetched to think that the arsonist was in the audience during Gould's speech, laughing with the rest.

Don't tease the arsonist. Rules to live by.

The auditorium had been decorated with twists of yellow and green streamers. There were two sparkling cut-glass bowls of Hawaiian punch, much improved, Addison said, by the clandestine addition of a local corn whiskey, known for its kick as white mule. Liquor (as well as sex) was forbidden to the residents of Holy City, but even at seventeen Addison had known they were screwing, and probably drinking too. Father Riker made a show of commenting that the punch tasted funny, while he helped himself to another glass. He grew loquacious. The property was no longer a convenient watering hole for tourists on their way to the beach; some in Riker's position would see that as sour lemons, he said.

But he was more the sort who took those sour lemons and made lemonade. He floated the idea of turning Holy City into a retreat of some kind. Perhaps, just off the top of his head, a nudist colony.

The property was no longer Riker's, so the proposal was purely speculative. It had passed into the hands of someone from Hollywood, the music editor of *Sergeant Preston of the Yukon,* a guy named Maurice Kline. Jewish. Suddenly Riker was convinced that Jews were practically white—he'd never had anything against the Jews, he said—and he gave Kline half the property as a gift, and designated him the Jewish Messiah of Holy City too.

Within the year, Riker sold Kline the other half, though there was a condition on the sale that Kline build a new Jerusalem on the site.

Within the week, Riker wished it all back.

Soon they were in court, Riker suing Kline, the other cultists suing Riker and Kline both, in separate suits for what they saw as their share of the property. The court's decision was that Kline owned it all.

This was when the fires began. Holy City was falling to pieces.

The night of the Fill Your Hole meeting, Riker wore a gray suit, a blue tie, and a red beanie. He had an enormous belly and he burped frequently. Addison had always heard what a charismatic, compelling young man he'd been. As an old man he was ridiculous. Another cup of punch had to be procured and drunk quickly, just to avoid picturing him naked.

But other reporters found much to like in the nudist colony plan. They turned on a dime from adult professionals into adolescent frat boys. Several volunteered to cover the story of the nudist colony's opening day. Or uncover it, if that was called for. Or go undercover to it. The key, they agreed, to a successful nudist colony was naked women. They raised their glasses to Addison. A couple of them winked. There were very few women in the room, and Addison was the only young one. Father Riker's wife had died nine years before.

Constance Wellington was among the cultists who visited the meeting. She stationed herself at the punch bowl, ladling it out as requested, but serving herself liberally too. She was perhaps fifty years old at the time. She and Addison spoke at length about the history of the cult and also about its current difficulties. Then, lowering her voice, Constance said she thought she knew who the firebug was.

"I was only seventeen," Addison told Rima. "And I had this ridiculous picture of me scooping all the boys on the arson story. So I gave it way too much credence. Also, I didn't know anything about Constance at the time. Riker came over, which shut her right up, just like something in a mystery novel, except that in a mystery novel she'd be dead later that night, which she wasn't, only drunk.

"And then she turned out to be the kind of person who always thinks she's solved the case, even when there isn't a case to solve. I'm betting everyone in Holy City knew who was starting the fires, and it was only a mystery to us on the outside."

Constance became flirtatious, and her flirting took the form of offering free kittens to many of the male reporters, until she fell,

ass over teakettle, off the porch. Riker was found the next morning passed out in a redwood grove behind the old firehouse. There
might have been a reporter or two as well, sprinkled like salt over
the ground somewhere.

Fortunately, Addison told Rima primly, the night had been a
dry one.

Chapter Nine

(1)

Rima's suspicion was that Addison had left out some important details, and she was more right about that than she would ever know. In Rima's mind, the story was primarily short on information about her father. Had he been one of the frat boys sniggering about naked women? Had he been among those offered free kittens? Had he and Addison fallen in love at first sight? The only question Rima could bring herself to ask was the one with kittens in it. Addison didn't remember the answer.

"He was allergic to cats," Rima said sadly. She herself had had a catless childhood as a result, even though her father was rarely home and she could have kept the cat in her own bedroom and you would have hardly known it was there.

"We stayed up that whole night talking," Addison said. "One of *those* nights. I told Bim things I'd never told anyone. I told him that I wanted to be a writer. You don't know, but back in those days, I could have been sixty instead of seventeen, and they'd still be calling me a girl. No one would have trusted me with a newspaper story, much less thought I could write a book. There was no reason to take me seriously.

"I read somewhere that behind every successful person is someone who believes in them. You don't need more than one, but you have to have someone. For me, that was your father.

"Later, lots of people believed in me. After I started to publish. But Bim was the one who believed in me when there was no reason to."

Addison finished the bit of her martini that remained. She paused a moment, staring into the empty glass. "Say," she said. "If your father didn't talk to you about Holy City, why did you want me to buy that book?"

"I didn't."

"How did it get on the top of my pile?"

"I don't know," Rima said.

Addison waved her hand for the bill. She paid it and they walked back out into sunlight. She looked old, or else Rima was noticing and usually didn't. Direct sunlight could do that. Make the plants grow. Make the snow melt. Show a woman's age. Addison's eyes were red, and the skin beneath them drooped like a hound's. "We were good friends until he married," she said.

"You're my godmother," Rima reminded her. By which she meant that the friendship had not, in fact, ended with her parents' marriage. So it hadn't ended because of her mother. Rima's best guess? It had ended because of *Ice City*.

"I guess Bim didn't talk about me much," Addison said.

(2)

Rima's emotions at this moment were really complicated. She felt bad for Addison. It would have been nice to be able to say that Addison had been important to her father, since the reverse was obviously true.

She felt defensive of her mother and her mother's generous, reasonable soul. She wanted to tell Addison that whatever had happened, her mother was innocent of it. But it seemed cruel to say this, given that the only other suspect in the destruction of the relationship was her father.

Rima had a sudden memory of the time after her mother's death, of her mother's sisters, swooping in with their luggage and their sobbing. Her mother was the baby of the family. She should have outlived them all. Rima saw her aunts in the kitchen, doing the dishes and making plans for guests to gather at the house after the funeral.

She saw Oliver on the floor under the breakfast table. He'd put the large dining room tablecloth over it to make a tent. Rima was trying to coax him out. Her reasons were selfish. She thought she could get through her mother's funeral if she had Oliver to take care of. If he stayed home under the breakfast table, all the weeping faces would be turned to her.

"She won't come." Rima's aunts were reassuring each other as if Rima and Oliver weren't right there, Rima crouched on the floor with a cookie, which might have worked if Oliver had been two years old and a dog. "She wouldn't have the nerve to come, today of all days."

Rima knew they were talking about the famous A. B. Early,

mystery writer and godmother. Rima's mother might not have been the jealous type, but the wicked sisters, on her behalf, had enough jealousy for the three of them.

Mostly, Rima didn't want to be the one talking. She wanted Addison to tell her about her father. She didn't want it the other way around. The truth was that Bim had mentioned Addison only rarely and, at the end of his life, not at all. So she told Addison that her father hadn't talked much about anything in his past.

In his defense, you had to note that Rima hadn't asked. When she was young, her father was her father, and no one to be particularly interested in. His stories, when he told them, usually reflected well on him. The details would change—he was working after school in his father's print shop, he was a volunteer tutor for underprivileged children, he was in high school, he was in college, he was abroad, he was at home—but the fundamental plotline was tiresomely predictable: He appeared initially to be wrong, but turned out in the end to be right.

These stories were told for their instructional content; useful things for Rima and Oliver to learn were hidden inside like candy in a piñata. Rima did her best to ignore the lessons. She'd never quite forgiven her father for living, while her mother died.

To that crime, he had now added dying himself.

It had been nothing like the clean and tender death scenes Rima knew from movies. No deathbed confession. No final words of wisdom. No mention of moving toward the light or seeing his wife and son waiting for him beyond it. No pale but translucent faces.

Early on, his doctor had talked to both him and Rima about the mind-body connection. Medicine could do what medicine could do, but a positive outlook was also medicinally prescribed. These instructions prevented both of them from saying aloud that he was dying, prevented Rima from asking him much of anything about his life (which would have amounted to the same thing), as she was finally interested enough to do, until he was so doped on morphine he could no longer speak.

A few days after his death, Rima found an envelope with her name on it in his desk. She opened it expecting—something. A letter with the good-bye that hadn't happened. Financial details, a memory, advice for her future. Something to show that he hadn't given up on being her father just because he was dead.

What she found was his final column, with instructions to pub-lish it posthumously. In the column her father wrote about what a beautiful and terrible world it was. He spoke of the great good luck enjoyed by his generation of middle-class Americans. How abundant their lives had been. Oceans and jungles still teeming with animals. Plenty of food and the whole world of cooking to choose from—Ethiopian one night, Thai the next, French the night after that. Medical marvels. Martian explorations. The blue ice of the great glaciers. How they had seen a man walk on the moon. Witnessed the creation of a whole new world in the Internet. He said that he believed (and feared) that they might well have been the luckiest people in the whole history of human-ity. Far luckier than their sons and daughters.

Her father moved then to his personal good fortune. He had seen the best and the worst of the world, but its treatment of him had been more generous than he deserved. He expressed his gratitude for the way he'd been privileged to live, thanked the people who read him and the people who wrote to him, all the people he'd never met who had allowed him to matter to them. He spoke of his own death only to assure them that he was at peace with it.

Thanks for all of it, the column finished.

It's been real.

Only it wasn't. It was a brave, and to Rima's mind unconvincing, performance. Would you, her father had asked her once, long before he was diagnosed, want to be remembered as you were? Or as better than you were?

As was often the case with his columns, Rima preferred the unedited version. She didn't much like the man in the column, with his peaceful, grateful death. She didn't like how he didn't say a word about the loss of his young wife, his only son, but claimed instead to have lived a lucky life. Or at least compared with most.

(3)

Rima was perpetually offended by the suggestion that luck should be graded on the curve. Of all the false comforts she'd been recently offered, the most poisonous was the one that told you to be grateful that you were better off than some. Why would anyone think that your own pain should be lessened by the thought of someone else's?

She loved her real father, a man who did not go peacefully to his death. (And if so many people hadn't conspired to make a lingering death look better than it was, would Rima have been so unprepared for how it turned out to be? All she had ever seen were the quick, unexpected ones. Naturally she'd imagined this would be an improvement.) At the end, her father had dreamt repeatedly of children, of the terrifying children he'd met in his life—the children of Pol Pot, Colombia, Sudan—and these dreams grew more frequent and more vivid with his rising dose of morphine. He sweated and sobbed, smells and liquids leaking from every orifice, as he begged invisible people to put down their guns. Rima couldn't decide if the morphine was worth whatever relief it might be bringing.

She'd held his hand and tried to take him somewhere else. She told him he was camping; they were on a camping trip she remembered from before her mother had died.

They'd rented a canoe and gone out on the lake, her mother in the front, her father steering from the back, and she and Oliver safe between the two, pretending to paddle sometimes, but mostly not. They'd seen a snapping turtle, four deer coming down the bank to drink.

There'd been a hammock near their tent for reading books in, and the food had been camping classic—roasted hot dogs on sticks, potatoes buried in the coals to bake. The potatoes had charred on the outside while remaining raw in the middle, but Rima and her father and mother had eaten them anyway.

Oliver had given his potato a name, which was his usual method for getting out of eating something. Imbue it with history and personality until you'd have to have a heart of stone to make him eat it. He'd made a hat for his potato out of the aluminum foil.

As Rima talked, her father had quieted. "I'm awfully tired," he said then. "Could you carry my pack for me?"

Apparently he was on a different camping trip. There'd been no backpacking on hers. But Rima said of course she would, she had it now, and they could stop and rest under a tree whenever he wanted. Before she finished the sentence, he was back to the horrors, and nothing she said could reach him.

Still later, Rima discovered that he'd assembled his own memorial website. He'd posted his favorites of his own columns, plus photographs and dispatches from his earlier career. The site could burn forever, like Kennedy's eternal flame. A hundred years from now, there Rima and her budding sexuality would be.

My father had been a public figure for so long," she told Addison, "I think he kind of forgot that he had a private life too." She hoped Addison wasn't hurt, but couldn't tell. Rima had tried so hard not to feel hurt herself when she realized that her father had, in fact, put a lot of thought and effort into saying good-bye. Just not to her.

The man she loved had worried about leaving his daughter alone, even if he never said so. If she ever wanted to get even, she would do so by remembering him the way he had wanted to be remembered instead of the way he was.

Part Two

Chapter Ten

(1)

When she was little, Rima used to play a game that she'd gotten from a book. You walked around the house holding a large mirror in front of you, pointing up. You weren't allowed to look at the ground beneath your feet. You looked only into the mirror. This transformed the terrain most familiar to you into something new and strange, a fantasy-land hidden in plain sight above your head in your very own house. You couldn't get anything like the same effect simply lying on your bed looking upward. You had to be seriously disoriented—up down and down up.

Rima had been playing the mirror game one day when she saw something on top of one of the kitchen cabinets. She had to put the footstool on the counter and climb onto both to reach it. Her mother walked into the middle of this. "For goodness' sakes, get down from there," she had said. "You'll break your neck. One more thing to charge to Addison's account."

The object turned out to be Addison's wedding gift to Rima's parents, an antique silver samovar. It was a wedding Addison had not attended. The samovar was engraved on the bottom. Rima ran her finger over this. The wedding date and then the words: *One is silver.* "What does it mean?" Rima had asked, and her mother sang to her. *Make new friends, but keep the old. One is silver and the other gold.*

This didn't exactly answer the question. Rima's mother put the samovar back on top of the high cupboard and, to the best of Rima's memory, took it out again only when she was cleaning the shelves, which is to say, never.

This maybe had nothing to do with Addison. Rima's mother disliked essential household chores bad enough, never mind the optional ones. Silver tarnishes. And Rima remembered her mother as distinctly not the jealous sort. Her father traveled so much. He'd covered Vietnam before Rima was born, and the Peace Talks in Paris. Cambodia later. Nigeria. The reunification of Germany. Baghdad. Madrid. Her mother never seemed to mind— always happy to see him come home, the two of them constantly touching each other in small ways, a hand on the back or the knee, a hand in a hand.

But her mother also seemed happy when he left. And busy. For Rima and Oliver, pancakes at dinner and a general relaxation of the house rules compensated for his absence. Not that they would have made the trade. Just that they were okay with it.

Their father went to dangerous places; he flew on planes; he interviewed murderers; he was much, much older than their mother. The chance that he would die someday had occurred to Rima, which meant the notion had been shared with Oliver. They thought of all the times he'd arrived like Santa Claus, with sugar skulls from Mexico, polished rocks from Thailand, wood clocks from Germany. Rima and Oliver would be so sad when he died. But they would be okay. What mattered was their mother.

Rima's mother was beautiful in a sixties sort of way—a Joan Baez with long, thick hair, nose slightly hooked, Gypsy eyes. Rima had the same eyes, which is why Martin had admired them. Her mother was a photographer who did portraits of families in front of fireplaces, brides looking out windows, kids under Christmas trees. She did dogs, birds, and horses, but her passion was old railway stations. On weekends the three of them would drive to Indiana, Illinois, Kentucky, so she could take photographs of people arriving, people departing, people waiting, or, if there were none of those, empty stations. Rima, Oliver, and their mother would stay in hotels, eat hamburgers, go to whatever movie was showing at the cinemaplex. They would sleep, all three of them, in a single room and often in a single bed. Her mother had seemed to need no one's company but her children's.

The reverse could not be said. As Rima grew older the weekend trips interfered with birthday parties or sleepovers, or with nothing at all, only Rima was increasingly reluctant to tag along. Kari Spector, a popular girl at her school, a high-status female if there ever was one, might call on a Saturday morning, ask whether Rima wanted to hang. If Rima was gone, Kari would move on to Siobhán McCarthy, and then all the next week at school there would be oblique references to things Rima had missed, jokes she wouldn't understand, boys she hadn't met. The next weekend it would be Siobhán whom Kari called first. Rima's whole life ruined so that her mother could take another stupid picture.

Stupid. Who was Kari or Siobhán to Rima now? What wouldn't she have given for one more trip with her mother and Oliver, one more night in a stale little room with one double bed, the mattress so scooped out that the three of them would wake up in a heap in the middle, push apart, roll together all night long.

At first Rima had kept the mirror game to herself. By the time she taught it to Oliver, it had become much more intricate. The world in the mirror was now an actual place. It had a name—Upside-down Town—and a history that Rima was always adding to. Queens, of course, in honor of Alice's *Through the Looking-Glass,* and also because who doesn't like a story with queens in it? Plus a mirror image of Rima (and now Oliver)—kids who looked just like them, but were otherwise opposite in every way.

Unlike most second children, Oliver was a games enthusiast. He played nonstop, even through dinner, until he fell down the stairs on his way to bed and Rima's mother said that was that and took the mirror away. Rima thought he might have fallen on purpose. Oliver was also a Band-Aid enthusiast.

Later that same night he came into Rima's room. He was supposed to be asleep, but sleep had always held little charm for Oliver. "How would you know," he asked Rima, "if someone who looked just like me took my place?" Rima couldn't tell whether he was agitated or merely philosophical.

"I would know you," she said. She too was supposed to be

asleep, but was reading in the time-honored flashlight-under-the-blanket fashion. The heroine had just been locked in her room by her evil governess. This was no time to be talking to Oliver.

Oliver lifted the corner of the blanket and, with his feet still on the floor, slid his face into her little lighted tent. "How? If I looked just the same?"

"I would smell you." As a child Oliver had smelled like oatmeal. Rima made sure her tone suggested something far less pleasant. She returned the flashlight to her book.

Oliver leaned on his elbows. He rocked slightly. The mattress creaked. "Go back to bed," Rima told him. He stretched his hand out, covered the flashlight bulb so his hand turned that neon red. He wiggled his fingers, and shadows rippled across the words in Rima's book. "Stop it," she said.

Oliver grabbed the hand with the flashlight in it, directed the beam into his own face so he was all lit up, a moon Oliver. "Hey," he said. "Pay attention." Like all second children, he was hypersensitive to those moments when no attention was being paid. "Listen. Which me would ask you that? The one before or after I switched?"

(2)

Jeopardy! April 5, 1990. "Books and Authors" for a thousand.

Answer: The only A. B. Early mystery with a dollhouse in it.

Correct question: What is *Ice City*?

(3)

Like Upside-down Town, Ice City is an imaginary place. Even in the fictional context of *Ice City* the book, Ice City is not real. Ice City is a made-up bar where made-up drinks are served to made-up people. Maxwell Lane is always one of those people. The others are whomever Maxwell wants them to be—people from his past, the famous, the infamous, the real, the fictional, the living, the dead. In every book, even those published before *Ice City,* Maxwell Lane spends some time in his imaginary bar with his imaginary friends. It's the closest we get to inside his head, although never presented as such.

Ice City is a state of mind, a psychological destination. Maxwell Lane goes there when he wants to drink more, feel less. He can't go to a real bar. Like most fictional detectives, Maxwell Lane has both a problem with alcohol and a problem with facing the world sober. Ice City the bar is the feeling-no-pain stage of drunkenness, but you have to get there without drinking, which is why it's imaginary.

Ice City the book is about betrayal, the unforeseen consequences of careless actions, the advisability of keeping secrets. These same things can be said about all A. B. Early books. But in no other does Maxwell Lane have such an intimate relationship with the murderer. In no other is the betrayal of one by the other so nearly equal. Maxwell goes to Ice City in every book, but *Ice City* is the only book that ends in Ice City.

"How do you deal with the things you've seen?" Rima once heard a friend of her father's ask him when he'd just returned from South Africa.

"I go to Ice City," he'd said.

So one of the many things Rima didn't know about her father and Addison was whether she'd gotten the idea of Ice City from him or it was the other way around.

Nor did she know how to get there.

Chapter Eleven

(1)

Everything will be better now that the Democrats have the
power of the subpoena, Addison had said, and sure
enough, such was the magic of the Democratic Party armed
to the teeth with the law that the very next time Rima put her
hand into the box of Maxwell's letters and rummaged around, she
found, crumpled against the side, the page-one onionskin she'd
been looking for. She put it together with the page two she'd
already read. This, then, was the whole letter:

21200 Old Santa Cruz Hwy
Holy City, California 95026
April 20, 1983

Dear Maxwell Lane:
    Have recently finished your Ice City. *Read it two times.*

Often reread books, but not so quickly. Appreciated the thought you gave to the whistling man's murder. As you know, I've gone back and forth myself ever since I first wrote you about poor old Bogan all those years ago. You'll remember the police ruled it a suicide. They call that a cold case if I'm not mistaken.

Anyway, there our agreement ends. Now, don't take me wrong. Have the utmost respect for you and your work. But something has been nagging at me. Sat at my dining room table, the book in front of me, and made a character list, a map, and a timeline. None of them disproved your case, but none of them proved it either.

The book starts with a series of "pranks"—the sawed suitcase handle, the missing hat, the fishing lure in the onion dip. Submit that some people plain crave excitement. They make a big mess and don't care who gets dirty and the only reason is they're bored. Is there someone like this in your book? The answer is obvious and it's not our boy Bim.

Poison, I hear, is a woman's weapon. So sayeth every man. Submit that it's even more female to paint your poison like fingernail polish on the claws of a cat. If your target was the cat's owner, this strikes me as a heck of a chancy way to go about things. Occam's razor. What if all you wanted was to kill the cat? One more "prank" in the set.

At the very least, you overlooked someone else with motive and opportunity. So here it is—I just don't believe Bim Lanisell would kill anyone. He always seemed like a pretty straight-up Joe to me. Think you got it wrong this time.

Bet if you put poison on a cat's claws for real, the cat would lick it right off, no matter how bad it tastes. Cats are very aware of their bodies. I know whereof I speak. I have twenty-two of them.

Of course, all this assumes Ice City *is a mystery novel. Can we be sure of that? Not clear from the cover. In a horror novel the cat could have acted alone. There is a larger world than you allow, Mr. Lane, and the truth you end up with often depends on where you are when you start. I knew your father about as well as anyone knew him. Not highly thought of today, but that much he had right.*

VTY,

Constance Wellington

PS. Joking about the cat, of course.

Rima read this letter over twice. Then she pulled her copy of *Ice City* from the nightstand drawer and thumbed through it until she found its first reference to the whistling man.

Ice City, pages 36–37

Maxwell Lane arrived on a typical summer day, which means it started hot and got hotter. I'd spent that morning picking up rotted apples. The orchard swarmed with black

wasps and the air smelled so much like wine I got dizzy on it. By the time I finished, the wasps were buzzing inside my head.

Part of me was surprised not to find my father at breakfast, mopping the egg from his plate with his bread and complaining about the weak coffee. I'd never been so popular. No one would leave me alone.

"Your father wasn't a man who expected much from life," Brother Isaiah started off.

Pamela was next. "Your father told me he never felt like he belonged anywhere."

"Why prolong what you don't enjoy?" asked Ernie.

And all the while, wasps were buzzing in my head.

When Maxwell Lane arrived, Brother Isaiah was just as angry as I expected. It was dangerous, he said, to bring a stranger into our little world, particularly during this intimate time of our mourning. He began an investigation into who'd hired Mr. Lane.

But there are advantages to being fourteen. No one ever suspected me. A second advantage: I was too young to guess what he usually got paid.

I'd gotten his number from the yellow pages at the gas station. We'd gone into town for groceries and to have the tires rotated. I stayed with the car. He answered his own phone.

"I heard my father," I'd told him. "Not more than five minutes before he died. He was whistling."

"You would know your father's whistle." It wasn't a question.

"My father was a good whistler. A fancy whistler."

"You told the police that."

"They said it happens. Sometimes someone is relieved to have finally made the decision. The big finale, they said."

"Is that the way your father was?" It was Mr. Lane's first actual question. It was the first I didn't know how to answer.

Well? my father whispered from somewhere inside me. Finish what you start, boy. "My father was the sort who did things. He didn't have much use for talk or plans or dreams."

"He doesn't sound much like a true believer."

"I'm the dreamer," I said.

I was running out of time and I didn't think I'd managed to interest him. Any moment now the women would come out of the store. "I know people thought my father was ridiculous," I said. Even if I never saw Mr. Lane or spoke to him again, I didn't want his pity. If my father killed himself, then he killed himself.

"No man whose children love him is ridiculous," Mr. Lane said. "I'll be there on Friday. Don't tell anyone I'm coming."

(2)

Though Addison was guarded now about her personal life, and almost everything else too, she'd once been more forthcoming. When *Ice City* was first published, she'd said openly that the cult in the book (not to be confused with the cult Maxwell Lane had grown up in—two different cults) was based on a real but obscure Oroville group once run by a man known as Brother Isaiah. The Oroville group had lasted only a short while, and little information about it was available. Addison didn't mind this. It was, she'd said, the best position a novelist could find herself in. It left her free to make stuff up.

In *Ice City,* she updated the cult from the '30s to the early '60s, moved it from Oroville to the trailer park in Clear Lake, and enlarged its numbers. These are the things she'd kept: the name Brother Isaiah and the cult's fundamental defining feature. Brother Isaiah had claimed to be immortal, and he'd promised his followers, each and every one of them, an endless life of their very own.

Time is money, always will be, world without end, so you mustn't expect that immortality will ever come cheap. Both Brother Isaiahs, the real and the fictional, got rich selling it. The Oroville group ended when, shortly after gathering and fleecing his flock, Brother Isaiah died of a massive heart attack.

In the *Ice City* version, the first death belongs to the whistling man. He dies in an apparent suicide. The *Ice City* Brother Isaiah responds by reassuring his followers that suicide is a special case, a door left open. Immortality, he tells them, isn't meant to eliminate freedom of choice.

But the man's son is not so sure his father killed himself. It is this son who brings in Maxwell Lane and sets in motion the chain that will end with two more deaths—the second belonging to Brother Isaiah himself, and the third to Bim Lanisell's wife.

In the real world, there was a tenuous connection between the Oroville cult and Holy City. When the Oroville cult failed, Father Riker had offered to take in the survivors. He attached a couple of conditions: There would be none of that living-forever nonsense. And they had to shave their beards, cut their hair, and generally clean themselves up. Holy City, Father Riker said, was not inter-ested in slobs. Among his own followers, Father Riker was known as The Comforter.

There is no record suggesting that any of the immortals accepted his offer.

(3)

Of course, the one night Rima came to dinner with murder on her mind, the subject was never raised. "Did you get one of the mur-ders in *Ice City* from Constance Wellington?" she'd planned to ask as soon as there was an opening. "Was there a real murder?"

Instead there was only pointless chat about Oro Blanco grape-fruits. Someone had told Tilda they were in the market now, even though she knew it was far too early for Oro Blancos, and sure enough, when she'd asked the clerk, his little eyes widened as if he'd never heard such crazy talk. "I haven't had someone cut me dead that way," Tilda said, "since I was on the street." She passed Rima the salad bowl. The salad was made of figs and mint and string beans. Tilda made a clicking sound, like castanets.

She was wearing an audible necklace. It was large as well as loud, a string of shells and acorns and feathers, the sort of neck-lace that Andy Goldsworthy might make. The sort of necklace, in Rima's opinion, that could cause a clerk in a grocery store to cut you dead even if you hadn't been overly optimistic about grape-fruit. Not that Rima minded the necklace herself. No one in such a necklace could ever come up behind you unexpectedly with a platter of roast chicken or an upraised carving knife. Tilda had been belled like a cat.

And just then Tilda asked, "Have you heard anything from Martin since the weekend?" So she'd sneaked up on Rima after all.

Rima thought it might be hurtful, if she'd gotten e-mails and Tilda hadn't, to say so. Then she thought it wouldn't be truthful to not say so. So she said she'd had an e-mail, but there was a suspicious pause between the question and the answer and, in fact, she'd had two e-mails, so though it wasn't a lie, it wasn't as truthful as it could have been.

It seemed she ought to go on to say what the e-mail had been about, but that was even more complicated. Would Tilda be pleased or upset to think that Martin might have come again to Wit's End if only Rima hadn't turned him down?

The whole thing put Rima off balance, so she never did mention the murder. That was the thing about a cold case. There was no particular hurry.

(4)

After dinner, the three women and the two dogs went up to the second-floor TV room to watch *Lost,* which Addison had Ti-Voed. There were two dollhouses in the TV room. *Average Mean*—botulism in the green beans—and *H₂Zero*—instantly recognizable for its under-the-sea death. *H₂Zero* was one of the weaker novels, but an excellent dollhouse, a functioning saltwater aquarium with real fish and the ceramic scuba diver often seen in aquariums, only this one's air hose had been severed. A toy octopus floated over the corpse, because Addison loved octopi. They were clever, clever creatures, she said, and because of this she never ate them.

The whole thing was the devil to clean, of course.

Addison's chair reclined. Rima and Tilda shared the couch, which had padded arms on which to put your head, and scarves and throws and dachshunds for added warmth.

Addison announced that she was having a glass of whiskey to celebrate what now looked to be the taking of the Senate. In truth, Addison had a whiskey most nights; if she wasn't celebrating, then the Bush administration was driving her to drink. "I'm going to enjoy this moment," she said. "Even if it proves Pyrrhic. All my life I've been locked in eternal struggle with the same people over the same things. Vietnam, Iraq. 'It's not a crime if the president does it.' Wiretaps, voter suppression. We lefties have to enjoy the few victories we've had."

Rima's father had said much the same thing. He'd written columns about it. Although he'd also noted the strange reconfiguration—the enemy of my enemy is my friend—that resulted in a new thaw between the old liberals and the CIA. Some things had changed and some things hadn't. Rima started to say this, but when she turned, Addison was wiping her eyes, which could have been a simple, sleepy gesture or could have meant she was crying. Drink sometimes did that to people.

A low-wattage lamp cast a circle of light onto the ceiling. There was the soft bubble of the aquarium, the unlikely threat of polar bears on the television. If Addison had had collies they would have been gathered anxiously around her, but she had dachshunds so they weren't. Stanford was on Tilda's lap. Berkeley had crawled under the couch so that only her tail showed. It twitched now and then.

"Cheney. Rumsfeld. Abrams. Negroponte, for Christ's sake. We seemed so young and they seemed so old when it all started," Addison said. "How is it that we got old, but they're still here? It's like something out of a Greek myth." There was nothing sad in her voice. Probably she wasn't crying, after all.

"It's a *Star Trek* episode," said Tilda. "I mean, I don't know that it's not Greek too. But definitely *Star Trek.* The black-white one."

Addison took a sip, and Rima could see her throat tighten as the whiskey went down. "It's a zombie movie," she said. "It's *Night of the* goddamn *Living Dead.*"

Rima left Addison locked in eternal struggle and went up to her bedroom, where she still didn't have the wireless key.

People in Cleveland claimed to miss her, but they were getting pregnant, buying rugs off the Internet, going to concerts, playing intramural sports anyway. They were coping.

There was a third e-mail from Martin. Subject line: Ice City. There was no telling what an e-mail tagged "Ice City" might be about. Rima was surprised to find herself nervous when she opened it. And then disappointed, so very disappointed that it wiped out both the previous friendly e-mails—the invitations to haunted wineries and mysterious gravitational anomalies, even the observation that she had cat's eyes, now seemed like ground-work for this. She went back to not liking Martin so much.

Martin had a plan for a bar in downtown Santa Cruz, a space as close as possible to the location of Maxwell Lane's fictional office and called, of course, Ice City. The decor would be from the

books, photographs of people Maxwell had had his imaginary conversations with, or else *their* books and paintings and what have
you. Martin hadn't worked it all out. But buying into the reality of
Maxwell Lane would be key. There would be no mention of A. B.
Early anywhere, which, given how much she liked her privacy,
Martin thought she would see as a plus. Martin wanted Rima to
talk A. B. Early into financing this. It was important the proposal
come from someone Addison liked.

But no pressure on Rima. Though she too could buy in early. It
wasn't a request so much as an opportunity. It was a surefire
moneymaker, in Martin's opinion. Did Rima even know how many
people came to Santa Cruz every year looking for the settings in
Addison's books, trying to find Maxwell's home and office? He
would love to talk to her more about it, either in person or by
phone, Rima's choice.

Rima's choice was none of the above. But she didn't e-mail
back. Her own rule was not to write e-mails after midnight and, if
you couldn't stop yourself from writing them, then certainly not
to send them.

This is an excellent rule. It probably should apply to paper mail
as well as electronic.

Chapter Twelve

(1)

That night Rima had her third dream about Maxwell Lane. She was walking with him on the beach below Wit's End. The sky was starless, but the water glowed with an eerie green light. The waves broke on the sand like emeralds.

Out in the middle distance, floating on that luminous green, was a boat. Rima could just make out the shadowy figure of a man on deck. He was sweeping the beach with a telescope, left, then right, as if he was looking for something in particular.

Even in her dream, Rima remembered hearing that boats represent death. Lincoln had dreamt of a boat before he was murdered, or so people said. She had a feeling the man on deck might finally be her father, come to say good-bye. But the telescope stopped its sweep, settled on her, and she knew he wasn't. The knowledge

that this man could see her face and she couldn't see his was terrifying. Around the boat the glowing waves rose in the air. The landscape turned to green towers with turrets, which became green
high-rises with windows, which became a photograph of the gray
buildings of downtown Cleveland.

Maxwell stepped into the photo, turning as he did so, holding
out his hand for Rima, so that was the way he stayed, with his
hand out like that. She tried to follow, even though she didn't
want to be in the picture, because she didn't want to be left
behind either. But whatever door had allowed Maxwell in was
closed to Rima.

She was still frightened, but now it was mostly for him.
Someone tried to kill him pretty much every goddamn book. Just
how long could his luck hold out? It wasn't as if Rima would save
him; there was no one she had managed to save. The whole thing
was so intense it woke her up.

She was in her old Shaker Heights bedroom, wallpapered with
climbing yellow roses, her mother calling her to breakfast. What
a horrible dream, she thought, happy it was over, and then her
mother called for Oliver to come down too, so she knew that
her mother didn't know about Oliver. The prospect of telling her
was so awful it woke Rima up.

She was in her bed at Wit's End and Oliver was still gone, but
now her mother was too. This was unbearably disappointing.
Maxwell's arms were around her. He whispered into her ear. "You
think I'm real," he said, "just because I'm here," but when she
turned in bed to find him, the pillow was empty.

This woke her up for sure and it was four in the morning, but when she actually opened her eyes it was only three. So there was absolutely no way to know when or if the dream had ended.

(2)

You think I'm real just because I'm sitting across from you.
—A. B. Early,

interview with Rolling Stone, no. 372

(June 1982)

(3)

The next morning Rima had breakfast with Scorch and Cody and the *Good Times* newspaper. Scorch was wearing pants that were all shaggy around the legs as if one of the dogs had been chewing on them. Rima would never dare wear such pants; she was bound to lose her keys in the fray.

Scorch had been hit in the head with a tennis ball on the beach and was in a bad mood as a result. "The guy had one of those flippy things," she told Rima. "One of those flippy things for dogs so you can throw the ball harder." Those flippy things were called Chuckit!s. Rima didn't know how she knew this.

"Lots of people wouldn't apologize for getting hit in the head," Cody said.

Scorch told him to fuck off. "I'm *so* sorry if I say the wrong thing when I'm in shock and my ears are ringing."

"Sometimes 'I'm sorry' isn't an apology," Rima said.

"Thank you," said Scorch.

Cody's T-shirt was blue and had "Mr. Toots Coffeehouse" written on the front. Rima could see that he maybe might be black, though if she'd had to guess, she would have guessed Italian. She thought Cody would go well with a glass of Chianti, and not in the *Silence of the Lambs* way.

This week's *Good Times* featured an article on the male pursuit of personal beauty, complete with photographs. But if sex was on Rima's mind, the fault was not the *Good Times'* but Maxwell Lane's.

"I dreamt about Maxwell Lane last night," she said. She remembered lying in bed with him, his whispering into her ear. "A bad dream," she added, just in case they were picturing the same thing.

Cody and Scorch had given up eggs in deference to the dogs. Scorch was eating nothing but toast and marmalade, and she didn't even like marmalade because of the orange peel, but the gesture was unappreciated. The dogs sat at her feet, keening their bewilderment. "I'm sorry," Scorch told them. "But could you please shut up?"

Cody turned to Rima. "You're living in his house. I don't think it's too surprising he'd put in an appearance." Cody had written a term paper on Addison. He'd read all the books, and he had theories. One was that the real mystery of the Maxwell Lane mysteries was Maxwell Lane. Each book had its murder, of course, and each was organized around the solution of same. But the overarching mystery was Maxwell himself. "It's what keeps people reading," Cody said.

Scorch scraped some of her marmalade back into the jar with

her knife. "Lots of them haven't kept reading. She was selling less every book. She told me so herself."

"Because she stopped advancing the Maxwell Lane story. It's what I'm saying," Cody said. "She got so secretive, it's like she doesn't think Maxwell's life is anybody's business anymore. He's hardly there in the last two books."

Scorch swallowed her toast and shook her head. "That's not it. They don't like the way she'd been writing him. You should read the forums."

Scorch said the chatrooms were well aware that Addison was getting older and that the day would come, though everyone hoped not soon, when one of the Maxwell Lane books would be the last of the Maxwell Lane books.

"Harry Potter has everyone worrying about endings," Cody said. "And there's suspense because she hasn't published in so long."

There was a woman who'd been in several Maxwell Lane novels now, sexual tension building delightfully, and then, three books ago, a consummation. Maxwell seemed to be opening up, letting someone in at last, which was very gratifying. The happy ending was so close people could taste it.

And then, in the very next book, the girlfriend was gone.

But there was still hope. The path to true love, et cetera, and she hadn't, in the time-honored tradition of detectives' girlfriends everywhere, been murdered. She'd merely dumped him. Even the news, one book later, that she had gotten married, didn't destroy all hope. Wasn't there also a tradition of ex-girlfriends' husbands' being murdered, so that they found themselves not only bereft but in need of a private detective?

Time passed with no new book, and the last couple of novels were reexamined. They hadn't been popular when published; they grew less so. Maxwell had done things in them, small things, but things people couldn't see him doing. Addison didn't seem to be on the same page as her readers; in fact, she seemed a little tired of Maxwell, or else she didn't know him as well as people had thought. On Addison's own site, someone posting under the tag LilLois was all but accusing her of character assassination.

"She doesn't want him to be happy," other posters agreed. "She'll destroy him first." LilLois said that Addison wanted to take Maxwell with her when she went, like some Indian rajah who made his wife burn herself alive on his funeral pyre.

Rima remembered how, in her dream, she'd been afraid for Maxwell; he'd seemed imperiled. How she'd thought that someone (not her) needed to save him. In her defense, she'd been asleep at the time. Awake, it was all a little too Stephen King.

She was momentarily distracted by the description in the paper of Le Pétomane, a professional farter who played the Moulin Rouge in the late 1800s and outearned Sarah Bernhardt by a ratio of three to one. Someday that fact would surface in Rima's mind, and she wouldn't have a clue how she knew it. Not that this had anything to do with Addison's readership. Rima was confident that Addison's readers would be the ones buying tickets to Sarah Bernhardt.

Of course, in a perfect world, you wouldn't have to choose.

"Have you ever heard of Holy City?" Rima asked. And when she could see they hadn't, "Old cult in the Santa Cruz mountains." She didn't mention the white supremacist stuff on account of Cody's maybe being black. And its being too early in the morning for white supremacists. "Do you think Addison used a real murder when she wrote *Ice City*? I mean, did she do that sometimes?"

"I don't think you could really murder someone with a cat," Scorch said.

"Not that murder," said Rima. "The first one."

"Here's what I know about that. If she did, she'll never tell you." Scorch ate her toast. The part of her hair that was pink fell in a feathery web against her cheek. The part that was red took on a deep honey color in the sun. You couldn't tell by looking that her ears were ringing. She was a transitory Rembrandt, the leaves in the window behind her just turning to yellow and a sparrow cavorting in the birdbath. The fig tree had a sweet sap smell.

Outside, of course. Not in the kitchen. The kitchen smelled of butter and tea.

"There's a new site on the Web," Cody said. "Some fan is trying to collect her obituaries. Of course, nobody signs an obit, they're just guessing. But might be worth a look, go see if your Holy City murder is there."

"She'll go nuts when she finds that site," Scorch said. "She'll make them take it down. God forbid that anything get on the Web without her approval."

So Addison had had that little word with Scorch about her blog. Rima tried not to feel guilty about this. Scorch had no business laying Rima's drunken breakdown out on the Internet for anyone and everyone to see.

Still, no one likes a tattletale, as Oliver used to say preemptively whenever he was planning something worth tattling about. Stanford was whining again, and higher; it was an awful pitch. Berkeley came and laid her head on Rima's shoe, the picture of deprivation and despair. Was there anyone in the room not suffering because of Rima?

"I'm sorry," Scorch said, and Rima had no idea what she was apologizing for, but it probably wasn't the thing she should be apologizing for. It made Rima feel even guiltier.

The feeling receded when she put her own knife into the marmalade and found Scorch's toast crumbs there. Rima hated toast crumbs in the jam. They were just plain thoughtless.

Chapter Thirteen

(1)

```
www.earlygraveblogspot.com
July 21, 1959. After a long, brave battle, Dr.
Julius Mackler succumbed on Tuesday to cancer.
The Morrison Planetarium has lost one of its
brightest stars.
```

Rima was on the second-floor computer, where connection to the wireless was automatic. She'd decided to check out the Wikipedia Holy City entry, but accidentally found herself on the Holy City Zoo entry instead. Apparently someone had taken the sign for the zoo to a 1970s San Francisco comedy club, which was then given the same name. Any number of famous comedians—Robin Williams and Margaret Cho—had performed there.

Rima spent half an hour googling the Holy City Zoo, reading postings about its closing night and also a reminiscence from one of the emcees about how he once bought a drink for a beautiful woman, only to have some other comic move in while he was fetching the second drink, so he told the interloper to reimburse him for the two drinks he'd already bought, and the club owner backed him up, but the woman left during the ensuing kerfuffle over the six dollars, so in the end nobody got any *value* for the money spent. It was all quite sad.

Eventually Rima remembered what she was about and that it had nothing to do with San Francisco stand-up or the expectations of men who bought women drinks. She found then:

```
http://en.Wikipedia.org/wiki/Holy_City,_California
Holy City, California, is located at
37°09'25"N, 121°58'44"W (37.1568904,
−121.9788476)GR3, in the hills above Los Gatos,
off Highway 17 on Old Santa Cruz Highway. The
current ZIP code is 95026.
   From 1919 to its disincorporation in 1959,
this was the site of a religious community
founded and run by William E. Riker, a salesman
turned palm reader turned cult leader. During
his 96 colorful years, Riker was charged with
numerous crimes—bigamy, tax evasion, murder,
and, in 1942, after writing several admiring
letters to Adolf Hitler, sedition—but was never
convicted of anything. The philosophy on which
Holy City was based was called The Perfect
```

Christian Divine Way. Its defining principles
were celibacy, temperance, white supremacy, and
segregation of the races and sexes. Followers
turned all material possessions over to Riker,
who was known to his flock as "The Comforter."
Exempt from his own rule of celibacy, Riker
lived on the property in a private house with
Lillian, one of his wives.

The town incorporated in 1926, with all
property and income held in Riker's name. Its
heyday came during the 1920s and 1930s, when it
was a popular stop for motorists on their way to
and from the beach. Holy City offered the
traveler a place to gas up, grab dinner or a
soda (William Riker claimed to have invented
Hawaiian Punch), see a peep show, look through a
telescope, and visit a petting zoo. The annual
take from this sideshow is estimated to have
been around $100,000.

From July 1924 to December 1931, Holy City
operated its own radio station under the call
letters KFQU. Though the call letters appear
obscene, they were simply sequential. The
programming featured several musical offerings,
including a popular Swiss yodeler. Its license
was later revoked for "irregularities."

In 1938, Riker ran for governor of California
for the first time. He ran again in 1942,
despite the sedition charge. His defense

attorney was the famous San Francisco lawyer
Melvin Belli, who won an acquittal by reason of
insanity. In lieu of payment, Riker offered to
procure a seat in heaven for Belli. When Belli
demanded cash instead, Riker sued him for
defamation of character—Belli had named Riker
the "screwiest of the screwballs"—but lost.
Riker ran for governor again in 1946 and 1950.

In the 1940s, Highway 17 was opened and
traffic on Old Santa Cruz Highway dropped
suddenly, sending Holy City into rapid decline.
The town disincorporated in 1959 after Riker
lost the property in a complicated real estate
deal. This was followed by a season of arson, in
which several of the buildings mysteriously
burned.

Riker died on December 3, 1969, at Agnew State
Hospital, having converted to Catholicism three
years before. There were, at the time of his death,
only three disciples still living in Holy City.

Holy City promised a world of perfect
governance. A sign welcomed all visitors. "See
us if you're contemplating marriage, suicide, or
crime," it said.

The popular fictional detective Maxwell Lane,
creation of mystery writer A. B. Early, is
widely believed to have grown up there.

(2)

Addison was working at the breakfast table on a speech for the library; the studio was reserved for her real work, her books. She scribbled on a yellow pad, writing a few words, striking them out, writing a few more. Rima had come downstairs to ask her about the reference to Maxwell Lane on the Wikipedia Holy City entry. Instead she found herself listening to a story about Addison's uncle, who was her father at the time, and how he worked on a commercial fishing boat but sometimes borrowed a friend's boat and took little Addison out fishing or whale-watching or something.

In this story he shot a sea lion. Addison had all the tender feelings of a child toward sea lions, their faces so much like dogs', intelligent, unfathomable. With a look at Berkeley and Stanford, who were sitting at her feet hoping for crumbs, because it was the breakfast table, even though no one was eating on it just now, Addison clarified that dogs weren't unfathomable, dogs were all too transparent in their hopes and dreams, but a sea lion had the sea in its eyes. So to see such a creature shot, especially by a man she loved, was horrible to her. Yet so ordinary to him that he hadn't even stopped to think how Addison would take it. To this day, she told Rima, she could still see the body, blood floating on the surface of the water like a veil.

Rima recognized the veil image from *H₂Zero* and also *Absolution Way*. It was an image Addison was fond of.

In Addison's story, her father/uncle woke her before dawn the next morning. They drove to the wharf and cast off, and there, in the dark, a hundred pairs of glowing orange eyes opened around them. Demon eyes.

He was trying to make her love them less. There were too many of them, he said. They were picking the ocean clean, and the hungrier they got, the more aggressive they became. They'd follow the fishing boats, swim into the nets, eat their fill, and then destroy the net in the process of escaping it. "You have to take sides sometimes," her father/uncle said. "The fish or the sea lions."

You can argue that a fisherman is on the side of the fish, but it's a nuanced case. "I learned something from the whole episode," Addison said. "I learned that even the people you love most are capable of murder."

The theme of Addison's library talk was supposed to be the impact of the coast on her writing. She wasn't using the story she'd just told Rima; it seemed dark for the library. (Though Rima's father had always told her never to underestimate librarians. The Patriot Act, he'd said, had made the mistake of underestimating librarians, and now they were the only thing standing between us and *1984*, and they weren't all spineless the way Congress was. They read books. His money was on them.)

Addison was trying to use the ocean as a metaphor for the imagination. As a child, she'd thrilled to stories about the SS *Palo Alto*, a concrete ship grounded off Seacliff State Beach in Aptos, and the USS *Macon*, a dirigible downed during a great storm before her birth. She'd followed avidly in the 1990s, when, with advances in infrared technology, pieces of the *Macon* were mapped off Point Sur. Every life had its wrecks, either right there in plain sight like the *Palo Alto* or dimly sensed somewhere below like the *Macon*.

And then there were those messages the ocean left on the sand—the shells of things long gone, wood from forgotten ships and trees, now polished into something more like stone. Addison made a note of the way that sea birds didn't sing like land birds, but called and cried instead. *The flukes of whales,* she wrote. And then, *Sea lions = mermaids.* With a question mark.

It was all a tangle. Addison was reaching for something lucid—something about living on the edge of an unknowable, unreachable world. A world stranger than anything any writer would ever imagine. A deep, deep place, and you could see only the surface. But she couldn't make it cohere.

In that old *Ellery Queen* interview, when Addison was answering questions about Holy City, she'd also tried to talk about the imagination. What she'd said then was that fiction is always some sort of mix of the real and the made-up. "We live in gossipy times," she'd said. "There's a type of critic who reads only to search for hidden autobiographies. For whom the story and the writer are one and the same. The imagination gets short shrift. But that's the interesting part—the part you can't explain or understand. Or teach or talk about. That's where the abracadabra is."

The interviewer had responded that we live in a time of science. "What if," she had asked, "the imagination turns out just to be those memories you don't remember?" And then she offered a compromise. "Or it could all be chemistry? Neurons firing?"

"Ka-pow," Addison had said, another answer best described as evasive.

(3)

Many, many times before and many, many times after that interview, Addison had told the story of her first dollhouse and the unfortunate late little Mr. Brown. She'd told it so often that the story had replaced the memory, and there was, by now, no memory of little Mr. Brown, only the memory of telling the story.

Here is a different story about her first dollhouse: it takes place before Mr. Brown, when Addison was three years old. This was back when they'd lived on Pacific. She'd never told anyone this story, because she didn't remember it. No memory, no story, no memory of a story.

Her mother had had a headache, so Addison had been told to play outside. She was collecting snails in the plastic bucket she took to the beach. She had vague plans for these snails—something thespian, a family drama they would star in. She'd found five so far by following their slicks into the ivy. When it comes to escaping, the whole game is rigged against the snail.

A black car stopped in front of the house and a man got out, came into the yard. He left the car engine on. Bing Crosby was singing Christmas songs on the car radio. The man knelt beside her. He wore gray wool pants, the knees stained with grass, mud, and motor oil. "I'm here to take you to see Santa Claus," he said.

Addison knew that she wasn't supposed to wander off by herself, but to leave in a car with a grown-up to go see Santa Claus was another matter entirely. The man helped her put the lid on her pail and weight it with a rock so the snails wouldn't escape. Then he put her in the passenger seat. When she rode in the car with her parents, she sat in the back. She had a wooden Budweiser box with crayons and books inside, and she could sit on top of the box and see out the windows. The novelty of being in the front seat wore thin after a while, since there was so little she could see.

The man driving didn't speak to her, but he smiled and winked and sang along to the radio. The road began to climb and wind. Tree branches slipped by overhead. By the time the car stopped, Addison was asleep.

The man slammed the door, came around, and woke Addison by lifting her out. He carried her through a shaded yard, up three steps onto a porch. He knocked on the door and set Addison down next to a rocker with a spider web between the arm and the seat. The paint on the rocker was peeling. Inside the house, a dog barked.

A woman opened the door. "I got her," the man said.

"Well, she's just a little peanut." The woman's voice was hearty. She stood aside to let Addison in. "Hello, peanut." She was wearing stockings that bagged around her knees, and a pair of embroidered Chinese slippers on feet as small as a child's.

The man saluted Addison smartly as he left. There was no sign of Santa Claus, but an excited terrier danced around Addison and licked her face.

"I don't want any accidents," the woman said. Her voice was less friendly now. She took Addison by the hand into the bathroom, removed her panties, and set her on the toilet, toward the back since she was so little she might fall in otherwise. "You're a big girl," she said with an admonishment in her tone. "You wipe yourself and call me when you're done." And she closed the door behind her, the dog pawing it from the other side.

Addison didn't have to go to the bathroom. She slipped getting down, so one of her shoes touched the toilet water, which splashed onto her sock. She dried the shoe with toilet paper and stepped back into her panties, struggling to pull them on. "I'm done," she said, but a long time passed before the woman came back and held her up to the sink to wash her hands.

"If anyone asks," the woman said, "you remember it wasn't my idea to bring you here. You say that if anyone asks."

The house smelled of hair spray and cigarettes. There were doilies on the backs of all the chairs, and ruffles around the bottoms that hid balls of dust and dog hair. A different man arrived, wearing blue pants with black shoes that tied. He was chewing gum. "Hey there, Buddy," he said to the dog, and, "Welcome, madame, to our humble abode," to Addison.

"She's just a little peanut," the woman said, all friendly again.

"Come here, little peanut," said the man. He lifted Addison in his arms, carried her across the room to show her a shelf with a dollhouse on it. He smelled like licorice. Addison had never seen a dollhouse before, and this was an elaborate one—three floors, twelve rooms—a hinge in the back to open and close it like a book. The man pulled up a chair for Addison to stand on, and he showed her how the grandfather clock kept real time. He let Addison hold it up to her ear to hear the ticking.

There were tiny china dishes in the dining room, painted white with blue flowers, and even tinier cutlery. "You could have a tea party," the man said. "Go ahead and set the table." He opened the icebox to show her a ham and a cake.

"I want to talk to you," the woman said, and she and the man left Addison on the chair. There was a nursery with a little crib, and a rattle inside. A dressing table with a mirror and a powder puff. A library with bookcases, only the books were painted onto the shelves.

Santa Claus still hadn't appeared, and by now it was lunchtime. Addison was called to the table and given a glass of lemonade and a tuna fish sandwich. The man ate quickly and left. Addison drank the lemonade and moved the sandwich from one side of the plate to the other. "I don't know what the rules are where you live," the woman said. "Here we stay at the table until we've finished our food."

Those were, in fact, the rules where Addison lived. But her mother toasted the bread when she made tuna sandwiches so it wouldn't get wet. She cut the crusts off and she didn't mix in sweet pickles. She didn't use so much mayonnaise that it soaked all the way through. Even so, there were plenty of times when Addison had to sit at the table until her mother gave up. This woman turned out not to have nearly her mother's staying power.

"I can't spend the whole day babysitting," she told Addison. "You go play outside now."

"I want to play with the house," Addison said.

"It's not for playing with," the woman told her. "It's for looking at."

"I want to look at it."

The woman sighed. She said all right, then, Addison could look if she took her shoes off so the chair didn't get dirty, and didn't touch anything, but then, when Addison took her shoes off, her wet sock left a spot on the chair that the woman saw. She shoved Addison's foot back into her shoe. "How did your foot get wet?" she asked. "Did you have an accident?"

She made Addison sit on the toilet again, and this time Addison did have to go. "Who lives in the house?" Addison asked as the woman washed her hands.

"They're all dead," the woman said.

Which suggested to Addison that the house was maybe up for grabs. The woman dried Addison's hands with a towel that had little pink-cheeked angels on it. "Play outside," she told Addison, and Buddy wanted to go with her, but the woman wouldn't let him; she said he'd get dirty.

Addison sat on the porch steps because there was a spider on the chair. She collected leaves and pinecones to make tables and beds, but they didn't come out well.

Eventually her father arrived. He drove up in their old green DeSoto and snatched her from the porch. "Are you all right?" he asked. "Did anyone hurt you?" And then he put her in the car, where she sat on the Budweiser box and watched him talk for a long time to the woman. And then her father told her to climb into the front seat so he could see her while they drove all the way home.

There was a great fuss over her at dinner, and she sensed that if she asked at just that moment for a dollhouse she was likely to get it, even though money was tight and she'd been told many times that Santa had already bought her Christmas present.

That night her father and mother both sat on her bed and said that she was never, ever to get into a car with someone she didn't know, no matter what. Santa Claus would never want her to do such a thing, and anyone who said he did was lying.

The next day she was given a whistle to wear around her neck. If someone she didn't know asked her again to get into a car, she was to blow hard on the whistle and not to stop blowing until her mother or father came. She was made to practice until the sound came loud and clear.

She'd forgotten about the snails in the pail, and they died. Usually Addison saved empty snail shells if she found them, but there was too much guilt associated with these. They were buried in their shells in the backyard beneath the rosebushes. She tended their graves until, within the month, she and her parents had moved to the house on California.

Addison wore the whistle until she was six. She took it off when she started school, since no one else there wore a whistle. By then she had forgotten why she had it. The only residue was an odd suspicion attached to Santa Claus (which made it strange that she had so many of him up in the attic). And, in the backyard on Pacific, the graves of the snails.

Chapter Fourteen

(1)

Addison's metaphors were running aground on the facts of global warming. Instead of the inspiration of the edge of wonders, the way she had seen the ocean for most of her life, what she now envisioned was the ocean empty, the waves rolling on like a great, lifeless clock, dead water curling over dead water. It seemed that was what she should be talking about, except it wasn't what she'd been asked to talk about.

Rima watched as Addison wrote and scratched out and wrote again, and she could see she was in the way down here, even though she wasn't the one doing the talking.

She went upstairs to her bedroom, but Tilda was already there, cleaning, sweeping, mopping. Judging. (To be fair, Tilda had not once mentioned how Rima's shoes had appeared like magic under Martin's bed. She'd been polite enough. It was maybe just Rima's imagination that Tilda felt the need to clean her room often and with great vigor, as if you never knew what might have been going on in it.)

Rima came downstairs again. She decided to get out of the house, and took the unprecedented step of asking Addison if she could borrow the car. The keys were by the back door in a little dish shaped like a scallop, and if Rima remembered to put them back, that was where they'd be next time she wanted them too. Or so it would be pretty to believe.

Now what? Where to? She sat, engine idling, and considered her options. She could take a hike, there was supposed to be great hiking in Santa Cruz, but that would require going inside again, asking Tilda where to go and how to get there. She could go back downtown, look in the shops. Yet even in the best of moods, she wasn't really a shopper, and she wasn't in the best of moods and she planned to get worse.

All these days, she'd been looking out her window at the tops of roller coasters and some ride that looked like a radio tower, and Oliver would never have let so much time pass without making the scene at the boardwalk. (*Killer Klowns from Outer Space* had been filmed there! Also some Clint Eastwood movie Rima couldn't remember, but Oliver would have known it. *The Lost Boys,* of course. *The Lost Boys!* Back when Kiefer Sutherland had been a perfectly respectable vampire and not the detestable government agent he'd become.)

Plus it seemed a suitable place for a virulent bout of self-pity— the boardwalk in autumn, all deserted and haunted by its summer gaiety.

She thought it would be easy to find, since its drops and roller coasters remained visible at most points in the drive. It wasn't. She passed the *Lost Boys* railroad trestle, crossed and recrossed the river and overshot and doubled back, and finally she turned onto a street of brightly colored stucco buildings—yellow, pink, and blue, with arches of a faintly faux nature, and tiled roofs. The blue-and-white roller coaster loomed above her, seagulls flying in and out of the coils of track. It was all a lot cleaner than she'd expected.

She parked in the parking lot and followed the painted bare footprints to the street. To her right were an arcade, a surf shop, and a blue building identified as "Neptune's Kingdom," with a painted shark grinning down from one side of its door and an orange octopus floating on the other.

She walked past the empty ticket booth, through an archway to an alleyway to the boardwalk. She was facing a ship. Behind her, a row of gargoyles leered down from the façade of something called the Fright Walk. Entry to the rides was blocked by a chain across the stairs, and the blue-and-white roller coaster was being worked on by a couple of mechanics. This was probably a good thing, roller coasters being maintained this way. And yet, Rima was less inclined to ever go on one as a result of seeing it. It raised the question.

She stopped at a booth called Remote-A-Boats. This featured a miniature lagoon made of algaed water with some tiny islands, a lighthouse, and an inn called the Rusty Rooster. It was like something Addison might have made, if only there'd been a body somewhere. Rima felt the lack of one. She could see just where it ought to be floating, blood like a veil around it.

She turned right, went down a covered walkway, the beach a flat

expanse seen now through a row of fat purple-and-yellow pil-
lars. On the inland side of the walkway were a restaurant, a
candy store, some shop whose windows were filled with carousel
horses. Seaward, the sun came through the clouds in a great
golden shaft. Lovely, but it made the day no warmer or brighter.

Two women sat at an outdoor table drinking coffee and discussing, presumably, a third woman. As she walked by, Rima
heard one woman say, "She doesn't sparkle."

And the other—"*You* sparkle."

And the first—"*You* sparkle too."

Rima felt a wave of sisterly solidarity toward the absent,
unsparkling woman. This was followed by an image of Scorch,
dancing in the black light of the bar, sweat and body lotion glittering on her bare shoulders. There'd been an undertone in Scorch's
blog, maybe even in a few comments Addison had made, or
maybe Rima had imagined it. You weren't supposed to love your
brother more than anyone else in the world. Maybe in a Dickens
novel you could get away with that, but not today. Not here at
the start of the twenty-first century, when the whole world of
MySpace friends lay before you. Rima's eyes began to sting and
she had to wipe her nose.

She heard laughter. The entrance to Neptune's Kingdom was
past a glass case that held an enormous, cacophonous automaton
named Laffing Sal. Laffing Sal wore a green jacket and a dress with
a ruffled collar. She had stiff red hair under a straw hat, freckles,
and a tooth missing. Inside her glass box, Sal writhed and bel-
lowed, and Rima could still hear that asphyxiated laughter after
she had gone indoors and was listening to the added sounds of
shooting from the arcade, old-school rock and roll on the speak-

ers, and from somewhere undetermined, the screeching of parrots. Neptune's Kingdom couldn't have been noisier, even though there were only a handful of other people in it.

A mural stretching two stories covered the wall opposite Rima. In it a pirate stood at the base of an erupting volcano, the eruption artistically depicted in blinking red lights. Above her, a second pirate, another automaton like Laffing Sal, shimmied up and down a rope that hung from the ceiling. A third popped from a rum barrel like a jack-in-the-box.

Rima had that déjà-vu-all-over-again feeling. Neptune's Kingdom was ringed with arcade games and glass booths containing the heads of various fortune-tellers—Omar and The Brain and yet another pirate—but most of the first floor was taken up by an indoor miniature golf course. As if all that miniature golf lacked was pirates to make it nautical as hell.

It would be hard to imagine a more Oliver-type place. Rima decided to get a table on the second floor, above the battery of cannons. Her plan was to buy a beer and cry into it.

She reached into her back pocket for her wallet, which was not there. In her front pocket was a handful of change that fell considerably short of beer money. She had a faint hope that she'd left the wallet on her bed at Wit's End and not in the bar Saturday night, which was the last time she was sure she'd had it. This should have made crying easier, but now that she'd set the mood with miniature golf and pirates and volcanoes, the tears didn't come. Annoyingly, she felt better. Not sparkling, mind you, but not bad either. Not as bad as Oliver deserved.

Suddenly she realized why the scene beneath was unsurprising to her. In *Below Par,* Maxwell Lane had found the body right down there, right on hole seven, beaten to death with a golf club. (*Below Par,* Addison had said in interviews, had been a learning experience. Never title a book as if you were playing straight man to the reviewers.)

Rima added *Below Par* to the list of dollhouses she hadn't yet found. It would, of course, contain a miniature miniature golf course. If only a few more miniatures could be added! Rima had a momentary glimpse of infinity as a set of miniature golf courses, one inside another like nested Russian dolls.

She closed her eyes and someone came to stand beside her, which could have been Oliver but was Maxwell Lane instead. "I'm a good listener," he said, "should you ever want one."

On the pages of the A. B. Early books, Maxwell was a good talker too. Half of being a good listener is in knowing what to say to keep the talking going. But outside the books, listening was what Maxwell was best at. It didn't matter. Rima didn't feel like talking. She was just glad he was there. He stayed until she opened her eyes.

On her way back out she turned her pocket change into four golden tokens. She put one of them into Omar the Fortune-Teller. His eyes lit up like Christmas lights. *Omar sees great things for you,* he began. And then abruptly switched to *Coin Jam Error. Call for Service.*

The fortune-telling pirate cost two tokens, but you get what you pay for. Rima put the tokens in, and the machine spit out a ticket. *A mountain is composed of tiny grains of earth,* it said. *The ocean is made up of tiny drops of water. Even so, life is but an endless series of little details, actions, speeches and thoughts . . .*

and the consequences whether good or bad of even the least of them are so far reaching. Patience and thought will show you the right way.

Rima's first reaction was that this was a lousy excuse for a fortune. Now she had no idea what was coming next!

(2)

Rima read her fortune again and more carefully. This second time through, she was struck by the images of sand and water, by the part about the little actions and thoughts. This second time through, the message seemed clear.

She had been making a special effort to be the one taking delivery when Kenny Sullivan dropped off the mail. This was made more complicated by wild variations day to day in the time the mail was delivered. Rima had never seen a postman so unpredictable.

Today she had forgotten. It would be just her luck if today was the day Maxwell's letter came back. It was probably already sitting on the entryway table, in front of the *Missing Pieces* dollhouse (woman strangled, tiny pieces from a jigsaw puzzle of the Egyptian pyramids scattered over her body).

Rima should go right home and get that letter before someone else did. Find her wallet. Find and pay those dog tickets. Stop feeling sorry for herself. Get things under control.

As she pulled into the driveway at Wit's End, a woman approached the car. "I know who you are," the woman said. She was pale and thin, with a mole on her upper lip. Light brown hair, small, sharp incisors like a rat's. Stoned little eyes. Rima hadn't been a middle school teacher for nothing. The woman was maybe forty years old, but in California, who could tell? Might be fifty. It was the woman from the beach; there was no doubt in Rima's mind. I know who *you* are, Rima thought.

She locked the doors and raised the windows. "You need to return the doll you took, or I'll call the police," she said. She pretended to be searching through the car for her cell phone. Rima hadn't had a cell phone since she lost her fourth one two years ago. There was just no point.

Not that sometimes you didn't really need one.

The woman didn't appear to notice her pantomime. She put her palm on the window by Rima's head. "You're Bim Lanisell's kid," she said.

Now that Rima could see the woman's neck she revised her estimate of the woman's age. Definitely older than forty. "And you are?"

"Pamela Price. I'm sorry about your dad."

"Give the doll back."

And the woman smiled in a way that suggested her complete and enthusiastic cooperation. Then she walked off, down the slope of the drive toward the Pacific Coast Highway. By the time Rima made it inside, the woman was long out of sight.

Tilda was at the stove, stirring a pot of something or other. Her hair was pulled off her face by a black band, and she was flushed from the steam of whatever she was cooking. Rima could have identified it by smell as onion soup and red wine if her mind hadn't been on other things.

"Where's Addison?" Rima asked. "Are we still not calling the police? Because the woman who took Thomas Grand was just outside on the driveway."

"Did she have red hair?"

"No."

"Could her hair have been colored?"

"Who's Thomas Grand?" someone asked. Rima stepped farther in until she could see the breakfast table, where Martin was sitting, ignoring the cup of tea his mother had made for him. His feet were on his overnight duffel. "Are alcoholics allowed to cook with wine?" he asked Rima.

"Look who's here," Tilda said gaily. "Look who came to surprise us." She gestured toward Martin with her wooden spoon.

"We were just talking about you," Martin said, and Rima didn't have to see the little flick of Tilda's shoulders to know otherwise. Sometimes when you enter a room, you kind of know you weren't being talked about.

None of this was to the point. "She knew my name," Rima said, and then—since this wasn't necessarily true—"She knew my father's name. She left fingerprints on the car window."

"You've watched too many cop shows," Tilda said. "They're not going to break out the fingerprint kits for one tiny little missing corpse. Cooking removes the alcohol. All that's left is the flavor."

"Dad and I sure didn't eat like this when I was growing up," Martin said. "I don't remember many home-cooked meals." Martin's father was a lawyer who had thrown Tilda out when she couldn't stop drinking, sued for and won sole custody of Martin, and then married a much younger woman. In a different kind of story, he would be a thoroughly unsympathetic character. In this one, he's quite a nice man.

"You should have dinner here tonight," Tilda told Martin. "I can always throw another steak on. There's plenty." She looked surprisingly motherly with her hair back, a spoon in her hand, and red meat at the ready. Even the snake tattoo could be a sort of Eve-in-the-garden, mother-of-us-all image, assuming you even saw it, which you couldn't just now, as Tilda was wearing a plaid shirt with long sleeves. No necklace, which was a shame.

"I could give the police a good description," Rima said. "I was really paying attention this time."

"Good for you," said Martin. "Who's Thomas Grand?"

Tilda put down her spoon and joined him in the breakfast nook. She filled him in, pointing out the *Spook Juice* dollhouse, making note of the fact that it contained no body. When it had contained a body, she told him, that body was Thomas Grand. She was just getting to the heart of the story, the break-in, and doing Rima the courtesy of making her sound more imperiled than stupid—"Did I mention that Rima was here? Alone?"—when Martin waved her through to the end of it.

"Would that really be worth something?" he asked. "Just one of the bodies all by itself? What would a whole dollhouse go for?"

"I'd pay you to take the lot of them," Tilda said.

Rima heard the sizzling sound of soup boiling over. Tilda leapt to the stove, and there was some brief excitement concerning broth and flames. When everything was quiet and the room filled with the smell of burnt onions, Rima spoke. "Okay, then," she said. "Did I mention that the woman told me her name was Pamela Price?"

"Good to know," said Tilda, fussing with the stove dials.

"Pamela Price." Rima looked from Tilda to Martin. Nothing.

Was she the only one who read the books that Addison took so much trouble to write?

"Who's Pamela Price?" Martin asked.

"A character in *Ice City.*"

"So. Probably not her real name, then," Martin said, just as if Bim Lanisell was no one's real name. He sounded disappointed. Rima could think of no reason why any of this should be a disappointment to him.

He rubbed his fingers over the little scrap of hair above his chin, and Rima suddenly remembered the name for a beard like that. Soul patch. She couldn't imagine why. "Is Pamela Price a good character or a bad character?" Martin asked. It was clear which answer he expected.

(3)

The woman Rima had encountered on the beach and by the car was considerably older than the character in the book, and had made no obvious effort to look the part. Nor had she bothered to look like someone who might at some point in the past have looked the part. Pamela Price was a bottle blonde, a plastic woman with lush curves and a pink complexion. The woman from the beach was gaunt, with bruised eyes and skin so thin she was practically blue.

It seemed to Rima that Pamela Price was an odd character to choose of your own free will to be. She was *Ice City*'s Miss Scarlet, a tired flirt with an eye for Bim Lanisell. Bim discovered the limits of her infatuation when he tried to use her as an alibi.

Ice City, pages 52–53

That my father killed himself was our new article of faith. Without that, Brother Isaiah was a liar and every one of us was going to die someday. I was the only one with doubts.

So Brother Isaiah sent me Pamela. She began to touch me whenever we spoke. She'd lean against my shoulder, her hair falling into her face. "You should come by," she'd say, her fingers floating across my upper arm. "I can't bear to think of you all by yourself. I can always find a use for a big, strong, lonely boy."

She figures to manage you, my father warned me from his throne inside my skull. Her with her dyed hair.

The truth was, she was frightened of me. All of them were—terrified of what I might do or say that would stop them believing. That kind of power is no good for anyone, much less a young man.

I behaved badly and the results were disastrous. But I chose to believe that my father loved me too much to kill himself, even when that choice cost me my immortal life. I'm not ashamed of that.

"I don't understand why she's got you all, even Mr. Lane, eating out of her hand," I said to Bim one afternoon. We were standing outside the trailers. Kathleen's laundry was on the line. Her old blue dress billowed suddenly, as if there were a body in it. I'd just heard that Pamela had told Mr. Lane my father couldn't keep his hands to himself, and I was angry. My father was so uninterested in women my life is something of a miracle.

Bim said that when a woman flirts with you, it's rude not to flirt back. But he also said that it's rude for two men like us, two men of the world, to discuss a woman in this way. So he moved from the particular to the general.

"Okay, then," he said. "Some men don't require imagination. Some men are turned on just by the effort. They don't ask themselves if it's real or not, because they don't care. They don't see a difference between a woman trying to be sexy and a sexy woman."

Someone was walking in the gravel behind us. I lowered my voice. "Is that the kind of man Mr. Lane is?"

"I think Mr. Lane's more the polite kind," Bim said. "Don't you worry about Mr. Lane."

(4)

Addison was on the second-floor computer. Rima found her there, her neck thrust forward like a turtle's toward the screen, her shoulders rounded if not downright hunched underneath a gray shawl shot with green threads. Nothing remotely ergonomic about the setup; maybe the studio was arranged better.

"The woman who took Thomas Grand was just outside," Rima told her. "I can't get Tilda or Martin too interested." It occurred to Rima that if this were an A. B. Early book, Martin and his mother would be suspects. In a Daphne du Maurier novel, the actual perps. Martin had the motive, Tilda the opportunity. This whole estrangement could be an elaborate performance to cover a nascent operation in the fencing of tiny corpses on the Internet to unsuspecting fans of Maxwell Lane. It would explain their unconcern.

But it would also make the fortuitous forced entry of Pamela Price too contrived to believe. Bad plotting there. "It seems like I'm the only one who wants to solve the case," Rima said. Me and Maxwell Lane.

"It's not a case." Addison pushed back from her desk, turned to Rima. She had a shallow scratch on her chin. The people at Wit's End, at least that subset who slept with dachshunds, often awoke with shallow scratches on their faces. Rima had done so herself about five days earlier. You could hardly see her scratches now. "We know who done it. It's just some fan who went off her medication. I still can't believe the Democrats have the Senate."

"Counting Lieberman," Rima reminded her. Why be happy? Life was short. And then, just to deliver all the bad news in a single go: "I think Martin may be joining us for dinner."

Chapter Fifteen

(1)

Given that it was a small group with at least one open hostility and several hidden ones, dinner went about as well as could be expected. The food was good.

Addison wanted to talk about politics. The last two candidates to concede had been Burns and Allen; it tickled her. Time for the Republicans to say good night now, Addison said. Rima got the joke, but had no idea how. How did she know the tagline to a show that ended years before she was born? Martin, she assumed, was mystified, but he gave no sign of it, caught up as he was in the complicated maneuver of asking for seconds without appearing to be enjoying the meal.

Tilda was keeping the conversation light. "This beef is grass-fed," she said. "Usually everything you eat turns out to be corn-based. We are a corn-made people, in general. I try to include some things that aren't corn in every meal."

Martin wanted to talk to Rima. "You must be awful glad not to be in Cleveland anymore," he said. He was the second person this week to tell her this. She felt an unexpected wave of patriotism. What was so great about Santa Cruz? The pirates? The clowns?

"Do you think we don't have miniature golf in Cleveland?" Rima turned to look at him. "We have miniature golf."

Rima wanted to talk about Pamela Price. "What should I do the next time she shows up?"

"Never talk to a stalker," Addison said. "It only reinforces the fantasy that you have a relationship."

"Then how will we get Thomas Grand back?"

No one answered. Rima hadn't realized that Pamela Price would be coming back until she said it. But why stop at two visitations? Of course there would be a third. Rima tried to figure out if she was frightened by the prospect or not. She decided she was. But only slightly, so for a few moments she barely attended to the conversation around her; that's how focused she was on making sure it wasn't some other emotion instead, like exasperation or fatigue.

"We could go play miniature golf this weekend. If that's what you'd like."

"I remember once when you were about four years old. We went out to eat and you told the waitress you wanted a petite filet mignon. She just about dropped her pencil."

"I was always saying something cute after you left. Hardly a day went by."

"This puts the Democrats in very good shape for 2008."

"There's even corn in toothpaste now. Did I mention that?"

Something wet landed on Rima's ankle. Stanford was drooling; it brought her back to the moment. "How did she know my father's name?" Rima asked, just to make the point that the answer was obvious. The information about the lovely house-guest and her connection to Addison was carelessly strewn about Addison's blog, where anyone, on or off her medication, could read it.

Thinking of the blog reminded Rima that she hadn't told Addison about Wikipedia yet. She did so now, in the form of a question. "Did Maxwell Lane really grow up in Holy City, the way it says on Wikipedia?" ("I knew your father," Constance Wellington had written to Maxwell. If he had grown up in Holy City, maybe she wasn't as loony as she seemed.)

"That shouldn't be there," Addison said, in what was clearly not an answer. "Everything on Wikipedia is supposed to have been published and peer-reviewed somewhere else first. It's not the place for grad student theories." Addison's knife scraped her plate with an irritated sound. "That must have been posted quite recently. I'll take it down after dinner."

This led to a story about an assistant she'd had a year back, a young man from the UC English Department who, among other duties, kept an eye on the websites for her. His name was Tom Oppenfeld. Tom and Addison parted messily one day after she came home from a movie matinee to find him stretched like a rock climber over the ice plant on the cliff face below the studio window. He was trying to find a gap in the blinds. Or else he was planning to kill himself. Either way, he needed to be sacked.

In retaliation, he e-mailed everyone who'd asked, and said

Addison would be happy to: speak, write a blurb, write an intro-
duction, teach a workshop, critique a manuscript, officiate at a
poetry slam, auction off the naming rights for a character, do an
online interview, host library donors for a literary-progressive dinner, get all dressed up and attend a fund-raiser. Tom Oppenfeld
was as much to blame as anyone for the fact that Addison was so
far behind on her new book. She'd spent so much time being a
writer there was no time left in which to write. "An assistant is
always a mistake," Addison said. "Would anyone know anything
about Margo Dumas's sex life if she hadn't hired that assistant?"

This was the second time Margo Dumas's sex life had been
mentioned in casual conversation. The repetition was intriguing.
Rima made a mental note to google Margo Dumas's sex life and
see what was what.

"I can monitor the Web or I can write a book. Can't do both,"
Addison said.

Rima put "That must have been posted quite recently" together
with "Can't do both" together with Addison's minute-by-minute
information concerning political matters. She thought she knew
which of the two Addison was doing.

"Did you want to go play miniature golf?" Martin asked.

"I don't like miniature golf," Rima said. This wasn't true. There
were few things Rima liked better than miniature golf. But you
had to be in the mood. You had to be with Oliver.

"Oh!" said Tilda. "Holy City! I completely forgot. Maxwell Lane
got a letter from Holy City today."

And then Addison said that seeing as how Rima was the one so
interested in Maxwell's mail, Rima should be the one to go and
get that letter.

She should bring it back to the table.

She should open it right there.

She should read it out loud so that everyone could hear.

Wouldn't that be fun, is what Addison said.

"And you got a letter from Animal Control," Tilda told Rima. Her voice was carefully uninterested. "That's on the table too."

(2)

This would have been a good time for a diversion. Where was Pamela Price when you needed her?

Or Scorch. A few days before, Scorch had burst into the kitchen with the dogs, all three of them in a state. These dogs, Scorch was saying, so angry there was spit, these dogs are the worst dogs ever. The worst dogs ever! Stanford and Berkeley made themselves busy, chewing their own rumps and paws, and not meeting anyone's eyes.

Scorch said that she'd been taking them to the beach, where they would have all had a lovely time if everyone had behaved in a civilized manner. Except there were two women on stilts, wearing bustiers and tricorne hats, sword-fighting on the stairs while someone took their picture. Before Scorch knew what was happening, the dachshunds had pounced. They harried the women, nipping and snarling at their stilts and ignoring Scorch, who was shouting herself hoarse. It was just God's mercy, Scorch said, that no one had fallen down the stairs and broken her neck. The women stumbled about on the uneven steps, and one of them screamed. Plus the man with the camera shouted at Scorch for not having leashes on her two nasty little dogs.

"I'm sorry," Scorch said angrily to Rima, "but don't you think the stairs are probably private property? And not part of the state beach?" And to the dogs, "What is wrong with you?!"

This would have been a good time for something like that to happen.

In fact, Rima had never seen a place to beat Santa Cruz for the sheer number of people determined to provide you with free entertainment. There were always drummers at the beach, drumming the sun up and then drumming it down. There were buskers who played the guitar or the flute or sang. There was that man, or else it was a woman, dressed like a donkey outside the Bad Ass coffee shop. And the body piercings! Don't tell Rima a person would go through all that for only selfish reasons if it weren't also so very crowd-pleasing.

Addison had told Rima once about being in a bookstore in Malaysian Borneo and how two kids from Santa Cruz, with their earlobes stretched and their teeth filed, had walked in. The Dayaks, Addison had said, were very entertained.

There were clowns on the streets! And now stilt-walkers in push-up bras. It was wonderful. Suddenly Rima was all about Santa Cruz. Cleveland had nothing.

"Am I the only one who sees that clown downtown?" Rima asked. "With the pink umbrella?"

She could tell that she had startled them all with this wild segue, but not so much that they forgot Maxwell's letter. They blinked at her obstinately. There was nothing for it, then, but for Rima to rise, letting her food go cold, and walk through the kitchen and down the hallway to the entry table by the door, where the mail had been stacked in the front yard of the *Missing Pieces* dollhouse.

Rima took a moment to notice the workmanship of the *Missing Pieces* murder scene. She felt she'd not sufficiently appreciated how meticulously the dollhouses were assembled. There were teacups painted in the same poppy pattern as Addison's dishes. A half-smoked cigarette stubbed out in the ashtray under the lamp. Rima suspected that if she gathered up the tiny, tiny puzzle pieces, some would actually fit together. She felt the impulse to do this. Right now. Even if it took all evening.

Addison was very good with her hands. If the writing hadn't worked out for her, there were lots of other things she could have done. Hairdresser. Brain surgeon. She wondered whether Addison had made the entire jigsaw puzzle or just the corner of it she needed.

The letter to Maxwell Lane was on top of the stack of mail. The envelope was business-size, the address in blue pen. The words were printed in capital letters. The return address was for Holy City Art Glass. This was not the letter Rima had written. And someone had already opened it.

Rima took it to the table. " 'Dear Maxwell Lane,' " she read aloud.

> *"I'm very sorry to tell you that Ms. Wellington is no longer with us. She was the last surviving member of Holy City (by a great many years), and the only one I ever met. She died in 1997 in a nursing home in San Jose at the grand age of eighty-nine.*
>
> *"I tried to find an heir for all the books she left here, but*

eventually donated them to the SPCA thrift store. Her cats I took in, and the last of them, Mr. Bitters, died only a year ago. Although I gather you weren't close, perhaps you know if there are surviving relatives. I still have her letters. I kept them for their possible historical value.

"As old as she was, her death can't come as too great a surprise. Still, I'm sorry to be the one telling you.

"Yours, Andy Sheridan"

There was a flyer enclosed. On December 1 the factory was having an open house, at which a collection of glass Christmas ornaments would go on sale.

"How very mysterious," Addison said. "Maybe Pamela Price has struck again?"

One of two things had just happened. Either: Everyone knew that Rima had written a letter to Constance and signed Maxwell's name, but they were too polite to say so. They were using Pamela Price as a convenient fiction. It was possible they didn't even believe Pamela Price existed. Why should they? No one but Rima had seen her, and Rima was already seeing clowns and such wherever she went. The only real evidence was the missing doll, and Rima could simply have lost that. This would explain why everyone was so casual on the subject of Pamela Price.

Or: Rima had gotten off scot-free. Of course, it wasn't right, letting an innocent thief take the blame like this. Rima should confess. Now was the moment to do so. If she let this moment pass and had to confess later, how much worse that would look.

Addison held out her hand for the letter and Rima gave it over. "People are really interested in Maxwell Lane," Martin said, which could have been the perfect opening to talk to Addison about his bar, but he took it no further.

"Does anyone want dessert?" Tilda asked.

And just like that, it was done, the blame settled on Pamela Price, who, Rima suspected, Tilda at the very least thought she'd made up. She vowed not to use Ms. Price again this way. She could see how it might get to be a habit. "Okay, then. I'll just put this letter in the box with the others, shall I?" she said.

Call Rima crazy, but if she confessed to writing letters to dead people and signing them "humbly yours, Maxwell Lane," she doubted that her courageous honesty would be the thing people noticed.

(3)

Martin wanted Rima to come to the movies with him. There was an old-fashioned drive-in down in Capitola, one of the few left, and *Borat* was playing, and *Borat* was awesome. Martin had seen it twice already. When Rima said she was too tired, Martin took his duffel and drove home.

She started to clear the table, but Tilda told her not to, said it sharply, said that Rima should go to bed, given she was so very tired. Clearly Martin would surely have stayed the night if Rima had been nicer to him. Probably he'd packed a bag hoping this would be the case. Probably Tilda, unhappy when she thought Rima was sleeping with Martin, was now unhappy that Rima wasn't.

The wind was rising sharply, filling the hush of the earlier evening. It whistled about the eaves. Rima went to her room, turned on her laptop, planning to connect the phone line, but then, all of a sudden, an unsecured wireless network, Unchained Melody, manifested like a ghost on the screen. It must have belonged to one of the neighbors, blown here by the wind.

Rima connected quickly, checked her e-mail, which was all spam, but you could hardly blame her friends for this. She was the one who'd spent the last week being unresponsive.

Then she googled Holy City and suicide. The only thing that came up was the Wikipedia site:

"Holy City promised a world of perfect governance. A sign welcomed all visitors. 'See us if you're contemplating marriage, suicide, or crime,' it said." Rima clicked on the link and saw that the sentence concerning Maxwell Lane had already been removed.

She googled Holy City Art Glass. According to its own website, the company occupied the corner where the Holy City post office had once stood. Andrew Sheridan was listed as the artist and owner. He'd recently done a series of windows based on Celtic runes. Rima saw the spaces where these windows should have been displayed, but before the pictures could load, the wireless connection disappeared and she was left with the Art Glass website and the blank spaces. The bottom of the screen showed an ad for eHarmony. Now I'm meeting people that really get me, the ad said.

Rima moved her laptop about, on her knees and off, a foot to the right, a foot to the left, searching for Unchained Melody, but it was gone.

She shut down and got ready for bed. Off in the distance there was an odd sound, like someone blowing over the top of a bottle, but very regular, every ten seconds or so. Rima wondered whether it was a foghorn, and if so, where. She had no sense of how far away it might be.

She pulled the comforter up so that it covered her mouth. The clock chimed the half-hour. She couldn't sleep. She might have stayed on the computer if the connection hadn't failed. She was tempted to get up, see if she could find it again. She would have liked to look for a website that discussed Maxwell Lane's history. This information had been spread out over many books, but surely someone had gathered it all together.

It was too cold in the room to leave the covers. So she tried to assemble the facts herself, from memory and as a soporific, like counting sheep.

Fact number one: Maxwell Lane had certainly grown up in a cult.

Five of the A. B. Early mysteries involved murders that took place within cults or communes. *Ice City* was one of those five. Addison began to write in the late sixties and to publish in the early seventies, when murderous cults were a more ordinary part of the zeitgeist, especially in California. Because of his upbringing, Maxwell Lane was often called in when cults were involved. He was a cult specialist.

But Rima saw little to suggest that Maxwell's cult was based on Holy City. Fact number two: It wasn't a compound in the mountains. It was a farm property, an almond grove on CA-128, halfway between Davis and Winters, wherever that was.

Fact number three: It wasn't a celibate, white supremacist cult.

When Maxwell was sent by the FBI to infiltrate it, he discovered that it was operating under the command of a South Korean corporation that was dedicated first to making unholy amounts of money and second to replacing the U.S. federal government with a foreign religious theocracy in which salvation was spread through sexual relations.

Fact number four (and most important): The cult Maxwell Lane grew up in seemed to be run by truly dangerous and competent people. In contrast, Holy City under Father Riker, in everything Rima had read and in everything Addison had told her, seemed like a version of the KKK in which the first two K's stood for Keystone Kops.

Six people had gone to jail on Maxwell's testimony (and none of them ever knew it was Maxwell who put them away), but these were his neighbors, friends of his parents, people who'd made him cookies when he was a child and babysat him. They were, none of them, the people he'd wanted to get. They were none of them anything but dupes and dopes. And they were, most of them, people who loved Maxwell.

Maxwell had cooperated with the FBI because they'd suggested that the cult was responsible for his mother's death first, and then later his father's. He'd never found any evidence of this. They'd also assured him they were after the big fish. Their decision to prosecute only the underlings came as an abrupt change of heart. It seemed to coincide with the prophet/mastermind's buying a newspaper whose editorial pages could be counted on to support conservative causes and Reagan's taking the presidency. (It was a puzzle to Rima how anyone could have missed the fact that Addison was a hippie liberal. But maybe if you hadn't read *all* the books.)

This explained Maxwell's usual state of mind, which was, simultaneously, that of the betrayer and the betrayed. Although he occasionally reopened the case of his parents' murders, or the file he still kept on the cult leaders, there'd been just enough progress over the years of his career to make some readers worry that the series would end with Maxwell's assassination. Surely even Addison wouldn't be that cruel.

Rima had lost track of what number she was on. The wind sawed at the shutters, which drowned out the clock in the hallway. Her door creaked open. She heard footsteps in the room, fast, light, and too numerous to belong to only two feet. Berkeley whined to be lifted into the bed, where she burrowed under the covers until Rima felt a wet nose against her ankle, the heat that radiated from Berkeley's little body. Soon Berkeley was snoring the snores of the innocent.

In the morning, Rima would have said that she hadn't closed her eyes the whole night, if this hadn't been contradicted by a clear memory of having sex with Maxwell Lane. The sex was powerfully satisfying even though Rima had slept through it. Compared with some of the bewildering people (him? really?) Rima had previously had satisfying sex with in her dreams, an entirely made-up man like Maxwell was a catch. Now I'm meeting people that really get me, Rima thought.

Chapter Sixteen

(1)

That morning, Cody and Scorch invited Rima to go with them to Steamer Lane, a world-famous surf spot. Cody needed to observe the short-board surfers for his term paper on primate behavior. The surfers at Steamer Lane, Cody said, were the most territorial pricks you'd ever hope to meet. But wicked good, and Rima should come along to see them. There was a great view from the cliff above, and always an audience.

Rima could tell that she was being asked only as an afterthought, simply because she happened to be at the table when they were leaving. There was an awkwardness about the invitation. Rima, who rarely wished to leave her room, who'd forced herself into the routine of joining them for breakfast as a sort of unpleasant medicine you took to get better, was a little hurt to think they might actually prefer if she didn't come.

"Cody surfs," Scorch said.

"Wicked bad," said Cody.

Rima said yes to punish them for not wanting her along if they didn't want her along. If they did want her along, then she was saying yes only to be polite. She was so much older than they were. There was no reason for them to want her company.

She wondered exactly who would be her age. Most twenty-nine-year-olds hadn't buried their whole families. So how old was she? It was no easier to calculate than the ages of fictional characters.

Rima went upstairs for her shoes and remembered that Martin had cut the laces in her sneakers. Every morning she remembered this, and every morning she planned to buy new shoelaces, and every morning she forgot to do so. So she'd have to wear her pumps. They had a low, thin heel, all wrong for walking in sand, or anywhere else.

Rima half expected to run into Pamela Price now every time she went out. She wasn't frightened, not in the daylight, but it would be good to have Cody around if Pamela showed. Cody was a big guy, even if not a scary big guy.

She climbed into the backseat of Scorch's car and they wound their way through town, past the boardwalk, past the statue of the unknown surfer, who Cody said really should be Hawaiian but wasn't. There he stood, his board upright, his hair curly, his very straight back to the ocean, and just beyond him, a parking lot beside a lighthouse, where they left the car. This was not the tiny lighthouse close to Wit's End, but a larger one, and it wasn't a lighthouse anymore; it had become the Santa Cruz Surfing

Museum. It was situated on a grassy point with the ocean on both sides and the wind slashing about.

The museum was closed for the day, which was a shame, Cody said, because there was a lot of good stuff in there, especially about the battle between Santa Cruz and Huntington Beach for the title of Surf City. "It should really be Santa Cruz," Cody said loyally. "The first surfing outside Hawaii was right here, right at the river mouth." The fight for the title had been a long one, involving the courts and the legislature up in Sacramento. Rima had never pictured surfers so litigious. Territorial pricks indeed.

There was a beach on one side of the point, and a large rock straight off it, covered with cormorants, pelicans, and sea lions. The sea lions were barking. It made a nice change from the high-pitched dachshunds.

Holding her hair back with one hand, Rima read an informational marker that showed the line of the coast all the way up to San Francisco. Although she'd seen the curves of Monterey across the water almost every day now, she felt she'd never completely understood that Santa Cruz was on a bay. There was nothing bay-like about the large waves of Steamer Lane. The cliffs were a tumble of rocks, and it looked to Rima as if here was the place a ride would end, and end badly.

A three-foot-high restraining grille ran along the cliff edge. Beyond the grille was a sign saying that since 1965, ninety-two people had drowned along the coast.

Don't Be Next.

Respect the Ocean.

Stay Inside the Fence.

Beyond the sign, two boys in baseball caps were smoking something that had to be passed from cupped hand to cupped hand. They couldn't have been any older than middle school. Kids in middle school were very self-absorbed, in an I'm-an-immortal-with-bad-skin-so-don't-look-at-me kind of way. They probably hadn't even stopped to think how someone like Pamela Price could come up right behind them and give them a push.

The air was cold and the sun bright. There were maybe twenty wetsuited surfers in the glittering water, and at least a dozen spectators watching from above. One of the surfers was an old man with white hair and a long white beard. He looked like Santa Claus in a wetsuit, if Santa Claus ever got himself seriously into shape.

Cody found a spot along the railing. He'd brought binoculars, and occasionally he pointed to something, gave Rima the binoculars to look. She never knew what she was being shown. She trained the binoculars on the waves themselves, the explosion of white, the sculpted curve, which magnified like this had facets like a jewel.

"What an asshole," Cody said. Apparently he could see assholery even without the binoculars, while Rima, with them, could not. She gave the binoculars back. A surfer stood, went down. Another paddled to catch a wave that slipped from beneath her board. Rima saw several rides that defied belief. Who would look at the ocean, the crashing surf, and think, I bet if I had a plank I could stand up in that? Rima added surfing to her list of heroic firsts. The first person to swan-dive. The first person to eat an artichoke. She watched the surfers, all of them dressed like seals, rising and falling in the water.

Eventually she tired of awesome athletics, as one inevitably does. The wind whipped her hair against her cheeks, and the light was too bright. She went to sit on one of the nearby benches, but there were words carved into the seat and back; she ended up reading it instead. *Mark David Alsip. Sit on a happy bench.* This last sentence was punctuated with happy faces.

There were several more annotated benches. Rima worked her way down the sidewalk, reading them all.

Arnette, Sam, Scott, Cindel. Forever.

Judy Maschan: Mother Teacher Friend. Do Your Dream.

Robert "Camel" Douglas: Feel free to love—appreciate the beauty and wonder in life.

Bob Richardson: You will always be with us in beautiful memories.

In Memory of Ron MacKenzie. He Knew How to Keep Christmas Well. Illustrated with holly.

The cliff was one long, copacetic graveyard.

A hand on her shoulder made her jump, but it was only Scorch. They left Cody at the railing and walked across the curve of West Cliff Drive into Lighthouse Field State Park. Over here the eco-system was completely different. On one side of the road, gulls and kelp. On the other, crows, eucalyptus, and pine.

They followed a muddy path past trees whose branches formed caves in which homeless people could leave their blankets during the day. Scorch told Rima that this was an off-leash area for dogs in the mornings, and also a monarch butterfly sanctuary, two uses that didn't seem to go happily together. Rima should come back when the butterflies came, Scorch said.

Because she was from Cleveland, Rima assumed the monarchs

would come in the spring. She couldn't possibly impose on Addison that long. She felt a momentary panic at the thought of leaving Wit's End.

They crossed over a creek on a little wooden bridge. "Addison took the line about Maxwell Lane off Wikipedia," Rima told Scorch. "Just like you predicted. But this morning when I looked, it was back again."

"An edit war," Scorch said. She sounded pleased. "Not Addison's first! I'm sure she's set things up so she gets e-mail notification whenever a change is made. Probably the other person has too. That line will go in and come out and go in and come out."

The path led from the dark wet under the trees into a bright, brittle field. Rima saw how it would all turn to green. She saw how spring would spill across the fields and spread into bird nests and wild flowers. And there Addison would still be, hunched over her desk, locked in her eternal struggles, just like *Star Trek,* while the world went green around her.

"At least until someone appeals to admin to lock the page. And everyone involved has egg on their faces," Scorch said.

They were headed back now, toward Cody and the cliffs.

"I checked the history page," Rima said. "It's someone calling themselves Hurricane Jane."

"Yeah?" Scorch shaded her eyes with her hand to look at Rima. "She's a poster on Addison's site. Active. Kind of a troublemaker, but I guess you don't call yourself Hurricane Jane for nothing."

Down by Rima's ankle was a rock with a plaque embedded in it. Rima stopped to read. *This rock is dedicated in loving memory of*

Rita Collier-Micuda. My wife and best friend. She was temporarily forever mine. January 9, 1962–December 17, 2000.

Such a short forever mine. But longer than Rima had had Oliver. Rima wondered if Oliver would like a rock. Or a bench. There was a world of memorial possibilities she'd never considered.

"Did you check out the Wikipedia talk section?" Scorch asked.

"No."

"You're supposed to explain your edits in the talk section."

"The thing is," Rima said. "The thing is. I don't get it. There's really no reason to think Maxwell Lane grew up in Holy City. And lots of reasons to think he didn't."

They paused to let two cars go by before crossing the street. There was a passenger in one of the cars, a woman who seemed to be staring at Rima, but was no one she recognized. A man in a blue windbreaker was on the lighthouse lawn, feeding French fries to the gulls. They circled him, dipping and shrieking.

"Then it shouldn't be on Wikipedia," Scorch said.

(2)

Rima had been eleven years old when the Maxwell Lane TV show called *The Mind of Maxwell Lane* first aired. It was scheduled opposite *MacGyver*, which meant Rima had never seen it. Now it was in syndication. She told Addison at dinner that she thought she'd like to watch it.

Addison paused, a forkful of salad suspended in air over her plate. She shook her head. She had never liked this star. He was, she said, less like Maxwell Lane than any other Maxwell Lane

ever had been—too cleft-chinned and square-browed, too South-
ern Californian, too emotionally fragile, too unsuspecting. Really,
what passed for cynicism in the mind of a screenwriter wouldn't
get a novelist past chapter two.

But there was nothing else on. Rima was certainly welcome to
see for herself.

That afternoon it had begun to rain, and it rained harder as
night fell. Rima had always loved hearing the rain from someplace
warm and dry. Wit's End was hushed and lovely, the windowpanes
and gutters singing, the ocean pulsing like a giant heart. Rima had
pictured an intimate evening, just her and Maxwell and a dead
body or two.

Instead, Addison and Tilda joined her. Addison drank a shot of
whiskey, which tonight she said she needed because of the show.
By the first set of ads she was snoring.

Tilda went to bed. The Maxwell Lane who was less like Maxwell
Lane than any other Maxwell Lane ever had been was trapped in a
sauna with the door jammed shut from the outside. This happened to be a particular phobia of Rima's, which was why you
never saw her in one.

The actor was campy and sardonic. Sarcasm without wit. Rima
had once taught middle school; she'd had enough sarcasm without wit to last a lifetime.

She would never have wasted a minute dreaming about this
Maxwell Lane. When Addison had been awake, she'd made snarky
comments about the dialogue, the clothes, even the camera work.
Minus these comments there was nothing about the show for
Rima to enjoy. She turned the TV off and left Addison sleeping in
the chair. Maxwell had been rescued from the sauna by a young

woman wearing only a towel, but a faint claustrophobia clung like perfume to Rima. In the attic above her head, the ghostly foot-steps circled.

Rima turned on the reading lamp in her room, sat in the chair, and opened the box of Maxwell's letters, looking for more of Constance Wellington's onionskins. She felt closer to her now that she knew Constance was a dead person. At the same time, Rima felt a loss. She hadn't expected Constance to be alive, but she'd hoped. She had such an impulse to like her she had to keep reminding herself that Constance was a white supremacist. Cody wouldn't have forgotten for a minute, nor should he have.

The postcard with the Watsonville Cowboy Wranglers was still on the top. Rima read it again.

Regarding my letter of July 2, you know how cats sometimes engage in heroic battles with imaginary enemies? Am per-suaded I've done the same. Please disregard.

"What you need," Maxwell Lane suggested, "is the letter of July second."

Rima dipped into the box, stirred through the papers. She caught sight of the Holy City address on a yellow envelope. Inside was a card. Underneath a picture of a little birdie were the words: "A little birdie told me." And on the inside, the little birdie's beak was opened wide. "That someone special is having a special day. Happy Birthday!" it was saying. Followed by Constance Wellington's signature.

Rima found a second onionskin letter, still in the envelope, pulled it out and read.

21200 Old Santa Cruz Hwy
Holy City, California 95026
April 2, 1978

Dear Maxwell Lane:

  Did you forget me? Been a while. Kitten season in the mountains! From where I sit, can see a pretty little Siamese minx climbing up the curtain. Two babies, one ginger, one black, wrestling under the reading lamp. Another black dozing on the paperback Roger Ackroyd. *Two calicos nursing on mama. Interest you in any of the above? Perhaps the bookish one? They do lighten your mood.*

  Finished Average Mean *on Tuesday and have been thinking about it ever since. Excellent, excellent work. I salute you! Bet there aren't many men who know as much about putting up vegetables as you. We used to do some canning here. Old days. Over and gone. Move along, as our boy Bim used to say.*

  The police came through last week and rousted the hippies again. No doubt they'll come creeping back like ants. Maybe lucky so many buildings were burned at the end; fewer places to squat. Can't help but wonder what old Father Riker would have said about these dirty young men with their bare feet and long hair. He would have had kittens. (Ha, ha.)

  Back to your book! Clever of you to notice the mysterious traveling umbrella. Excellent work on the dead ficus. Got lucky on the dry-cleaning stubs, had those practically

handed to you, but you saw what you had. Really cannot
fault you at any point. Bravo, Mr. Lane! Bravo, indeed!

VTY,

Constance Wellington

What I need, Rima thought, is some organization. Tomorrow she would go to an office supply store, buy some folders or those clear plastic envelopes, get methodical.

Of course, that would cost money. This reminded her that her wallet was missing, so she put the letter and cards back in the box and searched all through her room, the closet floor, the drawers, the bedclothes.

She went downstairs to look in the TV room, even though there was no way it could possibly be there. It was late, so she moved on the stairs as quietly as she could. The rain outside was louder now. Wit's End creaked and cracked. She pushed open the door. The blue light of the aquarium shone dimly.

Rima turned on the lamp. Tilda was sitting in Addison's chair, holding Addison's empty whiskey glass. It would be hard to say who was the more surprised. "What are you doing?" Tilda asked. There was a snappish tone to her voice.

"I lost my wallet," Rima said. "I'm just looking everywhere I've been."

Tilda stood. She picked up her own teacup with the hand that wasn't holding Addison's glass. "Did you check the pockets of the pants you wore yesterday?"

The house shuddered suddenly. The rain fell. Air bubbled into the aquarium; the murdered diver swayed like a dancer in the water. Tilda remained standing, holding the dirty cup and glass, until Rima turned and went back up the stairs. She was left with the distinct impression that Tilda had prevented her from searching the room.

Even though the pocket of the pants she'd worn yesterday was exactly where the wallet proved to be.

(3)

The clouds dipped lower and lower all night, and by morning Wit's End was wrapped in fog. Rima saw it drifting across the window and thought for the briefest moment that it was smoke, that there was a fire somewhere close by. She lay in bed until Berkeley heard Scorch and Cody arriving, and she made it downstairs in time to join the morning walk. Addison was out back. Tilda had gone to her twelve-step meeting.

Rima still didn't have shoelaces. She wore her pumps down to the sand and then took them off and left them by the steps. The sand was damp and cold under her feet.

She had never seen the beach look so dirty. She'd figured out that the color of the water depended on the color of the sky; today the sky was solid cloud and the water a surly green. Bunches of kelp had been left by the tide, and tangled up in one was a dead gull, breast up and bedraggled. Also two beer cans, half a tennis ball, and, not in the seaweed but nearby, a plastic bag of dog shit with a twist tie. *Good Times* had recently carried a claim that the water was full of *E. coli,* and Rima thought she could see that.

The storm had scattered the surf; the waves were short and

chaotic. Even so, there were people in the ocean. Two men in wet-suits and kayaks muscled their way through the chop to deep water. On the beach, a young woman wearing yellow shorts and a sweatshirt with the UC Santa Cruz banana slug on it jogged on the wettest sand. When a wave came in, she was in the water, kicking up a spray, and when it went out, back on the sand. She was run-ning at a truly impressive speed.

Rima had tried jogging after Oliver died. She thought it would be smart to get physically exhausted. She thought if she were body-tired instead of, or along with, feeling the heavy exhaustion of grief, she might think less. But the effort involved in lifting her feet over and over was too much for her. Later she tried again, but found she'd been mistaken in her primary assumption. All you did when you ran was think. She hated it.

A man scanned the sand with a metal detector. He paused, dug, pocketed something small. There was a Doberman on a leash, a bull terrier off. Two basenjis and a Bernese mountain dog. Rima was good with dog breeds. For a while, when she was about thir-teen and Oliver about ten, they'd shared an enthusiasm for the Westminster dog show. By the time he turned twelve, Oliver wouldn't watch anymore. He'd decided it was all about eugenics.

There was a little girl on the beach, wrapped like a starfish around her father's leg. She was wearing rain boots and a purple raincoat that had green scales, like a dragon or a dinosaur, stitched on the back and over the hood. Her face under the spiky hood was cross. She was the crossest dragon Rima had ever seen. When she saw Rima looking at her, she shot Rima with her finger.

Such were Scorch's powers that she had persuaded the dachs-hunds to shift their interest from the dead bird to the half tennis ball, which was now being reduced to smaller pieces. Half of a half of a half of a tennis ball. Zeno's paradox.

Scorch was doing less well with Cody. Her family, she told him, was going to Yosemite for Thanksgiving and he'd been invited, only he'd have to share a cabin with her two brothers and pretend he and Scorch had never had sex.

Cody shook his head. Nothing about that said Thanksgiving to him. "Where are you going?" he asked Rima.

She said she'd been trying not to think about it. In fact, until Scorch and Cody brought it up, she'd been completely successful in not thinking about it. It hadn't crossed her mind that she had to go somewhere. Was Addison expecting her to? Suddenly the holidays were descending like a foot on an anthill.

A dark man in a turban was facing the ocean, gesturing to the waves with one hand while holding several sheets of paper in the other. Rima couldn't hear him over the water, but he was saying something. From time to time, he glanced at the pages.

Rima could always go to one of her aunts', assuming there was an affordable airline ticket available. She really didn't want to. Too much family in her aunts' houses. The only Thanksgiving Rima thought she possibly could make it through was a Thanksgiving with no family in it.

They drew closer to the man in the turban, close enough that Rima began to hear him. His voice was trained and melodic.

". . . all spirits, and are melted into air, into thin air," he said. "And, like the baseless fabric of this vision, the cloud-capp'd towers, the gorgeous palaces, the solemn temples . . ."

Thanksgiving had been her mother's favorite holiday. Thanksgiving is the holiday, her mother used to say, when everyone gathers in the strays and orphans. Rima had never thought to be the orphan at the table.

"... the great globe itself, yea, all which it inherit, shall dissolve, and, like this insubstantial pageant faded, leave not a rack behind."

To Rima's horror, she was in full sob again before she knew it, and again the breakdown was occurring in front of Cody and Scorch, should they only turn to look. She spun about without a word and walked back quickly, climbed the stairs to Wit's End, climbed the stairs to her third-floor room. She closed the door behind her, collapsed soddenly onto the bed. She hoped Scorch and Cody would imagine some other reason for her leaving so abruptly, maybe simple rudeness.

In her own defense, Rima thought that lots of people would find themselves crying, blindsided by Shakespeare that way.

Chapter Seventeen

(1)

After Rima had cried for a good long while, she took a shower. She stood under the hot water, washing her hair with a shampoo that smelled of melon. She turned off the water, reached for a towel, and then froze. She was thinking about Constance's letter, the last one she'd read. The letter had been about *Average Mean;* it had talked about *Average Mean* as if that book had only just been published. And also mentioned Bim. What was it Bim used to say? Nothing to see here. Move along.

Rima didn't remember the year *Average Mean* had come out, but she did know it was before 1982, which was the publication date of *Ice City*. There'd been at least three books in between, enough time for Maxwell to send the wrong man to death row in one of those and realize it in the nick of time in another.

Rima wrapped herself in the towel and went to look for the letter again. If it had been written before 1982, as Rima felt sure it must have, then the Bim that Constance had mentioned could not have been Addison's character. The Bim that Constance had mentioned must have been Rima's father.

(2)

Ice City, pages 161–162

Brother Isaiah told Bim to take Mr. Lane and me fishing for bluegills. This got Mr. Lane out of the trailer park for a few hours at least, while making sure I was never left alone.

The air stank of algae. The water was green. An empty beer can floated past. My father used to say if you dropped a can into one of the shafts in Mount Konocti you would never hear it hit bottom. But a day or two later, it would show up on the lake.

Bim sat back by the motor. I was in the prow, Mr. Lane in the middle. There were already several boats out. Bim liked to make lists of things that would last forever. Tourists and cockroaches. He didn't see a difference between one-time tourists and the summer regulars. They were all cock-roaches to him.

We found a spot on the south shore and Bim cut the motor. A flock of mallards made soft, unhappy noises. Water slapped on the gunwale. There was a radio some-where off in the distance. I had a headache from getting up so early.

"This is the life," said Bim. "This is all I ever want to do."

I took a waxworm from the pail, put the hook through,

and rinsed the worm guts from my fingers in the lake. The sun was only now rising.

"Shame your time isn't your own, since you have so much of it," Mr. Lane said in a pleasant voice. He cast his line as he spoke. I heard it sing out. "Brother Isaiah seems to run a pretty tight operation."

"He takes every dollar we earn," Bim said.

Before I could stop myself, I'd made a little startled motion. We don't talk to outsiders about money. I don't think Mr. Lane saw. He didn't say anything.

"Your wife, whom you love, tells you she's found a way to live forever. She wants it. Can you say no to that?" Bim asked. The boat rocked. The radio played, tinny and far away. Mr. Lane said nothing.

I think Bim knew he'd gone too far. He made a joke of it. "I'm not the kind of man who will deny a woman every little thing."

It was Mr. Lane's method to find a crack somewhere and work it till it widened. That morning in the boat I saw for the first time what was coming. To figure out my father's death, Mr. Lane was going to pull us all apart. He was going to bring Camp Forever down. And I was the one who'd hired him to do it.

Part Three

Chapter Eighteen

(1)

Ice City, pages 202–203

The night was so hot even Maxwell Lane was sweating. Inside the trailer, the air was thick and wet. My father grew up in a house with a sleeping porch. When it got this hot, we slept outside.

I fixed the fan so it pointed out the door, took my top sheet and went to lie on the lounge chair. The green mosquito netting fluttered around me. I slept fitfully and woke to the sound of voices. Someone was talking to someone else in the narrow space between my trailer and Kathleen's, but I couldn't hear them over the fan. I couldn't even tell if they were men or women, but I could smell someone's cigarette.

The talking ended. A moment later Maxwell Lane ducked inside the netting, took the chair next to mine. He spoke to me in a low voice. "There are predictable dynamics," he said. "Sanity finds the lowest level. Just like water. If the group is small, if there's little contact with the outside, if one member of the group is insane, then soon everyone will be. It's like a sickness to which the group has no antibodies. This is just basic small-group theory."

When I was older and looking back, I figured out that this was one of the ways Mr. Lane had of lowering your guard. He would start as if it were all hypothetical. Then he would slide the blade in. "In any cult," he said then, "there's someone does the dirty work. Brother Isaiah needs something done quietly, who would he ask?"

"Ernie."

"That's what Bim said. Ernie." He was silent for a moment, stretching out his legs as if he were relaxing. His hand tapped on the arm of his chair. His voice was casual. "Who would you ask?"

"You."

He laughed. "Bim said that too."

(2)

Rima couldn't find the letter about *Average Mean.* She would have kept looking, but she was cold, wet, and dripping all over the box and the papers inside. Anyway, she knew what she knew. *Average Mean* was published before *Ice City.*

"You should solve the case," someone suggested, and she wasn't sure who, might have been Maxwell, but was probably Oliver—sounded more like Oliver, all hopped up by the fact that no one had guessed about the letter Rima had sent Constance.

Solve the case.

The more Rima thought about this, the better she liked it. She couldn't spend the rest of her life just lying around. She needed a reason to get up in the morning. Places to go, questions to ask, clues to uncover. What was missing in Rima's life was structure. Maxwell Lane never had to wonder what to do when he woke up in the morning.

Really, she should thank Addison for a lovely time and head on home to find a job. She could always substitute-teach. Her father had once devoted an entire column to her decision to get her teaching credential. Nothing had ever made him prouder, he'd said, because the world needed good schoolteachers a sight more than it needed Pulitzer Prize–winning journalists.

Nice touch of modesty there, to mention his Pulitzer in that dismissive manner. Apparently Rima's getting a Pulitzer would hardly have pleased him at all. (So why bother? Oliver had asked. And if Rima wasn't going to get a Pulitzer, then Oliver wouldn't be caught dead with one.) But Rima hadn't become a teacher to make her father proud. She had become a teacher because she loved kids. Even the ghastly thirteen- and fourteen-year-olds, which virtually no one could do, and so, she thought, much to her credit.

Sadly, as it turned out, she loved them only one at a time. In the aggregate, by the classful, not as much. Solving the case would give her something to do that wasn't teaching "American History:

Growth and Conflict" to a rabble of conflicted and confrontational eighth-graders.

Here was the downside. What case?

It was all very well for Maxwell Lane to go around solving cases when A. B. Early did the heavy work of providing a body, suspects, and clues. That was case-solving with training wheels. Rima, by contrast, was on her own. She would have to do it all.

What case? Not Bogan. She didn't imagine she could solve the mystery of his death, with no witnesses, no information, and all these years later. She'd have to leave that one to Maxwell Lane.

Not Pamela Price. Pamela was obviously up to no good, but Rima would rather not see her again if it could be helped.

The case Rima thought she could maybe solve involved her father and his connection with Holy City. Maybe the mystery of his estrangement from Addison. In an A. B. Early book, these things would turn out to be connected somehow. Maxwell Lane would tease loose a single thread and watch as the whole mystery sweater unraveled.

Rima dried her hair and dressed. This was the moment she realized she had no shoes. They weren't technically lost, she remembered where they were. She just didn't have them. Her face was still the patched red of someone who'd been crying, and she would still have preferred that Cody and Scorch not see it. But she had that case to solve. Could she solve a case entirely in her bedroom slippers? She didn't see how.

The longer she put off retrieving the shoes, the more likely they'd vanish into the ether like sunglasses or cell phones. So she went downstairs, creeping past the kitchen, where Scorch and

Cody were eating in the breakfast nook, the dogs watching every bite. So far so good. The whining covered the sound of her footsteps, and she made the beach unseen.

Her shoes were already gone. In their place someone had left, in honorable trade, a pair of old red Converse high-tops. The right one had a large hole in the toe, and they were at least a size too small for Rima. But they had shoelaces, which was what she really needed. She picked them up.

Back inside, she made it to the second floor, where she helped herself to several sheets of paper from the printer. Her past was littered with no end of attempts to keep a journal, or a dream diary, or a calendar, or a to-do list. Even if she lost the actual paper, writing things down had always helped her remember them. This paper was for her notes on solving the case. Maxwell always kept notes.

Since she was on the second floor anyway, she took a quick look at her e-mail—nothing of interest—and then punched up the Wikipedia Holy City entry, thinking to make a list of the important details. She saw that the line concerning Maxwell Lane had been taken out, then returned, since she last looked. She checked the site history, clicking through the archived pages. The person inserting the line was still Hurricane Jane.

Rima recorded the date of Riker's death. As far as Wikipedia was concerned, that date marked the end of Holy City. Yet there were still three disciples (eight if your source was the *San Jose Mercury News*) on the property who had lived there almost thirty more years.

Rima wrote: "Who were the last disciples?"

And then: "When did Bogan die?"

In the time it took to do this, the line concerning Maxwell Lane had disappeared once again.

Rima went back to her room and upended the box of Maxwell's letters onto the unmade bed. Now there was dust on the quilt and between the sheets. In retrospect, thoughtlessly done.

But done—no point in regretting it now. One by one, she put the letters back in the box, keeping out only those that seemed to be from Constance. When Rima had finished—and this took some considerable time—she had fifteen letters and four cards.

Several of these had no envelopes, and two of the cards had no dates. Rima made a list of the dates she did find. The earliest had been written on March 23, 1972. The last on September 30, 1988. Six of the letters had come in 1983 and 1984. None of the letters was dated July 2.

Rima picked the two with the earliest postmarks and read them. Constance had introduced herself first as an employee of the federal government, then as a fan of the mystery genre, and then as something of an amateur detective in her own right. As such, she congratulated Maxwell Lane on the excellent sleuthing he'd done throughout *Our Better Angels*. It was her first exposure to Maxwell's work, but she predicted she'd be seeing more of him. She believed he'd fingered the right man, and noted that while to some the full confession would have erased all doubt, she had found in the course of her own quiet but not uneventful life that human nature was complex. Reason took you just so far. She applauded Maxwell for his fluid, intuitive approach.

The only part of this letter that Rima jotted down took the form of a promissory note. "Perhaps when we know each other better," Constance said, "I'll share some of my own sleuthing with you. Some old business from the old days. Think the professional perspective might prove helpful."

The second letter had been mailed shortly after the publication of *Below Par.*

21200 Old Santa Cruz Hwy
Holy City, California 95026
June 22, 1973

Dear Maxwell Lane:

Not an athlete myself. Still, can't help but wonder if the clubs for mini-golf are smaller than the regulation clubs and if so, how much. Reminding you that Jeff Strubbe is a golfer. (Know this from Better Angels.*) See no sign that you ever considered him as a suspect, but if the clubs are smaller, maybe you ruled him out on forensic evidence you didn't share with us. (Not fair, if so.)*

Also note that the body was left at the seventh hole. For a certain kind of person, the number 7 is a meaningful one. The Bible tells us 7 is the perfect number. The number of days in the week, the number of notes in the scale, the number of stars in the Big Dipper, the number of bones in the human neck. The seven deadly sins. I'm sure you know that most people, when asked to pick a number between 1 and 10, choose the number 7. See no evidence that you considered any of this. Goes to the psychology of the killer.

Not suggesting that you came to the wrong conclusion, only that there were other fruitful lines of inquiry. If I left a corpse on a golf course, it would be on the ninth hole. Leave you to figure out why. (Joking, of course.)

VTY,

Constance Wellington

PS. Believe that a hole in one is much more common in mini-golf than in regulation. Could be wrong. Never played either.

Rima heard the doggy commotion that meant Addison had come in from the studio. She put the letters she'd read back in the box, and left the unread ones on the bed. Washed her hands and went downstairs to conduct her first interview.

(3)

The fog had rolled up neat as a rug, and there was water all about the base of the birdbath. The sun was shining through the fig-tree window onto the wood table and Rima's hands. She was peeling an orange with her fingers. Nothing prettier than an orange in the sun. Addison had made herself a sandwich with leftover steak and was dipping the bread into the leftover soup. Her hair haloed her head as if she'd spent the morning running her hands through it, desperately searching for *le mot juste.* "I think we've all gone completely mad," she said. "I think we're suffering a nationwide psychosis."

This was surely a response to something in the political landscape. Rima didn't disagree, but she didn't allow herself to be diverted either. "Is the dollhouse for *Ice City* out in your studio?" she asked. She didn't mention her father, because her father was what she really wanted to know about. Maxwell Lane recommended this tactic. He called it coming in sideways.

"That one went in the earthquake. Along with *The Hat He Left Behind* and *Our Last Three Days.* The bookcase crushed them."

"I was just wondering which murder you put in the dollhouse. You remember the first one, with the whistling man?" Rima asked.

Addison looked up. Her sandwich dripped onto her plate. Tick, tick, tick. Tick, tick, tick, went Stanford's hopeful tail, hitting the table leg.

"Did you get the idea for that from a real case?" Rima didn't need Scorch to tell her how unlikely it was she'd get an answer. She'd read enough A. B. Early interviews. But Maxwell recommended asking some questions you knew wouldn't be answered. He called this upsetting the balance.

"Maybe," said Addison. "Could be. I don't remember. Why?"

"Constance Wellington," Rima said. "In one of her letters she wrote something that made me think there'd been a suicide like that at Holy City. And she'd maybe told you about it. Told Maxwell about it. But I don't find anything on the Web."

"Was this letter before or after she read *Ice City*?"

"After. But there might be something from before, too. I haven't been through all her letters yet."

Addison took a bite of her sandwich, chewed, swallowed. Stanford's tail moved faster. He was starting to whine, quietly, as if he knew he shouldn't, he knew the pointlessness, the hopelessness of it all, but was unable to stop himself. "Constance was a strange bird. I mean, everyone in Holy City was strange. But most of them were also quite dim. Not Constance. Constance was sharp as they come.

"Not so great at separating fact from fiction, though. I don't think we can rely on her. Or me." Addison tapped her temple. "Second law of thermodynamics. In today's performance, the role of entropy will be played by my very own brain. Oh, look!" She pointed suddenly across the table and out the window. "Hummingbird," she said.

Rima turned. The leaves of the fig shifted in the breeze.

"Gone now," said Addison. "Sometimes I can pull things back to the surface. Up from the muck. I'll let you know if that happens." She took another bite of sandwich. Stanford's whine grew louder. Rima nudged him quiet with her toe. The effort of not whining made him quiver. He began to whine again.

Rima finished peeling the orange. She separated the sections with her sticky fingers, laying them out on her plate in a fan. Maxwell Lane recommended doing something with your hands so you seemed a little distracted. Also, he said, people talk differently if you're looking at them from the way they do if you aren't. Sometimes you need the one, sometimes the other.

Don't you be the one to fill the silences. Don't you be the one to get uncomfortable because nobody is talking. And go ahead and let the suspect ramble. You learn a lot, Maxwell said, when you figure out why one thing has led to another.

"Riker had a son," Addison said, "from one of his earlier marriages. Bill Riker. He joined the Navy during the war, never had much to do with his father. But one day he was jumped in a bar in San Jose. Bones broken. And nose. The police found him by following the trail of blood. He said it was his father's men, trying to force him into Holy City, but he wouldn't identify anyone. He said they'd kill him if he did.

"There probably was a suicide in Holy City. I wouldn't be a bit surprised. They had everything else. Back in the twenties Riker was accused of murdering an ex-wife and burying her in quicklime. Not true, as it turned out. He'd never cared enough about the ex-wives to even take the bother of divorcing, much less murdering them."

Outside, the gate creaked open. The dogs raced to the kitchen door, Berkeley scrambling up and over Stanford to get there first. Through the window, Rima saw Tilda, bags of groceries (reusable cloth bags of groceries) in her arms. Tilda passed behind the screen of yellow leaves.

Addison rose to go to the stove, put the teakettle on. "Bill Riker sued for the land in the fifties. Argued that his father was incompetent and likely to just give it away. Which is exactly what happened, but he lost the court case anyway. Disappeared, then took off to Seattle, people said. There was a time I wanted to meet him."

"Which?" Rima asked. "Father or son?"

"Son. I did meet the father, remember? At the Fill Your Hole confab."

Maxwell would have managed things so as to keep an eye on Addison's face even while appearing not to be looking. Rima was too late for this complicated and delicate maneuver. Addison at the stove was a back-view Addison. "I still wonder about him from time to time," she said. The burner gasped into flame.

"Was that for a book?" Rima asked. "You wanting to meet him? Was that research?"

"Everything a writer does is research," Addison said. "Every breath you take."

Tilda came in, stamping her shoes clean. "My god, what a beautiful day! I would have stayed and hiked, but it's all mud."

"They really weren't nice people up there," Addison said. "Even Constance. Is my point."

"Who?" asked Tilda.

"The gang that couldn't shoot straight. Holy City."

Rima got up to help put the groceries away. She emptied one of the bags—tangerines, green olives, Irish oatmeal, and Goldfish crackers—all the things she liked best to eat. Rima's appetite had not been good since she'd arrived. She thought she was hungry, until someone put food in front of her and then it turned out she wasn't. She realized that, without asking or saying a word, Tilda had figured out how to cook for her.

Rima was incredibly touched by this. She felt something else, something she hadn't felt in so long it took her some time to recognize it. What she felt was mothered.

(4)

Maxwell never took notes during an interview, because he never wanted it to look like an interview. But he did make time as soon as possible after to write things down.

Rima's notes, made later that afternoon, read:

"Question leads to Bill Riker (son) and lyric from Police. Rest of song: *Every move you make, I'll be watching you.* Possible connection? Warning?

"Addison not so interested in senior Riker—just a dime-store hustler. More interested in the others. Why did they join the cult? What did they get out of it?"

(You join a cult, Addison had said, and people around you start doing crazy things, only no one reacts as if they're crazy. When there's no one from the outside, providing perspective, then you lose track of where the line is. Someone tells you to go beat a man half to death and you do it.)

Rima wrote: "What Addison wants to know: Were they all crazy first and that's what brought them to HC? Or could any of us be led there, step by step?"

"Check out *Ice City*," Rima wrote. So maybe Addison didn't remember everything about writing that book. But to the best of Rima's memory, what she'd said about cults and craziness was very close to what Maxwell had said. Maybe something could be learned from that context.

Tilda had noted that you saw the same thing sometimes when you were on the street. "Speaking of crazy," she'd said. She'd made her usual tea and come to sit at the table, stirring, stirring, stirring while the steam rose from the cup. She had a high color from being outdoors. She glowed with health. Or else drink. Hard to tell one high from another.

"Morgan's been picked to be part of another research project." She'd turned to Rima. "Morgan's a local serial killer. Sexual predator. He went on a yearlong spree that left about twenty mutilated bodies behind. All of them sexually molested. Bitten in the face, and then held underwater till they drowned. They finally caught him in Elkhorn Slough."

There'd been evidence, Tilda had added, of a second killer, a copycat who'd disappeared without a trace. Now Morgan had been outfitted with radio transmitters and trained to dive for food.

"Morgan is a sea otter," Addison had told Rima quietly. "The victims were all seal pups."

"Didn't I say that?" Tilda had asked.

It was like a novel by Thomas Harris. As written by Beatrix Potter. Apparently Morgan had been rescued by the Monterey Bay Aquarium as a youngster. He'd spent seven formative months in the rehabilitation facility before being released to begin his reign of terror. The case of the murdered seal pups had been solved by eyewitnesses. Still, it took a year to recapture him, and then he spent several months in solitary until the research was proposed.

"Same question, really," Addison had said. "I mean, these behaviors are unnatural. I gather they're unheard of. So probably there was something every little otter needs—some sort of feed-back or modeling or something—which the humans couldn't provide.

"But maybe he was abandoned by his mother because he was just wrong from the get-go. Maybe he looked like an ordinary otter to people, but the other otters, they knew better."

All of this was represented succinctly in Rima's notes:

"Very bad otter."

Chapter Nineteen

(1)

Addison went upstairs to take a nap. Tilda was in the laundry room. Rima knew because she heard the dryer door slam, the motor start. Rima finished her tea. The song from the Police was running incessantly through her brain. *Every yard you rake, every cake you bake.* She thought she should get right on those notes before she forgot the details of what had been said.

She was waylaid on the second floor by the sight of the idle computer. Her first stop was Scorch's blog, which had been friend-locked. Maybe this was a good thing. Rima wouldn't know what, if anything, was being said about her and her little breakdowns, but neither would anyone else, beyond the small and select circle of Scorch's two hundred twenty-seven friends. *Every friend you make, every hand you shake.*

Rima went then to Addison's blog. Several new pictures of the dachshunds had been added, so the load took its sweet time. It was the genius of owning dogs that Addison could post regularly and with a casual familiarity while revealing nothing about herself. A glamour shot of Stanford appeared, gazing out a rain-streaked window. Below this was a flirty shot of Berkeley shaking a small stuffed mouse. Stanford in a sweater. Berkeley watching the figure skating on ESPN Classic. *Every day you wake.*

Rima noticed considerable recent action in the forums. Given the length of time since Addison's last book, she thought this surprising. There had been talk of another movie, maybe Colin Farrell as Maxwell Lane. Perhaps there'd been some movement with that.

She clicked over to the message boards and went cold. Quite literally. She could feel the blood draining from her face and fingers. All this activity, sixty-seven postings in the last week, was confined to a single topic. The thread head? "Rima Lanisell: Is she her father's daughter?"

Rima clicked back seventeen pages to the beginning of the thread. The early postings were all about Oliver's death and/or Rima's drinking. A brief description of Oliver's death had been on Addison's blog, but Rima's drinking could have come only from Scorch's. Apparently the A. B. Early completist kept up with A. B. Early's dog walker as well as her dogs.

Oliver's death was a sad thing, the posters agreed, a criminally irresponsibly sad thing, but what Rima could and should do was make it matter. Make it count for something.

Wouldn't Rima be the perfect person to appear at school

assemblies on the topic of drinking and driving? How many young lives might she save, just as soon as she laid off the sauce herself and stopped making this be all about her. It was a teaching moment, and Rima was, by god, a teacher. What would Oliver have wanted? The posters on Addison's website were pretty confident they knew.

About a dozen postings in, someone self-identified as Beezer finally asked the other posters to show some sympathy. If my father killed my mother, Beezer said, I'd probably turn to booze. I'd probably add some pills to the mix. Cut her a break, you guys. She needs counseling not scolding.

Downstairs the dogs were barking furiously. Rima refused to even wonder at what. The chat had turned to O.J.'s poor children. They were reported to be in college now, and no one knew how they were doing, though no one could imagine they were doing well. Then a posting about L.J., the kid in the television show *Prison Break,* whose father had been falsely accused of killing the vice president's brother and who wasn't really relevant to the discussion except that the poster felt sorry for him too, and then the name L.J. was so very similar to the name O.J., which, the poster said, was probably the real reason L.J. had come to mind and not the murderous-father part.

Your father's being a murderer was conceded to be a hard thing to get over. Your father's murdering your mother? Forget about it! Rima was much to be pitied.

Not just pitied. Loved! Someone posting as Norcalgirl said that Rima was the best character in *Ice City.* Norcalgirl described Rima as touching and absolutely believable.

Maxwell Lane is the best character in *Ice City*, the poster LilLois riposted. And after Maxwell, Bim. And then, but only then, maybe Rima.

It fell to Hurricane Jane to point out, with admirable brevity, that Rima hadn't been a character in *Ice City*.

The dogs came racing up the stairs. They danced at Rima's feet, frantic with the need to communicate something to her. Little Timmy's down the well! Feed us ice cream and potato chips! Sometimes there's a benefit to not sharing a language. For all their noise, Rima hardly noticed them. Online, things had taken a nasty turn.

JBC242, a self-identified Ohioan (which probably meant that he [or she] had never left his [or her] Pasadena basement), posted that he (or she) had been in high school with Oliver. Never had a class with him, but their lockers had been close together, at least until senior year, when the school had gotten a series of bomb threats and done away with lockers altogether as a safety precaution. JBC242 said that Oliver had won the senior award for Most Likely to Talk Himself out of a Speeding Ticket.

JBC242 wasn't content with that. Although no one had responded, s/he posted again. This time s/he said that Rima used to pick Oliver up after school because Oliver had lost his license over a Minor in Possession infraction. JBC242 said that on prom night Rima had to drive Oliver and his date around and that somehow during the evening Rima had lost the car.

For the first time, Rima was tempted to post herself. She reminded herself that nothing good would come of it. She heard Addison warning her not to engage. But not one word of that post was true except the losing-the-car part, and the car wasn't so much lost as misplaced for a couple of weeks, and this had happened long before Oliver's prom and had nothing to do with Oliver, who had still been in braces, for god's sake. When would ancient history be consigned to the dustbin of ancient history?

The other posters were immediately deferential to JBC242. Weren't they right, they asked, when they said that Oliver would have wanted Rima to make his death mean something?

JBC242 didn't doubt it. That was certainly the Oliver s/he'd known. Heart of gold, even if he liked a party. Terrible dancer, btw. Like a chicken.

(Was this to be Oliver's permanent memorial? Was it too late to get him a bench?)

Hurricane Jane returned to pose the obvious question. How likely was it that Oliver would win Most Likely to Talk Himself out of a Speeding Ticket if he'd already lost his license over an MIP? JBC242, as always, she said, you are so full of it.

These were Rima's thoughts exactly. In spite of the Wikipedia shoot-out, she found herself liking Hurricane Jane.

Then there was a flurry of postings about *Prison Break*, which had maybe jumped the shark or maybe not. As well as *Battlestar Galactica*, another show on which generational guilt apparently loomed large.

On to *Bones*, which was about a female mystery writer/forensic anthropologist who solved her own cases, as if A. B. Early and Maxwell Lane had been mashed into a single really smart person. This really smart person's father had murdered a bunch of people too. It began to seem as if there was hardly a made-up father anywhere who hadn't. And this really smart person was having her own hard time with it, though she was too smart to turn to drink or pills the way Rima had done.

Woven periodically throughout, ignoring the TV chat and focused like lasers only on each other, Hurricane Jane and JBC242 continued to snipe:

You have some special expertise on the Lanisells? JBC242 asked. *Dazzle us.*

Hurricane Jane: *No special expertise. Just a good bullshit detector.*

JBC242: *I hope you don't keep that in the bedroom. I bet it smells.*

And two minutes later, another JBC242: *Well,* someone's *got her bitch on today.*

Hurricane Jane suggested that JBC242 would have been right at home in Nazi Germany, because Hitler's rule had also been based on gossip and innuendo. (Rima's only surprise was that it had taken so long to get to Hitler. In her online experience, this usually happened pretty quickly. Godwin's Law.)

Meanwhile LilLois was posting that it was too bad Oliver was dead, because a brother-sister detective team was a really great format and, in the right hands, could be gold. It wasn't clear whether what was being suggested was a book or a television show.

Nor was Rima sure the suggestion was serious. Some of the people who posted in response obviously thought so. Others did not. Jake and Maggie Gyllenhaal were suggested. It would be so cool, one poster said, to have an actual brother and sister playing the fictional Lanisells. It would be post-fucking-modern.

The final message, dated the day before at 3:17, was from Norcalgirl again: Okay, maybe it wasn't *Ice City,* Norcalgirl said.

But whatever that book was with Rima in it, Norcalgirl had really loved Rima in that.

(2)

Rima's imaginary adventures so tired her out that she decided to go upstairs and take her own nap. But when she got to her bedroom, her bed had been stripped. This disappointed, embarrassed, and irritated her all at the same time. She shouldn't have gotten the sheets dirty, dumping the box of letters out on top of them. Tilda had enough to do without Rima's thoughtlessly making a new mess.

On the other hand, who asked Tilda to clean it up? Rima was perfectly capable of changing the bed for herself. She'd had every intention of doing so as soon as she had a minute.

The notes she'd taken from Wikipedia had been moved to the dresser. She wondered if Tilda had read them. Tilda was always snooping around her room.

Luckily, so far they were pretty innocuous. Nothing Tilda or Addison had said at lunch was in them yet. Rima added that now. Then she folded the pages and put them in the pocket of her heavy coat. She realized that if she left them there, she wouldn't find them again until she put the coat on next winter in Cleveland. She moved them to the sock drawer, because that was where anyone in her right mind would look first.

Next she searched for the pile of unread letters she'd gone to such trouble to separate out and catalogue. They weren't on the dresser and they weren't in the sock drawer. She hoped Tilda hadn't simply dumped them back in the box, but sure enough, that was where they were, the letters Rima had separated out commingling once again with the letters she hadn't separated out.

It wasn't the problem she'd thought it would be. The sorted letters remained on the top, the only thing disturbed was the chronological order. Rima picked up a Christmas card with no envelope and no date. On the card, Santa Claus slept in his chair. He'd been knitting a stocking; his hands still held the needles. His beard hair was deeply tangled into the yarn and his mouth was open in a snore. The printed message—*It's the thought that counts.*

On the blank space opposite, Constance had written in her clear New Palmer cursive:

> *Merry Christmas, Mr. Lane!*
>
> *Don't know if you heard that the post office here has finally closed its doors. As has old Glenn Holland's Santa's Village over in Scotts Valley. Used to get a lot of visitors in December, driving through the mountains to have their Christmas cards stamped with the Holy City postmark. Very quiet this year; finding myself a bit blue. The good old days, end of an era, fa la la la la. Boring old woman. Don't worry about responding. You're probably real busy. Read about the arrival of your new adventure in the bookstores. Merry Christmas to me! God bless us each and every one.*

Chapter Twenty

(1)

About the same time Rima fell asleep, Addison woke up. She often took an afternoon nap, and sometimes it refreshed her, but sometimes it left her addled and logy. This was one of those second kinds of times. Addison had grit in her eyes and a nasty taste like spoiled cheese in her mouth. She brushed her teeth, washed her face, and went to be with the second-floor computer until she was fit for human company again.

She started by checking the Internet for the definitive word from some source she trusted that it was safe to eat raw spinach. President Bush had managed to send even the FDA off its rails. The government was now claiming the spinach problem had been caused by wild pigs. Truer words were never spoken.

Her eye was caught by an ad for something called an obituary hunter. Addison wasn't sure exactly what this was, but what she imagined was a search engine you could customize for certain kinds of deaths or for certain people's deaths. UFOlogists, say. Or nudists. Or the intersection of the two. She was sorely tempted. Decades had passed since the days when she worked at the *Santa Cruz Sentinel,* but she still took a professional interest.

Her e-mail contained a message from her editor in New York, saying she was going to call this afternoon. Just to check in, see how the new book was coming. Chat about this and chat about that.

Addison turned off the computer and went downstairs for her coat and car keys. She told Tilda she had to go downtown, which was true, and she wasn't so much avoiding the call as refusing to adjust the plans she'd already made in order to accommodate it.

After parking, she walked a few blocks to the used-book store to check out the bottom floor, as was her habit, see if any Peter Dickinsons had shown up. It was a crime that man was out of print. While in the mystery section, she ran into Carolyn Wallace, and Carolyn made the predictable ironic fancy-meeting-you-here noises. Carolyn had been a year behind Addison at Santa Cruz High School and was one of the few class of '61 Cardinals still in the area. The last time they'd run into each other was several Halloweens before, at a neighbor's haunted house. Carolyn had been wearing a black garbage bag over her regular clothes, cinched at the waist, with a top hat on her head. Addison had been carrying a whip and had forty plastic spiders glued to her back. Even though her hat was not right, Addison was clearly Indiana Jones, which maybe meant it was more in the past than Addison was thinking it was. She remembered that she'd had no idea what Carolyn was supposed to be.

Carolyn had put on some pounds since then, and also added an indigo skunk streak to her gray hair. "I figured if I'm going to be a little old blue-haired lady anyway . . ." she said. She told Addison that the tree in Addison's old front yard on California Street had had to be taken out, and it was only last week some guys had managed to dig the stump up.

Addison wished she'd heard this earlier; she would have liked to say good-bye. That tree was a great valley oak, at least a hundred years old—a spring chicken in oak years—and in the bloom of health as far as Addison had known. She'd had a tree house in its branches until a terrible storm had blown the boards two whole houses down the street, where they broke the Bartholomews' dining room window. Addie's nest, her father used to call that tree house. Addie's crow's nest, because from up there, she'd be the first to see whatever was coming at her. (About which, in retrospect, and specifically regarding her mother's marital status, ha, ha, and ha.)

Addison got in her car and drove up California, but the sight of her old house denuded of the tree that had lent the property its only grace was too sad. She turned around at the historic Weeks House without stopping and parked instead in front of the high school. She'd been editor of the student paper, the *Trident,* for about five minutes once, until her article on Hawaii's proposed statehood was censored of all references to imperialism and the American-led coup that deposed Queen Liliuokalani, and she'd been forced to quit in protest.

Shortly after, she'd gotten the *Sentinel* job. She had come home one day from school, was wheeling her bike down the driveway past the kitchen window, when she'd heard Aunt Joan, her father's new wife, talking with her mother. Aunt Joan had tried so hard to make things right with Addison at first. There'd been invitations to dinner, the movies; they'd even taken her along on a camping trip.

In return, Addison had been as unpleasant as possible. She remembered refusing to get out of the car because she was reading a Perry Mason paperback and preferred it to the breathtaking scenery everyone assured her she would see if she'd just look up. Her uncle told her to get the damn hell out of the car, and even though he was a fisherman, he was not a man who swore often, at least not in Addison's presence. The book was *The Case of the Hesitant Hostess.* The breathtaking scenery was the Grand Canyon. To this day, Addison still hadn't seen it.

In the kitchen, Aunt Joan was revealing her true colors. "She's eighteen years old," she was saying.

"Seventeen." That was Addison's mother.

"He didn't even tell me. I found the check stubs," Aunt Joan said. "He doesn't want you to think you can't still count on him. You can absolutely count on him. But goodness gracious, she's seventeen now! Almost grown up!" And then the conversation stopped because the women inside had heard the rattle of the bike chain outside.

Addison's mother had come to the window. "Hello, dear," she'd said. "We're in here having coffee. Come say hello to your aunt."

Addison did that, all frigid politeness, because she would never take another dime, now that she knew that she was taking a dime and that it was so grudgingly given. She hadn't thought about how her father's turning into her uncle and getting married might have financial repercussions.

She went to the paper the very next day and asked for a job. All they had for a starter was in obits, and no one wanted to give that to a fresh young girl who was still in high school and should be thinking about sock hops and soda pops, not deaths and deadlines. Addison had had to insist. It was just a lucky accident, the job's being exactly the one most likely to drive her mother crazy. When Addison was seventeen there was no one who loved her whom she didn't hope to drive crazy.

(2)

Rima woke up to the sounds of excited dachshunds. Possibly a dozen. Possibly two. Plus wood grinding on wood. Down the hall, in the *Our Better Angels* bedroom, someone was pulling down the attic stairs.

Rima seemed to have drooled on Constance's card as she slept. When she raised her head, it was stuck to her cheek. She made it to the *Our Better Angels* bedroom just as the stairs landed, her hair in a post-nap state, but her face cleared of all obvious debris. The dachshunds boiled up the steps, baying. "Do you need help?" Rima asked. She had to shout it, and Tilda shouted back no, she could manage. Tilda was wearing green cotton overalls, and Rima could see many things bulging out of the side pockets, one of which was the flashlight.

There was no way for Rima to pretend that she had been invited. She climbed the bottom steps anyway, stopping on the fourth with her head in the attic and her feet on the stairs. The beam from the flashlight skipped about in the gloom. Beyond it and by it, Rima could make out shapes she knew: the sphinx lamp, the plastic Santas, the old chairs, the shoe box with her father's name on it. The dogs' whining fell away into a delightful quiet of heavy breathing and claws on wood. Rima smelled dust. She climbed up the rest of the way.

Tilda had set the flashlight down, making the edges of the attic go dark. She rolled up her sleeve so the snake showed, took a Swiss Army knife from a pocket, and cut open one of the boxes. She removed a book, put it on the floor. "As long as you're here," she said. "You can tape the boxes back up when I'm done with them." She handed Rima a roll of packing tape. The book on the floor was the hardcover *H₂Zero*. Rima recognized the kelp on its spine.

Taping up the boxes wasn't the job Rima would have chosen. She would have been better at slicing them open; she had no gift for gift-wrap. She would try to lay the tape out flat, but it would curl, one sticky side drawn like a magnet to the other sticky side. When she set the roll down and tried to smooth the creased tape, the end would wrap around the roll so that when she picked it up again, she wouldn't be able to find the end. She would scratch along with her fingernails until they caught on something that would shred as she scraped it free. She would end up with only a small splinter of tape, and would have to go back with her fingernails, teasing another splinter free, and then another, until finally she'd freed the whole, but then, when she'd cut off the ragged edge, she'd lose the end of the tape and have to start all over picking at it with her fingernails. "Sure," she said.

They were up here in the attic to gather a dozen first editions. The libraries in New Orleans were holding an auction for Katrina relief; these were Addison's donation. Not that Rima knew this. She didn't ask and Tilda didn't say. But she could see the stack of books growing on the floor and assumed they were for *someone.*

Tilda was many boxes ahead of Rima by the time she finished. She took the tape back. "I'll pack up," she said. She pointed to the stack. "If you could just take those down?"

Rima didn't want to take the books down. Rima wanted Tilda to take the books down and leave her alone in the attic with the flashlight. She couldn't think how to make that happen. She picked up four, but put two back, playing for time. A faraway phone rang. "The machine'll get it," Tilda told her.

Rima looked off and away into one of the attic's dark corners. "Martin said he might call."

This was a mean and shameful lie. Rima would never have guessed she would stoop so low just to solve a case, and so quickly, too. No wonder Maxwell hated himself. Tilda went swinging down the stairs so fast it was pure luck she didn't break her neck.

But there was no point in telling a mean and shameful lie for nothing. Rima picked up the knife and the flashlight. She knew exactly where the shoe box was, and she sawed through the twine, which didn't snap as quickly as she'd hoped, so she had only a few moments with the box open before she heard Tilda coming back. She laid the twine over the box, hiding the severed ends underneath. When Tilda's head appeared, the flashlight was back where Tilda had left it and the knife was either where Tilda had left it or not. Since she couldn't remember for sure, Rima picked the knife up and handed it to Tilda as if she were merely being helpful.

"It wasn't Martin," Tilda said. She was staring at the knife in her hand as if she didn't know how it had gotten there. "Did he say when he was going to call?"

"No," said Rima, and how was that a lie? It wasn't. She picked up four books and made her way down the stairs.

When Rima was eight or so, she and Oliver came down with chicken pox, Oliver first and Rima a half-day later. They stayed home from school, which would have been great if they'd been feeling better, playing Sorry and Yahtzee every morning and watching the Zach Grayson murder trial on *All My Children* every afternoon from opposite ends of the sofa, their feet piled together in the middle so that they could communicate with each other through kicks. Between naps they called for endless cups of hot water with lemon and honey stirred in, which was the drink of choice for invalids in the Lanisell family.

After a few days, though, everyone involved had had enough. Oliver's case was light, but he acted as though he had just as much right to misery as Rima did, which was aggravating in the extreme. One morning they quarreled for hours over a geode their father had sent them from Brazil. Oliver wished to break it open with a hammer. Rima wished to throw it from her second-floor bedroom window like a grenade onto the driveway below, which, Oliver said, would break it too hard. There were tears (Oliver's), and their mother was forced to take the rock away from them.

At lunchtime, they fought again over who got to deal with the plastic seal on the new jar of peanut butter. Rima wanted to peel it off without breaking it, while Oliver wanted to plunge a knife through it so he could hear it pop, and Rima didn't even really care; she was just making Oliver cry now because she could. Their mother took the jar away and told them to go sit on the couch in the TV room and play a game in which they weren't allowed to talk or touch each other until she said so. If they managed to do this, which would demonstrate maturity and control, two things a spy needed, then she would teach them how to be spies. Like she was.

"You're not a spy," Oliver told her, and she asked him if he was sure about that.

"You're a mother." But there was already doubt in his voice. The woman on *Scarecrow and Mrs. King* was a spy, and her two little boys didn't know a thing about it, although honestly, they were dumb as posts. How many times did your mother have to miss dinner before you asked yourself what was what? (Their father, now, he could be a spy. He probably was. He was fooling no one.) Oliver followed Rima from the kitchen to the TV room and sat as far away from her as possible.

When their mother arrived, she was carrying a single tray covered with a red-striped dish towel. She told them that this particular spy training came from Kipling's book *Kim,* which she would read to them later at bedtime. Grandma had read that same book and taught her this same game when she was a little girl.

"Grandma's not a spy," Oliver said. "She teaches nursery school."

Rima could have pointed out that he had just lost the game in which they didn't talk until their mother said to. The only reason she didn't was that she was bored with making him cry.

The new game was to look at the objects on the tray when the dish towel was removed and then see how many of them you could remember when the dish towel was put back. To this day,

Rima could tell you many of the things that had been on that first tray. The peanut butter jar and the geode. Rima's charm bracelet and her toothbrush, Oliver's Obi-Wan Kenobi action figure and his Adam Bomb Garbage Pail Kids card, a vial of some oil to help you meditate, a pearl drop earring, and a postcard from their father in Argentina, where a few years earlier there'd been a dirty war. Rima had asked him why some wars were dirtier than others, and he hadn't had a satisfactory answer.

Oliver and Rima liked the game. They played several times that day and often afterward, making up trays for each other if their mother was busy. As Oliver got good at it, his enthusiasm for spying grew. He became an incorrigible eavesdropper, which lasted many years and maybe the rest of his life. Certainly he always knew more about Rima than she could easily account for.

Rima helped Tilda carry the books down until all twelve were on the first floor, ready to be wrapped for mailing. Then she went to her room, found her notes in the first place she looked, which was her sock drawer. She closed her eyes to help remember what she'd seen in the Bim box, and then opened them and wrote what she could recall:

Old newspaper clippings; the top one, at least, with her father's byline.

Ticket stubs for a movie.

A small spiraled shell.

An invitation to her parents' wedding.

A bar napkin with something sketched on it.

A tiny plastic dollhouse birthday cake, three layers, chocolate icing.

A ruby-colored shot glass.

Rima read over the list. Perhaps a real detective would want to find out what was written on the bar napkin, exactly which newspaper stories Addison had chosen to save. But Rima had seen enough to know what she had seen. And she had seen the things a person in love collects when she's not loved in return.

She put her notes back into the sock drawer. It was all so long ago. Addison was a different person now. A rich, outrageously successful writer. A rich, outrageously successful unmarried writer. In all the interviews and society columns Rima had read, there'd never been any suggestion of a long-term partner. Or much information of any kind concerning Addison's social life. It didn't necessarily follow that Rima's father had broken her heart for good and all. Addison was a very private person.

This detecting was for people made of sterner stuff. Already Rima had said something she wished she hadn't said in order to see something she wished she hadn't seen. She was finished. Case closed.

There was no case. Ipso facto pterodactyl, as Oliver used to say, there was really no need for Rima to solve it. She could find something else to do all day. Learn to play the guitar. Dust off her conversational French. *La plume de ma tante est sur la table.* Take over those secretarial duties, the way she and Addison had once discussed. Make her bed.

Rima went downstairs to the laundry room to fetch her sheets before Tilda did it for her. She came upstairs with the pile, all soft and smelling of soap, in her arms. On her way back to her room, she stopped to send an e-mail to Martin.

By evening she was able to tell Tilda he would be coming again. He would join them for dinner and spend a night at Wit's End, if someone at the store would switch shifts with him.

Chapter Twenty-one

(1)

The next morning Rima skipped breakfast with Scorch and Cody in order to read the rest of Constance's cards and letters. She gathered them up and climbed back into bed. Downstairs, she heard the dogs returning from their walk. In the hall, she heard the clock chime the half-hour. Before she had finished reading, it had chimed three more times.

She'd found five other mentions of Bim, which she sorted into Real Bim and Fictional Bim.

"Had a Christmas card from Bim," Constance wrote one January. "You probably already know he's a daddy. So nice of him to remember me when we haven't seen each other in so long." (This was Rima's father. Real Bim.)

On March 17, 1978—"We're as old as the hills here and creak when we walk. Hasn't been a fresh young face around since the days that Bim used to drop by. Donkey's years. Father Riker wasn't thinking of the long term when he decided we were none of us to do the necessary to have children." (Real Bim.)

On September 14, 1983—"Will never be persuaded of Bim's guilt. There are other ways to get out of a marriage." (Fictional Bim.)

On February 7, 1984—"I'm afraid the matter of Bim still lies between us, Mr. Lane. Have remembered something pertinent. Bim was extremely allergic to cats. Could never have held one for the time required to paint its claws without suffering hives and severe shortness of breath. Very much doubt that his wife would have even owned one. Unless she was maybe trying to kill *him!* In which case she deserved it." (Some combination of Real and Fictional.)

And on September 30, 1988, the final reference—"Ghastly dream last night about poor old Bogan. He was fixing Father Riker's roof and I climbed up to tell him to be careful. He came at me with his hammer and his eyes black and dusty like a toad's. I pushed him away and he went cartwheeling off the roof. And I thought that I could go look, see if I'd killed him. Or I could wake up, which is what I did. Upset me the whole day.

"You had it wrong about Bim, you know. He liked Bogan and Bogan liked him back." (Real Bim.)

Constance had gone on to complain that her arthritis was so bad her fingers were curled like claws. She could hardly dress herself, she said. She doubted she would ever hold a pen again. No one should feel sorry for her, though. She had so many pen pals. She would learn to type with her nose! But this was the last date Rima could find.

(2)

Rima's period had been irregular since her father's death. Now she realized it had arrived. No wonder she'd been so tired the day before, so reluctant to get up this morning. She peeled back the covers. Her nightgown hem was smeared with blood, and also the sheets. In short, everything that Tilda had just washed would have to be washed again today. Possibly there was a lesson in that. Rima bypassed the lesson in favor of the observation that when it came to removing incriminating stains women had every advantage over men. One of those secret-women's-wisdom things. Meant to be used for good instead of evil, of course.

She stripped the bed, showered, dressed, and carried the whole mess downstairs, because there was no way she was letting Tilda do any of this. But Tilda had beaten her to the laundry room and was already loading the machine with sheets for the bed Martin would be using. Tilda took the bloody pile from Rima, adding them to the load. "I have a great tea for that," Tilda said. "Raspberry leaves and catnip."

Rima had never been dosed with catnip before. It sounded dangerously frisky.

She followed Tilda to the kitchen and waited for the water to boil. There was a new fan letter stuck to the refrigerator:

"Dear Mrs. Early," it read. "I bought a used copy of *Hospital Beds* at our Friends of the Library sale. I like books that contain recipes, so I was pleased that you'd included one for the Butter Tarts, but when I came across 'one and a half sticks of butter,' I was quite surprised that you wouldn't provide a more accurate measurement. We don't all buy our butter in sticks. What is a butter stick?

"Unfortunately this lack of consideration tainted my enthusiasm for the book. I don't plan to finish it until some explanation of the measurement is provided." It was signed by Candace Adams of Paterson, New Jersey.

Natalie Merchant came on the radio, asking the motherland to cradle her. Rain spattered the walkway, pocked the pool of the birdbath. Rima took her tea to the breakfast nook, where Tilda's cup was still on the table, along with her plate, the tea ball leaking into her toast crumbs. Rima wondered idly what tea would be just the thing for your-estranged-son-is-coming-to-dinner-but-not-really-to-see-you-so-much-as-some-girl-you-don't-approve-of.

Next to Tilda's plate was the *Sentinel,* a little damp around the edges and folded so that a photo of Addison was on the top. The caption under the picture identified her as "A. B. Early: The Grande Dame of Murder." By some trick of the light or the angle, her teeth seemed as big as a horse's.

Rima realized that she was looking at the breakfast nook as if it were something to be figured out—the informational content of the plate, the cup, the paper. How exhausting it would be to go through the world seeing everything that way. How hard it was, once started, to stop.

Despite her late-night revelation, despite her early-morning letter-reading, Rima was sticking to her decision to give up the detecting game. She was pretty sure she was giving it up. She gathered some clues and put them in the dishwasher. Then she went back to the table to read the article about Addison.

Although its ostensible point was to advertise Addison's

upcoming library speech: "The Edge of Imagination," the bulk of the article was biography. It stressed Addison's lifetime ties to Santa Cruz, her fisherman father who, as every local knew, had turned out to be her uncle, her stint at this very paper. The only paragraph of the article in which Addison was quoted directly appeared shoehorned in. She had said that 9/11 was a test that our system of government had failed. One more such attack would wipe away all remaining traces of democracy in this country. And if people didn't think the men currently in power were capable of producing this attack if their power was threatened, then where had they been for the last six years?

"Does Maxwell Lane share your politics?" the *Sentinel* reporter had asked.

"Like any good patriot, he misses his inalienable rights," Addison had answered.

The sound of the gate brought the dogs down the stairs, a tangle of bark and snarl. Rima looked up to see who was being warned off this way. Kenny Sullivan was coming through in his mailman poncho and pushing his mailman bag. He saw Rima looking at him, gestured her to the door, but by the time she got there, Tilda had already let him in. He was shaking the rain off, the dogs bouncing happily at his feet, and handing Tilda the mail.

On the top was an unstamped wet envelope with no address and no name. "It was in the mailbox," Kenny said. Rima picked it up.

Something bulkier than mere paper was inside. Rima ran the envelope between her fingers: there was definitely something bumpy there.

"Cup of tea?" Tilda asked Kenny.

"Won't say no. Terrible cold and wet out." He chose the blueberry tea, removing his wet poncho and joining the women at the table. "Terrible picture of Addison," he said. Rima had returned the newspaper to its original folded state.

"Martin is coming," Tilda told him. "For dinner and to spend the night."

Kenny appeared to understand the significance of this. "What will you serve?"

"Mac and cheese. He used to love that horrible instant stuff with the orange powder. I thought I'd make the real deal. Maybe throw in some crabmeat. Crusty bread. Big salad. Homey, but with crabmeat."

"Perfect," Kenny said. "Only maybe save the crabmeat for a breakfast omelet. With avocado. Maybe a salad with jícama and blood oranges."

Meanwhile Rima had opened the envelope. It was wet enough to unpeel the flap without tearing it. Inside was a folded piece of paper, and inside that was an odd scrap of material—a small black grosgrain ribbon, tapered at the ends where it had maybe once been knotted. Printed in block letters on the paper were these words: I KNOW WHO YOU ARE. Nothing else.

Tilda reached over and picked up the ribbon. Kenny took the envelope and the piece of paper.

"At least it's not anthrax," he said. "That's the first thing a postman thinks of, letter like that."

Anthrax was not the first thing Rima had thought of. If it had been and Kenny had been the one opening the letter, she probably would have mentioned it before he did so.

"Good lord," Tilda said. "It's a cummerbund. It's Thomas Grand's cummerbund."

"At least it's not his ear." Rima noticed how Kenny the postman didn't even have to be reminded who Thomas Grand was. Of course, Rima had been there when Addison told him about the break-in. She knew he knew who Thomas Grand was. It just seemed odd that he'd remember the name all these days later with no prompting.

This was what it was like to be Maxwell Lane—suspicious of everyone and everything! Always on the lookout! As far as Rima was concerned, Kenny Sullivan was a perfectly ordinary postman with a somewhat cavalier attitude toward schedules and anthrax.

Kenny blew across his cup of tea, took a sip. "How freaky would that be," he asked, "to get a letter with a little plastic ear in it?"

As if getting a letter with a little grosgrain ribbon in it weren't freaky enough.

(3)

When Addison came into the kitchen around lunchtime, she was more startled by her newspaper picture than by the cummerbund. "Jeebus," she said, flipping the folded *Sentinel* over so that the text was on the top, "it's hard to capture my beauty these days." She was shown the note. I KNOW WHO YOU ARE.

"That's what Pamela Price said to me," Rima told her. "Those exact words."

"Never engage with a stalker," Addison said again. "She tries to talk to you, you just walk on like you don't even hear. She offers you something, you don't want it." She was shown the cummer-bund. "See?" she said cheerfully. "We'll get him back yet. One lit-tle piece at a time. The trick is to not want him back. Wanting him back gives all the power to her. Not wanting him back gives all the power to us."

Tilda had embarked on a take-no-prisoners round of house-cleaning. She was even washing the dogs, a periodic cataclysm in their lives that made them sulk under the sofas, asking them-selves what kind of a god would allow such things, until their fur dried and they forgot it had ever happened. Addison offered to take Rima out for pizza, and Rima could see it would be best to leave before Tilda dusted her.

So Addison took Rima to a small place in Seabright where she knew the owners. There were wood tables and silver chairs, and on the wall huge pictures of trucks and also the Roman Colosseum. The menu was on five blackboards over the bar. Beer on tap, and a lot of pizzas with feta cheese. And cashews. Apparently they put nuts on the pizzas in Santa Cruz.

Rima followed Addison past the ovens and the bar to a side room barely large enough for the Ping-Pong table it held. Addison chose a seat by the windows.

A woman with her hair in a buzz cut came over to say hello. She and Addison agreed that they'd not seen each other since the very beautiful Night-Light peace event on West Cliff Drive back in September. Rima was introduced as Addison's goddaughter from Cleveland.

"You must be loving our weather," the woman said. Perhaps

she hadn't been outdoors yet today. Rima was damp and she was freezing. The cuffs of her sweater had stuck out from her raincoat, and now they were glued to her wrists. She kept her thoughts to herself and joined Addison in ordering a Fat Tire ale.

The table next to them was occupied by an older man and a younger woman who might have been his date or might have been his daughter. Rima was guessing daughter, because her hair was in pigtails and his tone was patronizing. "You need to make a plan and stick to it," he was saying. "There's no value in making a plan you don't stick to." Not only did Rima dislike his tone, she doubted his position. In her experience the making of the plan was always the best part, and often its own reward.

The day before, with the vision of that sad Bim box lodged in her mind, Rima had made a plan not to press Addison again on anything concerning her father. Now, with Addison all to herself, an ale foaming in front of her and a pizza on its way, she was asking, "Did you and my father ever go back to Holy City? After that first night?" This was not detective work, which she had given up. This was just an idle question. The main difference was that no notes would ever be taken.

"Why?"

"Constance seems to have known my dad. Not just met him once. Met him several times. Had Christmas cards from him."

Addison was looking at her own hands, which allowed Rima to look at Addison's face. There were elegant hollows below her cheekbones and thin blue shadows below her eyes. She was lucky to have good bones, since they were all so prominent. Instead of softening and blurring the way some faces did as they aged,

Addison's had grown more dramatic. She should have been easy to photograph. There was really no excuse for the big teeth in the paper.

"I told your father the night of the Fill Your Hole event that Constance knew who the arsonist was. She seemed pretty susceptible to the charms of a nice young man. I know he went back a few times," Addison said. "I didn't know about the Christmas cards. I expect she wrote him and he was too polite not to write back. That woman wrote everyone. Once there was a mystery convention in San Diego with a whole panel devoted to her and her letters." Of course, Addison had already told Rima that last part, only it hadn't occurred to Rima that everyone might include her father.

Chapter Twenty-two

(1)

Ever since her talk with Rima around Election Day, Addison had been remembering things. Once she'd started, she couldn't seem to stop. She hadn't thought about the night of the Fill Your Hole dinner in years, but there was a time when she'd thought of it so often that now she found the memories waiting for her, like snapshots in an album. She'd already told Rima how Riker had gotten so drunk he'd passed out in the redwood grove. How Constance had gotten so drunk she'd fallen off the porch. Now she remembered in considerable detail that she and Bim had helped Constance to her bed and then wandered a bit about the property, talking about their lives and their ambitions. Their stroll had taken them past the petting zoo, where the nocturnal animals made such a racket, they woke the diurnal ones—the whole zoo up and excited. They'd stopped at the telescope to look at the moon, clear and pocked instead of vague and pearly, and had an argument over which was the more beautiful, Bim preferring distant and blurred, Addison liking the pocks and surprising herself with how deeply she felt this was the right position. By then they were off the road and into the trees.

They'd come across Riker passed out on a bed of needles in a sunken bowl inside a perfect ring of redwoods. Bim had taken his pulse and covered him with his coat. Luckily it was a warm night. The fairies got him, Bim had said. He'll wake up about a hundred years from now. Bim had said that as long as Riker was sleeping for a hundred years, this would be a good time to check out his house.

Midnight was gone, and the moon was slipping from the sky. Stars were flung over the black like rice at a wedding. The doctored punch Addison had drunk was still spinning her head. She felt her heart rising in her chest. There was nothing she would have said no to.

She followed Bim back toward the Showhouse and Lecture Hall and then across the parking lot, across the Old Santa Cruz Highway to the house on the other side. They heard someone walking in the gravel toward the dormitories, and Bim pulled Addison with him behind one of the trees. It was a thin tree, and there was something cartoonish about the two of them pretending they could hide behind it. Addison started to laugh, and once she'd started, she couldn't stop. She was able to stay quiet only by biting her fingers. She was, she realized, hysterical. This struck her as extremely funny. Bim reached over and put his hand over her hand over her mouth to muffle her. She could smell the bay aftershave on his fingers.

The footsteps faded. "All right now?" Bim asked. "I can count on you?" His hand moved her head in a nod. "Okay, then. I'm letting you go." He took his hand away and Addison assumed a shaky control. Riker's house was a white two-story, set on top of a hill. They climbed up the sloping yard together.

Everything appeared dark, but the shades were down tight; there was no way to see in and be sure. The porch light was on, moths and smaller insects beating about it, a moment of unavoidable visibility through which Bim and Addison had to pass. "I'm going in," Bim told her, and he moved into the edge of the light, and quickly up the porch steps.

The middle step cracked like a gunshot when his foot hit it, a sound that made Addison jump. Then she was laughing again, and the effort of doing this silently brought tears to her eyes.

Bim tried the doorknob. It spun. He disappeared into the house, and Addison followed at a run, taking the stairs two at a time so that she skipped the middle step. She'd stopped laughing as soon as she hit the light.

With the front door open, she could see the entryway. There was a coat on a coat rack, an umbrella hanging from the same hook. Then Bim closed the door behind her and she couldn't see a thing.

He lit a match, cupping his hand around it so that his face floated above the tiny flame. Addison saw the shapes of a sofa and chairs. A bookcase. A lamp. They were in the living room. The match went out. The room smelled of pipe tobacco, which was pleasant, and cat piss, which was not. Bim sneezed three times, all in a row. Muffled pitchy sneezes.

Just because the dim starlight outside didn't make it in didn't mean a bright light inside wouldn't make it out. A whole night of darkness can be conquered by one small flame, as Addison's mother had often told her. Bim gave her a matchbook. Later she would see it was from a bar in the city. "You take that side," he said, directing her by touch to the interior wall while he took the wall with the windows.

"What are we looking for?" Addison asked.

"A story. Really anything we can get a few columns out of."

Addison took two steps in the dark. Her left foot landed in sand. She lit a match. She was in the cat litter box. She raised her shoe; the wet sand stuck to it. "God damn it," she said. She was seventeen years old. She never swore. She remembered vividly the bravado of doing so.

"Try not to break anything," Bim said. He sneezed again. "There are cats here somewhere," he said. "I'm never wrong about cats."

Addison's memory didn't really come like that, as a whole coherent narrative. It was more like flashes, a visual here, an audio there. Like a room seen one minute by matchlight, and the next dead dark.

(2)

Two young men in baseball caps, one brim backward, one forward, began to play Ping-Pong. The ball pinged on the table and ponged on the paddles. Stevie Wonder came over the loudspeakers.

One of the Ping-Pong players said something to the other in

Spanish. It did not sound complimentary. It did not sound like a thing a good sport would be saying. The ball skidded under Rima's chair. She reached down, tossed it back.

"Did my father ever figure it out?" Rima asked Addison. "Did he catch the arsonist?" Addison's face had an abstracted, distant look. Rima thought she was maybe eavesdropping on the people at the table adjacent. Addison had always maintained that eavesdropping was a professional obligation. Rima had read that in more than one interview.

Besides, the conversation one table over had become compelling; Rima was listening too. Perhaps they were not father and daughter, after all. The older man was suggesting that sexual innuendo was entirely a matter of tone of voice. The words were insignificant. In fact, any words would do so long as the tone was right.

"How about you and me *take the dog for a walk*," he said by way of example.

"I like a pizza with *some cheese on top.*

"What say you and me go back to my place and *play some bridge?*"

Addison's eyes were on Rima, but not so they looked at her. Rima leaned forward. "Did anyone ever catch the arsonist?" she repeated. Although her tone was unimpeachable, suddenly the words "catch the arsonist" had a lascivious ring that hadn't been there the first time she'd said them. What say you and me go back to my place and see if we can't *catch the arsonist*?

Addison answered slowly. "No." She picked up her ale, and her eyes focused. She was paying attention again. "The fires stopped.

Maybe they stopped because your dad was poking around," she said. "Maybe Constance knew that as soon as she gave your dad a name, he wouldn't be dropping by to see her anymore. She was a lonely woman. Maybe she made the whole thing up. Maybe nobody who joins a cult isn't pretty lonely to begin with."

"How do you know it wasn't Constance herself setting the fires?" Addison asked.

(3)

Suddenly it was strange for Addison to think that the young woman across the table was Bim Lanisell's daughter, who had Bim's mouth and Bim's smile, not that you saw it often on Rima's face. Addison looked at Rima, and what she remembered next was the wide-awake, so-alive feeling she'd had, standing in the dark next to a young man she hardly knew, in a house where they weren't supposed to be. She saw herself and Bim from above, the two of them bending over the little lights of their matches and the room large and dark and unseen around them.

She'd worked her way down the bookcase, leaving a trail of sand. She didn't think this would be too incriminating. It seemed like something the cats probably did. "Lots of pamphlets," she told Bim.

"Forget them. That's the public face. That's not what we're after."

On one of the shelves was a tiny bottle with a paper rolled inside and a price on the glass, so this was surely also the public face, something they sold at the arcade. The littleness of it appealed to Addison, and she put it in her pocket, as if this wasn't stealing, just because the object was so small and cheap.

She moved from the bookcase to the pictures on the wall. She was going through her matches very quickly. The pictures turned out to be framed photographs. There was one of Father Riker holding a world globe in his hands, captioned "The Wise Man of the Far West." Another picture was of the line of penny peep shows with a billboard at the end: "Good Things Are Bad Things for Some People. And Vice Versa." All this was the public face again. Addison moved on.

Whatever it was they were looking for was more likely to be upstairs in the bedroom than down here in the living room. She didn't say this aloud. Her bravado was already pushed as far as she could push it. A staircase would snap her last nerve.

She knelt by the coffee table and struck her final match. By its light she could see the dark spot that the oil in Riker's hair had left on the back of the easy chair. She could see that the coffee table was dusty and there were plates from someone's breakfast on it. Addison could see a crusting of egg yolk on one of the plates.

She heard the crack of the middle porch step and blew her last match out. "Bim," she said as quietly as she could, but the room was silent and completely dark.

Someone knocked. "Are you in there?" a man's voice asked. He tried the doorknob, but apparently Bim had thrown the lock. There was a long silence. Then Addison heard the crack of the step again. More footsteps, now receding.

A minute passed, maybe two. Addison noticed that she'd stopped breathing. She started again. Bim struck a match and came over to her, helped her up. He shook the match and the room went dark. "I'm out of matches," Addison said.

"Me too." Bim took her hand, turning away from her and putting it on his shoulder so that he led her as they went back through the room to the front door. They stopped there. "I have something for you," Bim said. "A birthday present."

"It's not my birthday."

"You have to promise not to open it till it is. I won't give it to you unless you promise."

Addison promised. Bim handed her a bundle made of his handkerchief, with something small inside it. She put this in the same pocket as the bottle. Now she and Bim were standing in the dark, facing each other, so close she thought he must feel that she was shaking. This would have been a good time for Bim to kiss her.

He didn't. Maybe this was because his nose was running and his eyes were puffed and swollen. Maybe it was because people who smell like cat piss seldom get kissed.

Addison got home around sunrise. She left her shoes at the door, tiptoed through the hall so as not to wake her mother.

Addison put Bim's handkerchief into her jewelry box and slammed it shut, because, when open, it was also a music box and quite noisy. The song it played was "Love Is a Many-Splendored Thing," which Addison's mother loved. Hated the movie. How hard is it, she'd asked when they saw it, to give the people in movies a happy ending? You're making the whole thing up. Why not make it up happy? The thing in Addison's handkerchief turned out to be the kind of little plastic birthday cake you might see in a dollhouse, but she didn't find that out for months.

She didn't wait to break the little bottle open. She did that as soon as she'd put the handkerchiefed bundle in her jewelry box. She fished out the roll of paper, smoothed it flat, and read it. In fancy, curly lettering, it outlined Riker's doctrine of The Perfect Christian Divine Way:

> No 1 No longer are those murderous wars needed because we now have the true solution to get rid of them.
>
> No 2 No longer are our imperfect governments needed because we now have the perfect one to take their place.
>
> No 3 No longer do our intelligent people have to tolerate terrible-God race crime blood mixing because we have the true solution to that racial problem.
>
> No 4 Also we now have the true solution to that spiritual religious problem as never before in history.

Of course, sitting there in the pizza parlor, Addison didn't remember it all word for word like that. She remembered just something evil and oddly vague. The only words she remembered for sure were "true solution."

What was the true solution? Riker neglected to say, but it had a Nazi ring to it. True solutions that couldn't be revealed seemed, to Addison now, to belong to the same family tree as secret plans to end the war, FOIA documents with everything but the verbs blacked out, secret prisons with secret lists of prisoners in them, secret methods of extracting information from those secret prisoners in those secret prisons, and all those things that for national security reasons couldn't be counted up, like Iraqi deaths and private contractors. Addison couldn't say any of this online, though she would have liked to. The myriad fallacious Hitler references had ruined it for the legitimate ones.

"Which is worse, competent or incompetent evil?" Addison asked Rima. "That's really the question of our times, isn't it? William Riker was the first man to make me ask that. How I wish he'd been the last."

At the next table, the older man was on his feet, helping the younger woman into her coat. He turned to Addison. "William Riker had some serious father issues," he said. "Sorry. Didn't mean to eavesdrop. I just heard the name and I'm kind of a buff."

"I didn't know that about Riker," Addison said.

"Oh, sure."

Addison was only being polite. She had yet to meet the person who didn't have father issues. It came with the standard package. She'd never supposed for a second that the exception would be a white supremacist cult leader.

The man flashed the Vulcan hand signal from *Star Trek* on his way out the door. He did it surreptitiously, shielding his hand with his body, so the young woman wouldn't see. This was puzzling. Not the fact that he'd hidden it—there are few situations in which Vulcan hand gestures add to a man's allure—but the fact that he'd made the gesture in the first place.

Neither Addison nor Rima knew it, but the man had confused William E. Riker with William T. Riker. William E. Riker was born in California in 1873 and ran Holy City from the 1920s through the 1950s. His followers sold gas, dirty pictures, and holy water to travelers on the Old Santa Cruz Highway.

William T. Riker was born on Earth (Valdez, Alaska) in 2335 and served as first officer on the USS *Enterprise-D* and *-E* under

Captain Jean-Luc Picard until his promotion in 2379 to the command of the USS *Titan*.

Two totally different people.

So my father never did write anything about Holy City?" Rima asked.

"No. A few months later he was offered a job on the sports desk at the *Chicago Tribune*. I never met the man who wouldn't give it all up to work the sports desk," Addison said.

Rima finished her ale and ordered another. She hadn't had breakfast and she'd drunk quickly, so maybe that was causing the pleasantly buoyant feeling on the edges of her brain. Or maybe it was a delayed reaction to the catnip tea. "Okay, then," she said.

She looked across the table to Addison, and was filled with affection for this woman without whom the world would have no Maxwell Lane in it and no one would even know what they were missing.

"What exactly was it that went on between you and my father?" Rima asked.

Chapter Twenty-three

(1)

Rima was instantly sorry she'd asked. Addison's face locked tight for a second; her cheeks had no color. But before she could speak, Rima became aware that someone was standing behind her. She turned to see a young Asian woman with tiny glasses and black hair just long enough to tuck behind her ears. "I don't mean to interrupt," the young woman said, "but I'm such a fan. I can't even fly on a plane unless I have one of your books to read. Otherwise I spend the whole flight expecting to crash and die." She had a preppy look—a powder-blue sweater set and jeans with embroidered flowers on the knees. Gold stud earrings, only two, and only in the lobes. Very un–Santa Cruz. But very pretty.

"Air travel has become impossible," Addison agreed. She'd

managed a smile. Unpersuasive, but high-wattage all the same. "I'm so pleased to hear I help."

"That's all I wanted to say." This was a lie. The woman's eyes were big and her voice nervous. More words came out, all in a rush. "I love every book you've ever written. I won't read anyone else. Until you write a new one, I'll just keep rereading the old ones. Will there be a new one soon?"

Addison stopped smiling. "I hope so."

"Does it have a title?"

"Not yet. Maybe when we get habeas corpus back." Addison gestured to Rima. "This is my goddaughter, Rima Lanisell."

"Oh!" The word came out in a gasp. "Bim's daughter? I love Bim! I'm the biggest M-and-B-shipper!"

A couple of weeks earlier, Rima wouldn't have known what to make of that description. Now she knew it meant that this woman was a fan of the Maxwell–Bim relationship. Possibly she wrote sex scenes and posted them on the Web. Probably she read them. Probably these sex scenes were lousy with deep emotional connection. Rima didn't imagine that anyone who wore sweater sets would be into meaningless sex.

"You do understand that those characters are under copyright?" Addison asked. (In point of fact, since Bim was not only a character in a book but also a newspaper columnist for *The Plain Dealer* and dead, the issue of copyright was kind of interesting. Addison wasn't doing the nuance.)

The woman took a step backward. "I'm not a writer," she said. "I won't interrupt you anymore. I just wanted to say how much I love your books."

"Aren't you sweet?"

The woman backed into one of the Ping-Pong players. The backswing of his paddle hit her right on the ass. This mortified everyone concerned, so there was a string of apologies in multiple languages. It brought the smile back to Addison's face. "Ping-Pong is a deadly game," she said to Rima. "Few survive it."

The cavalry arrived, a bit late, in the form of the owner with a water pitcher. "Are you being disturbed?" she asked in a whisper, topping off their already full glasses.

"By someone who reads my books? Never," Addison said. "She'd have to bite me before I'd find her disturbing."

The owner and Addison were both members of the Bonny Doon wine club. They discussed the latest shipment in such detail that Rima felt Addison was deliberately prolonging it. If enough time passed, she could pretend to have forgotten the question Rima had asked. Rima did her bit by excusing herself and going to the bathroom.

The rest room mirror was recessed, and framed by a wooden box painted with vines. The silver base of the sink matched the chairs in the restaurant. There was the usual sign about employees being required to wash their hands. No such requirement for customers. Rima washed her hands voluntarily.

Someone knocked on the door. Rima dried her hands quickly and opened it. The young M-and-B-shipper was standing outside.

"Oh my god," she said. "I was trying so hard not to babble and all I did was babble. I insulted her!"

"You didn't," Rima said.

"I gushed! I babbled! I got paddled! That's what she'll remember. I'll probably be in her next book."

"She was charmed."

"You're such a liar."

Rima stepped aside so that the woman could step in. It was that sort of bathroom, a single toilet, no stalls. One person at a time. But the woman blocked Rima's exit. "I actually wanted to talk to you," she said. She closed and locked the door with Rima still inside. "I'll only take a minute."

Rima didn't suppose she should let herself be locked in a rest room with a strange woman even if it was only for a minute. Any more than she should let one in the house to rifle through the shelves. And yet somehow, here she was.

"You're staying with her, right?" the woman asked. "I was just wondering if she ever talks about the new book. You've probably seen the dollhouse at least."

"No," said Rima. "And no. And why would I tell you, even if I had? She obviously doesn't want it talked about."

"There's this person," the woman said. "On the Web. Who's offered two thousand dollars to anyone who can find out what's going to happen to Maxwell. Of course, I'd share the money if you found out something. Fifty-fifty. I mean, you could just look around, right? The dollhouse has to be somewhere."

"When did this offer go up?" Rima asked. "The two thousand?"

"A few weeks ago."

"We had a break-in recently."

The woman brushed her black hair back nervously with her hand. Her eyes skipped from Rima's face to the mottled gray-and-white tile on the floor. "Yeah," she said. "Listen. That's the other thing I wanted to say to you. You know how on the Web you mostly can't tell who's crazy and who isn't? That woman's crazy. You should watch out for her."

"You know about the break-in?"

"She posted about it. She figured she had some leverage, now that she had something Early would want back."

Rima had been picturing Pamela Price as a drug-addled homeless type. Not, she corrected herself hastily and for Tilda's sake, that the homeless were usually drug-addled or even that there was a homeless type. But the thing Pamela Price had never struck Rima as being was a Web maven.

"What's her handle?" Rima asked.

"ConstantComment. Avatar of a teapot. But I think she uses a lot of other names and avatars too. But I think she's all over the discussion boards. Sock puppets here, there, and everywhere. Nothing I can prove."

"Thank you for the warning," Rima said, "and I'm going to decline your offer. Are we finished, then? Can I go?"

The woman let her out. "I really do love her books," she said apologetically. "I really do love Maxwell Lane."

"Don't we all?" said Rima. Halfway through the open door, she had another thought. "How did you know we were here?"

"She comes here all the time. I got a phone call," the woman said.

Poor Addison! So worried about governmental spying, while her fans were tracking her every movement. Every pizza parlor a nest of spies. Rima had changed her mind about the young woman's being pretty. Apparently they were letting just anyone wear a sweater set these days.

(2)

Martin had said he would come for dinner and would arrive around six-thirty. By seven, Tilda was so nervous she was practically airborne. She stood at the stove, stirring the mushroom soup and fretting that it was getting a skin.

Rima had told Addison about the woman in the rest room and the two-thousand-dollar bounty on Maxwell Lane sightings. Addison had gone upstairs to see what she could find on the Internet. Now she came back down. If she'd found anything out, she wasn't sharing.

"Just leave the soup," she told Tilda. "Rima and I are going to play Trivial Pursuit while we wait for Martin." This was the first Rima had heard of it. "Come join us."

"Which board?" Tilda asked.

"Lord of the Rings. It's a party in a box," Addison said temptingly.

Tilda turned the burner off and put a lid on the soup. She moved the baking dish from the oven to the counter and covered it with a dish towel.

"No one has ever beaten Tilda at Lord of the Rings Trivial Pursuit," Addison told Rima. "Not in the whole history of Middle-earth."

Rima didn't think of herself as a Middle-earth expert. But she did know that Gandalf's sword was named Glamdring and that Glamdring had once belonged to Turgon, the only Elf ever to be king of Gondolin. She had no idea how she knew this. But she thought she'd probably do okay. Like all first children, when she played games, she planned to win.

Addison got the board from upstairs; Tilda got the books from her room. Rima cleared some magazines that Addison would maybe read someday from the living room coffee table. There was a chair for Addison and the couch for Tilda. Rima would sit cross-legged on one of the deep pile rugs Addison had bought from the Portuguese widow whose shop occupied the address given in Addison's books as Maxwell Lane's. The rug was a Persian pattern in black and red, the red so vivid it glowed.

The living room contained three dollhouses—*Folsom Street, Native Dancer,* and *Party of None.* The largest and most elaborate was *Folsom Street*—San Francisco woman pushed from a balcony during the Gay Pride parade. The dollhouse was actually a street scene with three housefronts and two parade floats. The corpse lay on the sidewalk, head cracked open and flattened where it hit. The victim had missed a Nancy Sinatra impersonator by inches. This dollhouse took up most of the window seat that looked out on the yard toward Addison's studio.

On the opposite wall was a fireplace in white tile with white wood shelving on either side. *Native Dancer* was to the left of the fireplace and three shelves up—the tack room of a stable, plus two stalls, one with an arch-necked palomino inside. Hanging from a rafter was the corpse, western bridle around his neck.

Party of None was on the lowest shelf to the right of the fireplace—a long, narrow diner with a linoleum counter, tiny napkin dispensers with tiny napkins, and a shiny black jukebox. The corpse had bits of green foam around her mouth. She'd overdosed on caffeine.

The three women heard a car outside, and each stopped what she was doing for a moment to listen. The motor cut off somewhere down around the Morrisons' house. The door slammed. The women picked up where they had left off.

They gathered at the coffee table and the game began. Tilda took the wizard token, Addison the man. This left the Elven princess or the halfling for Rima. She made the obvious choice. The halfling's sword curved, but not like a scimitar, more like a mistake.

The game provided answers as well as questions; Tilda and Addison ignored the former. Too many of the answers were based on the movies rather than the books, and even when based on the books, they were often not based on what Addison called a deep reading. Who solved the riddle that opened Moria's West-gate? If Rima had answered Gandalf, she would have gotten the pie wedge. If she'd answered Merry, there would have been wiggle-room enough to count the answer, since in the book Gandalf credits Merry with being on the right track. But Frodo, the answer Rima gave and the answer listed as correct on the back of the card, could not be credited. It could not even be countenanced.

In addition to ignoring the official answers, Tilda and Addison had inserted a system of challenges into the game. Rima, for instance, was free to challenge the decision on Frodo. If she did so, Tilda would find and read the relevant section from *The Fellowship of the Ring.* If Tilda and Addison turned out to be right, as they had no doubt they would be, the challenge would cost Rima the only pie wedge she had so far—the green one for remembering that the name of the Elven bread was Lembas. She passed on the challenge.

The game was interrupted when Addison noticed that Berkeley

was chewing on something. It took both Addison and Tilda to pry the Ringwraith pawn from Berkeley's jaws, and it looked nothing like a Ringwraith by the time they'd done so. If Rima ever wrote a horror movie, the world would find itself menaced by gigantic dachshunds, dachshunds the size of semis. "Has anyone tried to reason with them?" the scientist would say, and before the scene was over he would look just like the Ringwraith pawn now looked.

Rima fell behind. She wasn't missing the answers so much as sucking at the die-throwing part of the game. This too had been made more difficult by the substitution of Addison's Dungeons & Dragons die for the normal six-sided one. With a single throw you might lose as many as three turns battling balrogs, or two turns for orcs, or one turn to stop and eat your second breakfast.

The clock upstairs chimed eight. Addison got up and went to the kitchen. She returned with a tray and three salads made of lettuce, jícama, and blood oranges. When they'd finished those, Addison went back to the kitchen and dished up the mac and cheese.

By eight-thirty, Tilda had all six pie wedges. "Pwned again," Addison said, handing Tilda her final wedge plus the ring of ultimate power.

Tilda wore the ring while she did the dishes, thus proving herself extremely unclear on the concept of total world domination. Rima cleaned up the board and cards. Addison poured herself a glass of whiskey.

Martin arrived a little after nine. "I kept dinner hot for you," Tilda said, but he said he'd already eaten.

(3)

Martin and Rima quarreled quietly at the top of the stairs. Things got about as heated as they could and still be whispered. A pen-and-ink sketch of an old oak was hanging on the wall behind Martin. By tilting her head, Rima could make the tree appear to grow straight out of his hair. This provided a small and cheap sense of satisfaction.

Rima started the fight, unless Martin started it by being so late in the first place, for which a case could certainly be made. "Your mother expected you for dinner," Rima said. Her tone was as unpleasant as she could make it.

Martin's was unperturbed. "My mother missed the teen years," he said. "I'm just filling in the gaps." He added that he didn't really think of Tilda as his mother anyway, and he wished Rima wouldn't keep calling her that. He stood, with the tree growing out of his head, stroking that stupid little stamp of hair above his chin in a way Rima could describe only as complacent. There were many reasons Rima would never grow a beard. Among them was all the annoying stroking.

Rima said that he did too think of Tilda as his mother, because no one would treat another person as badly as he treated Tilda unless that person was his mother. No one would treat a stranger or a casual acquaintance that way.

"I didn't say I wasn't her child," Martin said nonsensically. "I said she wasn't my mother." He'd taken a step backward, so Rima lost the edge that the tree on the wall had given her. Now she was reduced to winning on the merits.

She pointed out that his mother wasn't dead, the way some

people's mothers were. Dead to you, she said, was not at all the same as dead. Someday Tilda *would* be dead, and Rima could predict with absolute certainty that then Martin would be sorry.

By now his temper matched Rima's. How often, he asked, did Rima plan to play the my-whole-family-is-dead card? Could she limit it to once or twice a day, because it was getting tiresome.

And anyway, Martin said, any idiot could see that it was worse for him because his mother *wasn't* dead. Rima's mother would have stayed if she could, but Martin's mother had chosen to leave. His situation was much worse, and if Rima weren't so focused on herself she'd see this. "Just because she's back now doesn't mean she's here to stay," Martin said. "How do I know she's not already drinking again?"

Rima remembered Tilda with Addison's glass in her hand, sitting in the TV room in the blue light of the aquarium. If she hadn't been so angry, she might have conceded Martin the point. But what he'd said about her family was unforgivable. "I would give anything," Rima said, "to see my mother again," and Martin said, there, that proved it, because there wasn't a thing in the world he would give for that.

And how was any of it Rima's business?

They retired to their separate rooms, both in a state of substantial snit. The clock on the wall chimed ten.

Just after the chime at the quarter-hour, Tilda came knocking. In spite of the whispering, the argument had been overheard. "Please don't blame him," Tilda said. "Please stay out of it." And then, having just asked her to stay out of it, Tilda said that Martin was leaving and would Rima please come and talk him back into staying the night. Rima followed her down the stairs. Seeing

Martin and Tilda by the door together made her notice how much they looked alike. Same hair, same eyes, same sad, sad expression.

It took about a half an hour of insincere groveling to get Martin to stay. By the time it was done, Rima had agreed to that wine-tasting with ghosts in the mountains on the following day. Apparently there would be not only wine and ghosts but also a piano player.

Somewhere in the back of her head, somewhere in the midst of that jumble of Glamdring and Le Pétomane and British slang circa World War II, Oliver—or maybe it was Maxwell—had come up with a new plan, but Rima wouldn't figure that out until the next day. It would come to her slowly, as she sat in the passenger seat of Martin's car, cresting the mountains on the wet, twisted road.

You know what I could do now, she would find herself thinking, if only I wasn't me? You know what someone who wasn't me could do now?

You know what Oliver would do?

Chapter Twenty-four

(1)

Before Rima found herself on the slick, deadly Highway 17 in the passenger seat of Martin's old blue Civic, she'd had one more chat with Addison.

Just as she was going to bed, there was a knock that she immediately feared might mean Martin had confused insincere groveling with foreplay. He wouldn't be the first. But when she opened the door, it was Addison standing in the hallway, a glass in each hand, whiskey bottle under her arm. "You asked about your father and me," she said, and Rima let her in, let her take the seat by the window. Addison poured a glass and passed it to Rima. Then she stared for a while in silence at the black water, the string of harbor lights, the distant roller coasters.

"My uncle always wanted his own boat," she said finally. "When he was my father, he used to say he'd name it after me. The *Addie B.* Never could afford it, though."

"One of my favorite books when I was little was called *The Maggie B.*," Rima said. "It was all about a girl who took her little brother James out on her boat, and they ate a soup she made with fish and crabs, and then they slept under the stars. I don't think it was the boat I found so appealing. It was more how competent the big sister was. It was how she managed the boat and the supper and bath and bedtime. I used to love books where it was up to the big sister to keep everything together. Like *Homecoming.*" By "keeping things together" Rima meant mostly not losing people.

"I used to love books about big families," Addison said. "*Little Women. Cheaper by the Dozen. The Family Nobody Wanted.* I used to fantasize about brothers and sisters."

Rima sipped her whiskey without answering. This was an effort, because ordinarily Rima liked nothing better than to talk about the books of her childhood. In the conversation she wasn't having, she told Addison she'd also loved *Cheaper by the Dozen,* and what was up with the movie? She didn't know *The Family Nobody Wanted.* She asked if the Edward Eager books had been around when Addison was a girl. Because of those books, if Rima were a writer—which she never would be, Addison had nothing to worry about on that score—she would write books with magic in them.

But Rima said none of this. Rima said nothing at all. Her throat was hot where the whiskey had been. Addison too was silent, staring out the window for what seemed to Rima to be a long time.

Addison was thinking about her uncle's boat, the one he'd never gotten. After her new aunt had talked to her mother about finances and Addison had gotten the *Sentinel* job, she went to her aunt and uncle's house in their absence and looked for his canceled checks. Because he had moved so recently, things were unusually well organized. She'd found them in a box in the study closet, labeled "Canceled Checks." She wanted to know how much her uncle had been giving her.

She'd started back a year before his marriage. He'd paid the rent and utilities on their house. No phone payments, and nothing directly to her mother. Addison didn't much notice the first check to William Riker. She didn't know who he was. But the next month there was another, and the month after that another, and every month since, her uncle had sent him two hundred dollars, the last checks having been written and cashed in the months since the marriage.

There was no William Riker listed in the Santa Cruz phone book. Addison asked at work if anyone had heard of him. "Holy City," one of the reporters told her. "I'm sure his obit's already in hand. Look it up."

Her uncle's politics were straight-up union, left-wing labor, and he loathed racists; there was nothing in Riker's obituary of which he would approve. This was not a man Addison would ever have imagined her uncle sending money to. It took her a couple of days to figure out what any reader of A. B. Early books would have guessed instantly.

Of course, back then there were no A. B. Early books. "You don't know half the things your parents do for you," Addison said, and Rima didn't know quite where that was coming from, but she figured it was true.

Those checks were the reason Addison had wormed her way

into the Fill Your Hole banquet, an event planned for seasoned hard-drinking reporters and not callow high school girls with part-time or summer jobs.

Which is how she'd come to know Rima's father at just that time when she had a big secret and no one to tell it to. At just that time when Addison understood what the man who wasn't her father had sacrificed for her, month after month, year after year. Not just the money, not just his own boat, but his principles as well.

"I had an enormous crush on Bim when I first met him," Addison said finally. "Of course I was only seventeen. Prime crush years. I also liked a guy at school named Charlie Bailey, who led the debate club, and wore argyle sweaters. And the guy who bagged at the grocery. But especially Bim. And then he left and we wrote letters—he wrote great letters—and it turned into some-thing else. Something better. He was my dear reader," Addison said. "For a very long time, he was the first person to read every book I wrote."

Rima had her doubts. The box she'd seen in the attic was not the sort of box you put together for your dear reader. "And then what happened?" she asked. She didn't look at Addison's face. She looked at Addison's face in the window, her ghost face, just visible underneath the bright spot of the reflected table lamp.

"I was hoping you'd tell me," Addison said.

(2)

One day a letter Addison had written was returned unopened, along with a note asking her not to write again. She wrote again immediately, asking what she'd done, and that was returned unopened too, no note this time, just "Refused" written over the address. And then when she learned that Rima's mother had died, Addison tried again, and even that letter came back, though the handwriting on that envelope was different; she thought it might be one of Rima's aunts'.

"You must have heard something over the years," Addison said. "You must have a guess. I'd settle for a guess."

Rima pictured her aunts again, Oliver under the table, her mother dead and about to be buried. "She won't come," Auntie Sue was saying. "She wouldn't have the nerve to come, today of all days."

Auntie Lise had answered with a question. "Like she wouldn't come to the wedding?" she had asked.

Did Addison really want to have this conversation? "Were you at my parents' wedding?"

"No. Why?"

"Just something my aunts said."

"I flew out before the wedding. Behaved very badly. But I was forgiven. All charges dropped," Addison said. "That was a joke."

"So when did you stop being friends?"

Addison drank again. "The *Ice City* dollhouse wasn't really destroyed in the earthquake," she said. "It's the only one I ever dismantled. We stopped being friends after I published *Ice City*."

Which was what Rima had always suspected. "I think it was Bim killing his wife. My mother mentioned that pretty often." Even as Rima spoke, it didn't make sense. Her mother had mentioned it often, and just that often her father had said, "For Christ's sake, it's just a book. It's just a made-up murder in a made-up book." He wouldn't have lost an old friend over that. Her father had seen the real world. He had perspective on the made-up ones.

"But that woman is nothing like your mother. That Bim is nothing like your father," Addison said.

"Was my father your first reader for *Ice City*? Did he see it before you published?"

"No. He was off somewhere, back in the days of no e-mail. But he knew I was using his name. He said he was fine with it. He said he was tickled. I certainly meant it affectionately."

"I don't think he thought he'd be killing his wife." Rima wasn't as sure as she sounded, but she was more sure than she'd realized. Her mother had complained about the wife-killing, the zeal, the sheer electricity of it, and her father had told her not to be silly. And there had been an edge there. Every time the conversation happened, there'd been an edge.

Addison finished her whiskey. "The only man I ever truly loved is the one I made up," she said, and there was no reason not to let her remember it that way if she chose. In point of fact, couldn't you argue she'd made up Bim too? The real one as well as the fictional?

"Maxwell's taken good care of you," Rima said.

"Everything I ever wanted," said Addison.

(3)

There was an empty soda can on the floor of Martin's car by Rima's feet. It rolled one way and then the other as the road turned, until finally Rima stepped on it hard. They were just pulling into a parking lot at the base of a hill. The sun was out but not insistently so. The ground was still wet from the week's rain, and the breeze was cool, sometimes cold. A strand of hair blew into Rima's mouth. She took it out.

On the hilltop, in the sun, was a lovely old villa. The wine bar at its base was smaller and more rustic. Seven other cars were parked in the lot, three of them Priuses.

The door was heavy, with handles shaped like sheaves of grape stalks. Martin held it open for Rima, and she passed through into a large room with exposed beams and a gleaming copper counter. Her first impression was that it was crowded; on second look, though, she could see there were fewer than twenty people in the room. On a table left of the door was a gigantic chess set. Rima noted the novelty of seeing something scaled up rather than down.

The pianist was playing "Blue Skies" and pretending that some-one, anyone, was listening, despite the hubbub of voices and the clinking of bottles and glasses. She wore a sleeveless black sheath and had a spray of white flowers pinned into her wild, curly hair. "Blue Skies" gave way to "Blue Moon" gave way to "Love Walked In." Rima was good at identifying songs, even those popular long before she was born. But then she heard something that stumped her, though in another context she might have thought it was Kelis's "Milkshake," a song she knew because of all the times she'd heard it in the school yard and had to pretend it had no sexual subtext of any kind.

By now she'd already tasted the Blanc de Blancs. She'd had a pleasant exchange with a middle-aged couple from Kentucky who said they came every year and shipped wine home by pretending it was vinegar. Apparently there were states you could ship wine to and states that you couldn't, but vinegar could be shipped absolutely anywhere, which the couple thought made no sense at all, as so many people preferred wine to vinegar.

Rima couldn't quite see the outrage, but she shook her head disbelievingly to be polite.

Their server was a cheerful hippie with large brown eyes, a braid down her back, and moon earrings, the full moon in one lobe, a crescent in the other. Her name was Fiona. What were the chances, Rima asked, that they might see the ghost today?

None at all. There was no ghost, Fiona said, though the winery had once made a Syrah-Zinfandel blend and called it Pierre's Ghost after the winery's founder, so maybe this had caused the confusion. She consulted briefly with another server, a chubby man in a blue Hawaiian shirt who looked too young to be pouring wine, but presumably wasn't. He said he'd heard there was a haunted winery somewhere around Livermore. Footsteps, windows open when they'd been left shut, the air in the room suddenly cold—that sort of thing. No actual sightings, which would have been so, so much cooler. If there'd been sightings, then he'd be working there instead of here.

Martin shrugged and changed the subject. He seemed untroubled to find he'd lured Rima with the promise of ghosts he was in no position to deliver. His sunglasses were pushed to the top of his head; his nose was in his wineglass. "Raisins?" he said to Fiona.

"Very good," Fiona told him.

Had Martin just been complimented for guessing that the wine was made of grapes? It appeared that way to Rima. The piano switched to "The Streets of Laredo." Martin reached over and took Rima's hand.

Rima took it back. "Martin," she said, but he'd already flushed, bright, distinct patches on his cheeks as if she'd slapped him. "I'm not in any shape for that. I'm not even missing that right now," she told him. "I'm too old for you."

"Okay," he said. "Whatever. One reason's plenty. Don't take my head off." He emptied what was left of his Pinot Noir into the dump bucket, returned the glass to the counter. "How about a Chardonnay?" he asked Fiona, and even though it was backward, going from red to white that way, Fiona said sure, they had one, which she poured, and pointed out its many notes and under-tones, berries and chocolate and pudding and tomato sauce or something; Rima wasn't really listening, she was too embarrassed.

But this was good, really, Rima told herself. Good to get it out in the open and avoid confusion. Still, very awkward.

Or maybe not. Martin was already flirting with Fiona, telling her there should be a wine named for her, something light and fresh-tasting. It was angry flirting, but Rima liked him for the effort. This seemed to be the pattern with Martin—she liked him and then she didn't like him and then she liked him. Not liking him would come next. She had only to wait.

The truly awkward part was that Rima wanted Martin to do something for her, and it wasn't an ordinary something, like drive her to the airport or pick up her mail while she went on a trip. It was something requiring not only a request but an explanation as well. And after he'd done that, she still needed him to drive her back and stay for dinner and be nicer to his mother. It was quite a list. She started at the top. "What I really need," she began, "is a little brother."

"So flattering, and yet no, thanks." Martin swirled the golden wine in his glass and sniffed at it. "Too late to start sharing Mother's love."

"All you have to do," Rima said in her nicest voice, "is tell a bunch of lies to someone I've never met." She felt how wrong this was as she said it, a bad idea, a bad thing to be talking Martin into.

Right would have been Oliver's talking Rima into it. Rima liked it so much better when she got to express her strong objections, go along reluctantly, predicting the worst, and then find herself completely validated when the worst happened. She was still certain the worst would happen, but now she didn't get to say so and turn out to be right. Now Martin got to do that part. Martin had been training for that part his whole life.

Rima had never appreciated how hard it was to be Oliver. "It'll be fun," she said, which was what Oliver always said, but he probably believed it when he said it. Oliver had an expansive idea of fun.

Fiona brought a dessert wine. Something about it—Rima didn't hear what, because Fiona was hardly bothering to talk to her now; it was all about Martin—made it just right for the holidays. Two men had replaced the couple from Kentucky at the counter. "My cat likes wine," one said to other. "But only the good stuff."

"That's a cat for you," the second man said. The pianist was playing "The Wanderer," hitting the notes hard to rock them out. "What's your cat's name again?"

"I can fill you in while we drive," Rima said.

Martin looked straight at her, moving his sunglasses from the top of his head to his eyes so she couldn't see in anymore, his face blank behind the lenses. His hair fell forward and he brushed it back. "So where are we going? Where is this person you never met?" he asked. The question had undertones of raspberries in it.

(4)

They missed Holy City Art Glass on their first pass. It was a low-slung building set into a deep curve on the road with no promi-nent sign and no prominent address and almost nothing but trees around it. Coming back from the east, Martin spotted the name in the window and pulled into the parking lot. Across the old high-way, behind a screen of birches, Rima could see part of a decaying house that had once been painted white with maybe a green trim on the windows. Next to that, an empty lot with the brick founda-tions of a vanished building.

The door to the Holy City Art Glass company led into a studio, an open-beamed workshop with long tables on which several proj-ects were in process. The windows were coated with dust, and the place smelled of wood chips and blowtorches. A man was bent over one of the tables, matching pieces of glass to a paper pattern of a mermaid under a low-hanging fluorescent. "Can I help you?" he asked without looking up. He had a bald spot on the top of his head, but he was so tall that normally no one would see this. Rima guessed he was in his forties or fifties.

"Are you Andrew Sheridan?" Rima asked.

"Last I looked."

To the left of the worktable was an open door into a second room. Rima could see through to shelves of Christmas ornaments, vases, and many rows of glass pumpkins, some orange, some purple, some mottled like pebbles. One of the larger ones was a Cinderella carriage with gold wheels, but no horses and no footmen.

"I got your letter," Martin said. "About Constance Wallace."

"Wellington," said Rima.

Martin held out his hand. The man took it, looking up at them for the first time. He was wearing a green shirt that advertised his own shop, and there was an old scar, barely visible, along the bone beneath one of his eyes.

"I'm Rima," Rima said. She gestured toward Martin. "This is Maxwell Lane."

Chapter Twenty-five

(1)

Andrew Sheridan released Martin's hand. "You have the same name as that detective. That's got to be weird."

"Named after," said Martin. "Take it up with my mom."

Sheridan stood for a moment, looking him over. "How old are you?" he asked. "You don't look old enough to have known Constance."

"Thank you," said Martin, which Rima thought was pretty good, and probably what Oliver would have said.

Maxwell Lane dealt with doubt by silence. Let the suspect talk himself through it, Maxwell said. Just keep your eyes directly on his, don't blink, and wait him out.

But Oliver advocated meeting doubt with effusion. Rima put herself between Sheridan and Martin. "Constance was my grand-mother's cousin," she said. "I'm the one who asked Maxwell to write. I'm putting together a family history, just for us, you know, not to publish or anything, and I wanted to include Constance. I didn't even know she was dead. Because of the cult thing. The family didn't talk much about her. Could you tell me about her? And Holy City?" While she was talking, Rima had made her way into the back room. "Did you make these pumpkins?" she asked. "I'd love one as a memento. Are they for sale?"

Sheridan was suddenly enthusiastic, not on the subject of the pumpkins, to which he barely responded, but on the subject of Holy City. He said they should call him Andy. "I only got here after it closed," Andy said. "Riker'd been dead for years. But Constance told me a lot."

Andy took them to the back wall where he'd stapled a bunch of newspaper clippings, since they weren't the first to come asking. He opened a drawer and drew out a folder of photographs so they could see how the buildings used to crowd this curve of the street, and where the billboards used to be. "William E. Riker," read one. "The only man who can keep California from going plum to Hell."

"Where we are now, this used to be the post office," Andy said, passing over a photo of the old interior. Rima looked at it closely. It was larger and more stately than the present building suggested. Just beneath a soaring ceiling was a mural depicting Jesus, William Riker next to him, and next to William Riker someone Rima couldn't identify. She pointed to him.

"Maurice Kline," said Andy. "Holy City's Jewish Messiah. Until he sold the property."

The final photo showed the eatery. Its flat roof was lined with Santa Clauses, and these were Santa Clauses Rima recognized. Currently, they were up in Addison's attic, or else those there were identical to these here. This startled her so much that she missed part of what Andy was saying, something about the pamphlets and how Father Riker couldn't spell worth a damn.

From the same drawer, Andy pulled a mimeo of the minutes from a meeting in which the governing board of Holy City removed Father Riker as its head (only Riker voting to the contrary) because he was running for governor and the rest of them believed in the separation of church and state. In the unlikely event that he lost the governorship, he was to be automatically reinstated at Holy City. The minutes had been submitted and signed by Constance Wellington, recording secretary.

Andy also showed them a recent map of the property lines done by the real estate company that was handling the current sale.

Then, "Come with me," Andy said, and he took them out the front, down the steps, and around the back of the building. They passed through a wire gate, walking over a track so wet that Rima's sneakers were soon heavy with mud. Farther on, the track dipped; the mud turned into a spongy layer of pine needles, and then they were standing in the same ring of redwoods, the same hollowed-out bowl of grass where, in a different season, in a different time, Father Riker had once spent a night in drunken sleep. "I think I know who built the wall," Andy said, indicating the high semicircle of stone that enclosed the far end, but not sharing his suspicions.

In an alcove under some tree roots someone had made a shrine. It held four pictures of the Virgin Mary and one of the Buddha, several colorful bits of broken glass from the glassblowing shop, some dusty silk flowers, seashells, and five red candles.

"There are nuns who come here sometimes," Andy said. "One of them is psychic. She talks to the trees."

"What do the trees say?"

"Bunch of boring shit. Lots of people come here. You wouldn't believe how many rituals I've interrupted—black magic and healings. And sex. High school students come here to have sex. There's just something about the place." (As if high school students were pretty picky about where they had sex.) "I worried a bit after nine-eleven," Andy said. "I thought we might be a target just because it says Holy City on the maps. But now I don't think we were attacked by the people everyone else thinks we were attacked by. I'm on to other theories now."

"I bet you'd like my mom," Martin told him.

Around them, the mountains rose green and quiet. Rima saw a radio tower in the distance, but no houses, no roads. She heard a car coming behind the stone wall, and then she heard it going away. They were in the middle of nowhere. Who would have thought California still had anyplace so remote?

She tried to picture how the Showhouse and Lecture Hall would have looked, her young, young father and Addison parking their cars and going inside to meet each other for the first time.

Andy told them that the only other Holy City building still standing was Riker's house, across the road. Constance had moved into it in her final years, though she'd confessed she never did feel right about that, as if she'd gotten above herself somehow just by surviving. Now it was vacant, except for the occasional squatter, and not in good repair. "I'd show you," Andy said, "but it's private property. I'm not supposed to go in. Anyway, there's nothing to see. Your cousin's stuff was all hauled away years ago." They were walking back to the highway now, picking their way through the mud.

"Constance wrote my father about a man who died here," Rima said. "It was ruled a suicide, but she was really troubled about it. Do you know anything about that? The man's name was Bogan."

"You name it, Holy City had it," Andy said. "Arson, burglary, murder. During World War Two there was some quarrel about putting emergency fire escapes on the buildings. Where or how to put them. One of the residents beat another to death with an iron bar. I don't think the police were all that interested in what went on here. Constance said that Riker had an eye out for troubled young women. All that no-sex stuff was for everyone else.

"She wouldn't quite say so, but I think she'd come to see him as a sort of predator. He specialized in girls who had no one."

Rima was a girl who had no one. She put this thought out of her mind as quickly as it had come in.

"He was a good-looking guy when he was young," Andy said.

Martin snorted.

"Okay, you can't see it in the pictures. But he'd have recruitment meetings with free food during the Depression. That's why Constance came, because there was free food."

Rima followed Andy and Martin up the steps. She stopped at the doorway. Her shoes were too muddy to go inside, but then so were Andy's and he hadn't stopped.

"Could I see Constance's letters?" Rima asked. This was the reason she'd come. Everything else, all the lies she'd told and made Martin tell had been to get to this question.

"See, that's the weird thing," Andy said. He stood, blinking down at her. Light from the windows glinted off the green glass of the mermaid's tail, threw rainbows on the walls. "I gave them to this other woman who said she was a friend of Constance's. Just two days ago. The whole box. I helped her load it into her car."

"Did this woman say who she was?"

"She said he"—motioning to Martin—"sent her. Older woman. Kind of wild-eyed. She said that she'd known Constance in the old days."

By holding open the door, Rima had let a fly into the studio. She could hear it, bumping against the dusty windowpane, again and again.

"Frankly, she was more believable than you guys are," Andy said pleasantly.

(2)

Martin told the story with great enthusiasm and in great detail at dinner. He did not forget to include: that someone had murdered someone else at Holy City in a disagreement over fire escapes; that we haven't gotten the full story on 9/11 yet and probably never will; that trees are boring conversationalists. There was very little left for Rima to add.

"Did I mention that I was pretending to be Maxwell Lane at the time?" Martin asked. He was teasing his mother, because he had not forgotten to say so; he had repeated this three times and counting. Granted, it was, along with the trees, one of the good parts.

Tilda had made scampi, rice pilaf, and broccoli amandine. Rima had never seen her as happy as she looked that night, listening as

Martin talked with so much animation, and laughing whenever he wanted her to. Though she did pause for a sober moment to note that the way the towers had come down was more consistent with an explosive detonation than with an airplane crash.

"What did you hope to get?" Addison asked Rima.

"Constance's letters."

"Why?"

Why indeed? Because that's what Oliver would have done, and the whole world can't change just because Oliver isn't here? "My father wrote her after I was born. I'd like to read that letter. And I was curious about the whistling man. Constance told Maxwell about him. You put him in *Ice City.*" Rima took a bite of shrimp and spoke around it. "Some of the letters she sent to Maxwell are missing." She hoped the shrimp muffled any sense of accusation the observation might have contained. She would ask about the Santas later, sometime when it didn't feel like a piling on.

Addison responded by noting that cataloguing and curating were better left to the experts. UC Santa Cruz had a standing offer for her papers. They had also acquired a set of letters Ted Hughes had written to his mistress while married to Sylvia Plath. Hughes had made it clear before his death that he didn't want the letters made public. On the other hand, scholars were interested. Scholars, in Addison's opinion, were just gossips with degrees. She was waiting to see how the university would handle the Hughes collection before she made up her mind about her own papers. She said most of this aloud.

Tilda gave Berkeley a piece of broccoli, because you should be careful what you wish for. Berkeley took it off to the living room and hid it under a chair. For the next two days, until Tilda found it, Berkeley would snap at anyone who tried to sit in that chair. She didn't want to eat it, but that didn't mean it didn't belong to her.

"You know," Addison said. "If I got that suicide from Constance, then I might have put the letters about it in with the *Ice City* papers instead of the Maxwell Lane ones. Tilda could get that box down for you. If you want. I mean, you still won't know any more than Constance knew."

Things were so amicable between Tilda and Martin that he actually asked for a cup of tea. Tilda got up to put the water on. "What kind?" she asked.

"Surprise me."

Tilda chose something caffeinated, something for staying awake. They'd eaten early, so that Martin wouldn't be on the road late, and now it was dusk, the light fading rapidly, the sunset colors turning gray. The day had been mild, but the night would be cold. At least the road had dried.

Addison chose a tea with chamomile for going to sleep. "I imagine"—she was dipping the tea bag in and out of her cup— "that if I'd thought it was a murder I would have contacted the police. Whatever Constance said, it can't have persuaded me."

"Andy said the police just didn't care what went on in Holy City," Martin told her. "Maybe you did contact the police and they didn't follow up."

"I'm not that old. I'd remember that."

It was the first snippy comment of the evening, and it passed without a ripple. Rima took a moment to congratulate herself for having brought this about. She was the one who'd invited Martin. She was the one who'd convinced him to stay the night. She was the one who'd dragged him to Holy City and made him pass himself off as Maxwell Lane so that he'd had a story to tell.

"So who did Andy give Constance's letters to?" Martin asked.

"Pamela Price," said Rima. "Obviously. The wild-eyed, more-believable-than-us Pamela Price."

(3)

In spite of the early dinner, Martin didn't leave until almost nine. He'd been strong-armed into taking the rest of the sherry cake home. The shrimp was gone, which made Tilda fret that there hadn't been enough, no matter how many times Addison and Rima told her otherwise. "It was a good dinner," Addison kept saying. "A good evening. I liked that Martin. That relaxed Martin." She went to her bedroom. She was in the middle of one of the biggest novels Rima had ever seen—something to do with magicians in the Napoleonic Wars, and Addison was anxious to see what happened next, if she could only manage to stay awake after all the sleepy tea she'd drunk.

Tilda rolled up her sleeves to reveal the snake's head, and Rima brought her the dishes to be washed. Then Tilda too went to bed. She hugged Rima when she said good night. It was a stiff, self-conscious hug, but Rima's was no better. They were both out of practice.

Rima sat for a while in the living room, Stanford on her lap. She didn't go upstairs, because she didn't want to wake Stanford and also because she wasn't tired. She fell asleep in the chair.

The phone rang. She picked it up and was speaking into it before she'd actually woken. "Hello," she said, asleep, but frightened, because late-night phone calls are frightening things. Stanford was gone and she was staring at the crushed skull of the *Folsom Street* victim as she spoke.

The voice on the other end was Martin's. "Don't tell Mom," he said. "I scraped the railing, and the front end is crap. And there's no cell-phone reception in the goddamn mountains so I had to walk about three miles before a car would pick me up. I'm at the Oakwood Saloon, down by the Los Gatos exit. The saloon is closed, but the guy who owns it is waiting with me. Could you come get me? There's a tow truck on the way, but they're coming from the Santa Cruz side. I said I'd meet them back at the car."

Rima heard the clock in the hall upstairs chime the half-hour. "What's the exit again?" she asked.

She took the keys from the scallop-shaped dish. The tank was nearly empty, so she had to stop for gas. She saw Martin's car as she drove past. It had been either driven or dragged to the side of the road. The left headlight was smashed, and the driver's door was so dented that Rima doubted it would open.

It was past eleven by the time she found Martin. He was inside the saloon, having a draft beer with the owner. He'd bitten his lip, which was swollen and had turned many exciting colors. "Now I don't feel so sorry for you, bro," the owner said, looking Rima over. "Now I think you maybe make up the crash."

The very divider Martin had hit prevented them from crossing the highway to get to his car. They had to go past it in the wrong direction to an exit and then double back. By now it was eleven forty-five.

Martin was sorry for the inconvenience. He wasn't sorry for the thing he should have been sorry for, because he hadn't thought about Oliver, about what it might be like for Rima to get a call concerning an accident. Rima was furious. She knew it wasn't fair, but there it was. She could hardly look at Martin, him and his fat lip. How dare he drive so badly? "Were you drinking?" she asked.

"Not until after. Jeez. I'm not my mom."

The tow truck was already waiting. Rima was working hard not to show how angry she was, because she didn't want Martin to think she minded coming to get him. She didn't mind that part at all.

A genial guy named Jerry loaded the car onto the truck. "I could make my whole living off the Seventeen," he said. "Never work anywhere else." He was wearing a Giants baseball cap and a filthy sweatshirt with greasy handprints on it.

And just like that, Rima stopped pretending. "Listen," she said to Martin quietly, so Jerry wouldn't hear. "Don't come back to Wit's End unless it's to see your mother. That's all I care about, that you be nice to your mother."

"So you don't want a little brother anymore?" Martin asked. It had taken Rima the whole way from Santa Cruz to get as angry as she was. Martin did it in an instant.

"Not one who can't drive," Rima said.

(4)

Rima had to go in the wrong direction again until she was back at the Los Gatos exit and could turn around. Eight or nine cars passed her, most of them going much too fast. There was no shoulder to the road. It was a miracle Martin hadn't been hit while walking to the saloon.

Finally she was headed back to Santa Cruz. She drove all the way to Scotts Valley, and then an exit came up and she took it, made another flip around, headed back to San Jose. She got off at Redwood Estates. There was a large sign for the Estates, and underneath that a small sign that read "Holy City." Inside Addison's glove box was a flashlight with the batteries still working. Some things are just meant to be.

The Old Santa Cruz Highway was as dark as dark gets on the California coast. There were no cars in the lot in front of the glass company, and no cars on the road either. Rima turned off the old highway and into the driveway behind the trees. She parked in front of the house with the peeling white paint. William Riker had lived here once, and after him, Constance Wellington. Rima dimmed the headlights and then switched them off.

She'd believed Andy when he said there was nothing to see there. Still, there could have been a box in a closet, a letter slipped behind the bathroom mirror and then forgotten. It would take only a short time to know for sure.

There were no stars overhead, so Rima assumed clouds she couldn't see. The air was damp, and she wished she'd worn her Cleveland winter coat.

She flicked the flashlight on and made her way up the sidewalk, up the steps to the front porch. The middle stair had rotted away and Rima narrowly avoided stepping through it. There was no bulb in the porch light, but she threw the switch anyway, because there is a larger world than Maxwell Lane allows for in his philosophies, and of course no light came on, because there was no bulb.

She directed the beam of the flashlight to the door. She tried the doorknob, which was locked. Above was a grid where nine panes of glass should have been. Two of these were cracked, four had been entirely removed. Rima reached through an empty space and unlocked the door from the inside. It was no warmer in the house than out.

The entryway was filled with dead leaves. Rima picked her way through them by the flashlight beam, nervous that they might be some sort of nest. On the entry wall, four holes suggested that a picture or a hat rack had been removed. Her light skipped over a dark stain shaped vaguely like a camel, as if someone had thrown a bottle of beer at the wall. Her feet uncovered something that might have been a condom had she looked more closely. Maybe just a plastic bag, but if so, very small. The place smelled of leaves and something else Rima could only assume were rabid bats.

This is another fine mess you've gotten me into, she told Oliver. The leaves ended and she was on the gritty surface of a wood floor. A few steps more and she found herself in what obviously had once been the living room.

She cast the light around, startled when it reflected brightly back at her from the black windows. The inner wall had been tagged with graffiti. She saw the initials PTC, fat and filled in, and under that someone literate had written, "Look on my works, ye mighty." Someone else had written, "I heart Amelia," in red marker.

A single chair, upholstered in a fabric that might once have been flowered, remained dead-center in the room. The seat cushion was gone, and one of its springs was sprung. Newspapers were piled next to it, tall enough to make a sort of table; a Starbucks paper cup was on the top. Rima stepped toward this, the room darkening around her as she narrowed the light toward the papers. There was the *Good Times,* the one with the article about male beauty. And underneath but not covered, a recent *Sentinel,* the one with Addison's picture.

Rima's heart was racing before her mind could catch up. I shouldn't have come, she was thinking, and even as she formed the thought, she heard footsteps in the entryway leaves behind her.

She turned.

The living room light came on.

Pamela Price stood between her and the way out, and she was holding the keys to Addison's car. Rima had no memory of having left those behind. This is the way car keys get lost sometimes, when you let yourself start thinking of other things instead of tracking their every movement—now I'm taking them out of the ignition, now I'm putting them in my pocket, and so on.

Chapter Twenty-six

(1)

Ice City, pages 313–314

Mr. Lane said that it seemed to him if there was anything I wanted from the house, I should take it. I was leaving the trailer park for a foster home up in Truckee. I was
telling myself that it would be all right, that I could do the
four years until I turned eighteen, no sweat. I didn't
believe it for a minute. What would high school be like for
someone like me? How normal could I pretend to be?

There was nothing here I wanted.

Mr. Lane stopped in front of the dollhouse. "Did you
never notice that he had you all represented here?" he
asked. "It was really the dollhouse tipped me off. This was
how he gave orders. To Ernie mostly, but also Kathleen and
Pamela and Julia when he wanted them in his bed. He

must have felt like God, looking down on his little king-dom, moving you all this way and that."

As he spoke, Mr. Lane took hold of the little man who stood for Bim.

I picked up several of the others. Here was Kathleen, who was in a home now and had to be fed and put to bed like a baby. Here was Pamela, who'd left after Brother Isaiah died, saying she was going to Hollywood, going to make it in the pictures, when we all knew she wasn't. Here was Julia, Bim's poor wife. I put them back.

Mr. Lane was still holding Bim. In that moment I saw his true face. When Bim had told Brother Isaiah about my father, he'd no idea it would get my father killed. I'd watched the guilt eat him up, and never known what I was seeing.

This time, I knew. Bim was no murderer when Mr. Lane first came to Camp Forever. It was Mr. Lane who'd made him one. Mr. Lane, who understood people so well, who knew just what to say and when to say it. Mr. Lane, who never saw that coming. Mr. Lane, who was dying inside. "Where will you go next?" I asked.

"Ice City," he said.

(2)

Pamela Price was dressed in a long coat, with an even longer nightgown showing at the hem. She had UGG boots on her feet, of a light and dirty blue. Her hair was loose and uncombed, tangled above one ear. Rima watched her put the hand with the keys in her coat pocket and keep it there.

"I was expecting A. B. Early," Pamela said. "Is she with you?"

"Yes," said Rima. She didn't have enough breath, and her voice sounded nothing like her voice. "She's waiting in the car." Don't engage with the stalker, Addison would have said, but perhaps, since she'd broken into and entered a house that was not hers, the usual rules didn't apply.

"No, she's not," Pamela said. Rima's score for the day on lies well told remained at zero.

Rima made a list of reasons she shouldn't be scared. No one knew she was here. No one would miss her until morning, and then they wouldn't know where to look. This wasn't the list she wanted.

She tried again. Pamela appeared quite sane, if a little sleepy. And maybe Addison had one of those OnStar systems. That would be money well spent. Tilda and Addison would be getting up, six, seven hours from now. Where did Rima go, they would ask each other, and discover that her bed hadn't been slept in, that the car was gone. Addison would call the OnStar company, and they would find the car in minutes. All Rima had to do was make small talk with the stalker for seven or eight or nine hours until help arrived.

"I didn't mean to wake you," Rima said. "I didn't think anyone would be here."

"Oh." Pamela waved her hand dismissively. "I don't sleep. Don't even worry about that. I really wanted to talk to Early."

"How about coffee tomorrow?" Rima said. "I could set that up."

"I planned on here. I have it all planned out. Like a scene from one of her books. I'll show you," Pamela said. She came toward Rima, which meant that Rima backed up, but not fast enough;

Pamela had Rima's sleeve in her hand. She turned Rima away from the graffiti. The room had once been wallpapered, and some bits of this remained, purple-and-gold fleurs-de-lis with a faded patch where a picture might have hung, and in other places an earlier, striped pattern. Rima realized her flashlight was still on. She turned it off.

"There was a shelf right there." Pamela pointed with her free hand. "Where the dollhouse was. I'll ask Early if she remembers the dollhouse. You be Early. Pretend I said that."

"Do I get Thomas Grand back?" Rima asked.

"Not yet. Then I point to here," indicating the faded patch, "and I say there was a picture of Father Riker with the globe here. 'I know who you are,' I say."

"Who am I?"

"Not yet. Now we go upstairs."

Pamela was pulling on Rima's coat. Rima reached over and removed her hand. Pamela's fingers were much warmer than her own. Rima had begun to shiver. Something rattled in the dry leaves by the door. "I'm not going upstairs. Just tell me this part," Rima said.

So Pamela told her the part about Riker's being Addison's father. Then she complained that she hadn't meant to say that yet; it was all coming out of order because Rima wouldn't go upstairs. Then she consoled herself that this here, with Rima, was just for practice anyway.

"How do you know that about Addison?" Rima asked.

The short answer was that Pamela had worked it out from the clues.

The long answer started back in 1970. Which did Rima want? Rima had those eight hours to fill. "Start in 1970," she said.

(3)

When she'd heard the story, it didn't seem to Rima so much that Pamela had put the pieces together as that Constance had outright told her. The only tricky part that Rima could see was that Constance had said it was Maxwell Lane that Riker had fathered. Which, in its own weird way, Rima guessed was true.

Pamela said that 1970 was not as bad a year as 1968, but it wasn't good. One day, after she'd had a fight with her mother, Pamela climbed out the window and hitched a ride into Chicago and from Chicago she got a lift all the way to Des Moines. She turned fifteen on I-80 in Wyoming, but she told the truck driver she was nineteen and he bought her a couple of beers for her birthday. Then she hooked up with a married couple who were on their way to San Francisco until they heard of a place in the Santa Cruz Mountains where the trees were big and the rent was free.

Pamela had lived in this very house for almost three months back then. If Rima would go upstairs with her—but Rima wouldn't (which, she had to be honest, was beginning to piss her off)— Pamela could show her the room she'd slept in, which wasn't the big bedroom, but more of a closet at the end of the hall. Riker was already dead when she arrived, but his things were still here. And there were four Holy City survivors—Elton Grange, Frank Mulligan, Paul Larson, and Constance Wellington—skulking about the place, all of them old and mad as Lear. At least it looked that way if you were fifteen and knew who Lear was. "I've always been a reader," Pamela told Rima.

She couldn't say how many young people were squatting; the numbers fluctuated. Mostly there was only one other girl. Her name was Harmony, or *so she'd have people believe.* She and Pamela didn't really get along.

Pamela got to know Constance because they both liked mystery novels and Constance had stacks of them. Pamela was always ducking over to return one book and borrow another.

Constance thought what was going on in Riker's house was another cult, as if the old one were renewing itself, only with white and black people this time. She worried about Pamela, but it wasn't like that, Pamela said. There were a couple of older guys who sometimes said who should do what, but mostly they were all on their own.

Constance thought that Pamela was sleeping with them all, when she wasn't sleeping with anybody, except that, of course, sometimes you had to. It was in this context that Constance told Pamela about how Father Riker had made girls leave Holy City if they got pregnant. She'd given Pamela a couple of names, one of which was Marjorie Early—easy to remember, Constance had said, because of Marjorie Morningstar. Constance had given Pamela *Marjorie Morningstar* to read, but Pamela hadn't finished it; it seemed kind of 1950s. A. B. Early had just published her first book, and Pamela was the one who told Constance to read it.

"Does Addison know she's Riker's daughter?" Rima asked, and she knew the answer before she'd finished the question. Why else would Addison have the Holy City Santas up in her attic?

"Read the books," Pamela said. "She's obsessed with cults and who joins them. I don't think she gives a fig about Riker. She's obsessed with her mother."

The living room light flickered briefly and noisily, off and back on. "What did you do with Constance's letters?" Rima asked.

"I burned them."

"Why?"

"So Early would know this isn't about blackmail. So there wouldn't be any evidence."

Pamela had been trying to get Addison to Holy City for weeks now. She'd left clues everywhere—in the bookstore, online, in the mail. She expressed surprise that it was taking Early so long, great mystery writer like her. But at least it had given Pamela time to work out exactly what she wanted to say.

Rima had done a good job of keeping Pamela talking; she had maybe only seven hours to go now. It was clear that Pamela was willing to go on. The story of her life, she was just telling Rima, would make a great book. Recently, she'd started living mostly online, where you could be anyone you chose, a new person every hour if you wanted. It was a lot like being a writer, she guessed. She'd made up a lot of characters by now.

Rima found herself actually interested in how Pamela had gone from hippie squatter to queen of the chat room. But her hands and face were freezing, and she couldn't stay on her feet a moment longer. Some time ago, she'd stopped being scared. Pamela's demeanor was so reasonable. Her story so linear. It was hard to stay focused on how insane she was. "I'm exhausted," Rima told Pamela, who said that she was exhausted too. Then she gave Rima back the keys. Just like that.

"All this just so Addison would tell you what she's got planned for Maxwell in the next book?" Rima asked. She and Pamela were walking together toward the door, and Rima didn't absolutely believe yet that she was being let go, even though the keys were in her hand and she didn't see how Pamela could stop her now, short of a brick to the head. She let Pamela through first, though. Better safe than sorry.

"Addison can do what she likes with Maxwell Lane," Pamela said. "I trust her. I just said that in the chat room. That's who I was pretending to be at the time." She pushed the door fully open. Rima was on the porch now, and could see the car down the slope of the yard.

"I just wanted her to see how I put the clues together," Pamela said.

Then Pamela realized she'd left the light on. She went back to turn it off, because of global warming. While she was inside, Rima got into Addison's car, cranked the heater up high as a promise to herself, even though it was blowing only cold air at the moment. She drove away without waiting for Pamela to come out.

It occurred to Rima to wonder where Pamela was sleeping. She'd come not from the upstairs, where she said her old bedroom was, but through the front door, and she was already in her nightgown when she arrived. Rima had seen no car but Addison's. She supposed this was the way it would always be—the closing of one mystery would only open another. What was the point, really?

Are you happy now? she asked Oliver.

He was. It was much better than his own bench, his own rock. It was everything he could have hoped it would be.

(4)

The lights were on at Wit's End when Rima got home. Tilda and Addison were sitting in the breakfast nook, arguing with themselves and each other over whether the police should be called, and drinking oceans of calming teas. "Where were you?" they asked Rima angrily, and that touched her; it was so parental.

"Was it Martin?" Tilda said, and of course it was, though Rima had forgotten.

Sometimes a story is best told in the wrong order. "He's fine," Rima said first off, and then went on to describe the call, the car, the tow truck. She didn't mention the big fight they'd had. She said nothing about Holy City and Pamela Price.

She avoided Addison's eyes. Rima was uncomfortable now that she knew so much more about Addison than Addison wanted her to know. Rima knew where Addison had come from. She knew whom Addison had loved. These were intimate things. It seemed rude to know so much about someone so private.

"I hate that road," said Tilda, but Addison said it was better than it used to be. In the old days there were two hundred fifty serious accidents on the 17 every year. That number had been slashed by almost a hundred when the dividers were put in.

Rima left them arguing the merits of the dividers and went to her room. She tried to sleep, but was too tired to close her eyes. Her brain throbbed in her hread. So she got up, plugged in the phone line, and waited to pick up her e-mail.

She had a message from Martin. "You keep telling me I'm not allowed to dump my mother. So if I'm your little brother, then you're not allowed to dump me. You can't have it both ways. Either we're all family and nobody leaves, or we're not and nobody stays. Your choice," he'd written. "Thanks for the lift."

He was no Oliver. He was no Oliver, but Tilda loved him and Rima could see he had his good points. There weren't many people, she supposed, who would have pretended to be Maxwell Lane just because she asked. Cody, probably, and Scorch for sure, and probably that fan from the pizza parlor, but not many others. "Nobody leaves," Rima wrote back, and it was so far past midnight that it was morning already, so she went ahead and sent it.

Chapter Twenty-seven

(1)

Rima came back from a walk on the beach to find a box labeled "Ice City Papers" on the floor by her bed. Inside, among the notebooks, early drafts, false starts, rejected scenes, plot trees, and bits of research on Brother Isaiah and his immortals, was one more letter from Constance Wellington.

21200 Old Santa Cruz Hwy
Holy City, California 95026
July 2, 1976

Dear Maxwell Lane:
    Had a man into the post office yesterday who runs a sta-
ble in Scotts Valley. Interesting discussion with him about
the different behaviors in prey animals (rabbits) and preda-

tors (cats). *All of which is to say that I finished* Native
Dancer *last night. Good job on the detecting front, but your
horses are too much like cats and not enough like rabbits.*

*Confess to being thrown by the hanging. You did your
homework there. I saw a hanged man myself, back in 1959,
good friend of mine. Man named Bogan.*

*That was the year Father gave the city away. Came to his
senses and tried to take it back, but the courts said no.
Maurice (the new owner, Hollywood Jew) promised to keep
it all as it was, and then right off had the telescope and the
old radio station building brought down.*

*That was when the fires started, when Maurice didn't
keep his promise. Father called us all together and carried
on something awful about how the burning had to stop, that
this was no way to settle the score, and I thought that would
end the fires, but it didn't. Bim said it wasn't supposed to.
Bim said that all that speech was for was plausible deniabil-
ity. I'd never heard that term before, but I knew what he was
saying. He was saying Father was behind the fires the whole
time, that he wanted to make Mr. Hollywood sorry he'd ever
heard of us.*

*We live too close here for secrets. Bogan warned me to
stay away from the print shop, and that burned to the
ground. Stay away from the ice plant, and sure enough, a
couple hours later, the smoke was rising. We lost the barber-
shop and a corner of the garage, and then I was the one
found him hanging in the restaurant kitchen, no warning
at all.*

I was the one called the police. Ruled a suicide. No more fires. Case closed. Bim stopped coming around, too, and who can blame him? Things were ugly here.

Never did sit right with me. Heard him just before, don't you see, whistling to beat the band. And Bogan would have said to stay out of the restaurant. Wouldn't have let me find him like that.

Which is man, predator or prey, Mr. Lane? Interested in your thoughts on the matter.

VTY,

Constance Wellington

(2)

The way Rima had found out she was expected for Thanksgiving was that Tilda had asked if there was anyone she'd like to invite. At first Rima had thought this might be Tilda's way of asking her to ask Martin, but it turned out Tilda had already done that. Martin wasn't coming; he would be with his father and step-mother. Rima thought this was just as well. He'd told her he was ready to broach the Ice City bar scheme and Rima couldn't guess exactly what Addison's response would be, but it wouldn't sound like thanksgiving.

Rima e-mailed her aunts to say she was staying in Santa Cruz for the holiday, and their responses managed to be simultane-ously shocked, hurt, disapproving, and relieved.

Scorch and Cody had also been asked, but Scorch had a family thing in Yosemite she couldn't get out of and Cody was going with her. One day at breakfast Scorch had gently let Rima know that she'd made her first appearance in the fanfic sex sites. "I'm sorry," she said. "But they're pretty hot."

"Tell me I'm not sleeping with Bim," said Rima, and Scorch said of course she wasn't; that would be perverted. It was all Rima–Maxwell. It was all a meeting of wounded souls.

"Good stuff. Classy," said Cody. "Not that I've looked."

If Rima had wanted to see, she could have done so on the new second-floor computer. Addison had sprung for something state-of-the-art, memory and speed added, and a larger screen. She'd also had a new computer installed in the outback.

On Thanksgiving morning, while Tilda cooked, Addison told Rima she had something to show her. They went to the second floor, where Addison launched a program, logged in, and then got up so that Rima could sit down. She was on a You.2 island called The Murder Capital of the World.

The Santa Cruz boardwalk unfolded before her. There was Neptune's Kingdom, complete with sound and color, the beach, the ocean behind it.

Rima found the body downtown, on Pearl Alley. A well-dressed woman had been stabbed from behind and lay on the ground, the knife a few feet away, blood like a veil around her. A fly circled the knife and occasionally landed.

Rima zoomed out until she could see the Farmers Market, the Bad Ass coffee shop, the used-book store. Over on Cooper Street, Maxwell's office had replaced the Portuguese widow's rug shop. The Ice City bar was close by, on Pacific.

"It's the new dollhouse," Addison said. "And the new book." She was going to New York in a week to have lunch with her editor and explain how the new book was a website. A print version would follow, but not until a few months after the site went up, even though the Democrats were taking charge in January and Addison assumed that restoring habeas corpus would be their first priority. By February, at the latest, we'd have our rights back and the book could go to press.

The print version had already been written. Finished, in fact, more than a year ago. Writing the book had been the easy part.

Even the virtual world, with all its detail, hadn't taken more than six weeks. She'd hired a team—A Million Red Sheep—to put it all together. The mystery on the island and in the book would be the same, except one would be a linear narrative and the other wouldn't.

The hard part had been Maxwell Lane.

Where was he?

"Where do you think?" asked Addison.

Rima walked into Ice City. An old man sat at the bar. He turned and motioned to the stool next to him. His eyes were dark and his hair gray. He was handsome, not in a presidential way, but more lifelike.

"He's an AI—avatar interface," Addison said, "connected to an advanced chatbot with a learning knowledge base. We've already uploaded all the novels. He knows those better than I do."

Addison had been working on him most of the last two years, helped by her tech wizard, Ved Yamagata. The technology wasn't quite there yet, but Ved was doing his best. There were constant modifications. Someday when the world caught up to him, Maxwell Lane would walk and talk to visitors throughout the You.2 world. In the meantime, he was a collaborative project, something like Wikipedia. Parameters had been set. There were things he would not do; things he would not say. But anyone could enter Ice City and talk with him, and every interaction would potentially refine and deepen him.

A certain few, a very few (Rima was surprised and flattered to learn she was one of these), would be given a password that allowed them to train him. Someday he'd be as real as the character in the books.

Rima's password was "biggame." The prompt "Suggest an improvement" appeared in the corner of the screen when she entered it.

Addison was called away to the phone. Rima's avatar took the stool next to Maxwell. "I thought you'd be younger," she said. She typed this.

"Did you really?" he answered. His facial expressions changed when he talked, but not when he listened.

Rima clicked on "Suggest an improvement." This opened a special text field into which Rima typed, "Come back in a few years and I might be."

"Can I buy you a drink?" Maxwell asked.

"Thanks," she said, and a bartender appeared at the far end of the bar, poured her something that foamed, and slowly disappeared.

She took a three-sixty look around her. The counter was a dark, polished wood with copper edgings. One of Picasso's Don Quixotes was on the wall. Rima faced Maxwell again. "Come here often?"

"I'm always here," Maxwell said. "Tell me something about yourself. What's your name?"

"I'm Addison's goddaughter. Would you call me Irma?"

"I won't talk about Addison."

She made a guess. "Politics?" she asked, and he offered to name every congressperson who had voted away the great writ if she wanted, but she said she already knew them.

Instead she typed in a long message about Oliver, and her mother and her mother's photos of train stations, and her father and how Addison and her father had once been close—"I won't talk about Addison," Maxwell said—and then about Constance, who used to write him letters that Rima promised she'd read to him someday. One of these letters, Rima said, was about a man who maybe hanged himself or maybe was murdered in Holy City.

"The Santa Cruz cult," Maxwell said. It was not a question. "Established by Father Riker in 1919."

Rima told him about Pamela Price, trying to make him understand that she wasn't talking about the *Ice City* Pamela Price, but someone else she was sure he'd be meeting soon, though who knew what name she'd be using when that happened, maybe ConstantComment, maybe Hurricane Jane. Maybe LilLois. Who knew?

The door to the outside opened. The day was turning to dusk. A clown came in, dressed in pink and carrying a pink umbrella. He took a seat at the far end of the bar. Maxwell gave no sign of noticing, and Rima ignored him.

"Tell me more about the hanging, Irma," Maxwell said.

She told him the little that she knew. He recognized the parts that came from *Ice City*. It was easy to solve, he said.

Constance had told Bim that Bogan was the firebug, and Bim had told Riker, who had Bogan killed. For starting the fires, if that wasn't all at Riker's instructions, or more likely because it *was* on Riker's instructions and now the word was out. Bim never meant for Bogan to die, Maxwell said. Though he blamed himself, of course.

Rima began to explain that Maxwell had confused the real Bim with the fictional one. She started to type this, but stopped, deleted it. What if?

What if Constance had given Bogan's name to Bim? What if Bim had taken it to Riker? Bim was in Holy City to get a story. He wouldn't be the first reporter making something happen just so he could write about it. He wouldn't be the only person to make the mistake of believing that since Riker was ridiculous he wasn't dangerous.

It made sense then that Constance would be so insistent about Bim's innocence. If he was innocent, so was she.

So Addison had picked up enough from Constance's letters to write the book just the way it had happened, without even knowing she'd done so. While Rima's father had read the book as a threat and a betrayal.

What if the rift hadn't been over the third murder, after all? What if it had been over the first? She should probably give more credence to Maxwell's opinion. He was the professional.

"Are you still there?" Maxwell asked.

"Yes," said Rima.

And then she went ahead and told him that there were two Bim Lanisells and that one of them had been a good husband and a good father and a good man. Don't confuse Holy City with *Ice City,* Rima said. Her father had spent most of his adult life in the world's worst places. If he'd caused Bogan's death, then he'd never gotten over it.

Would you want to be remembered as you were or as better than you were? her father had once asked her, and Rima chose as he would have wanted. She gave Maxwell the wise, brave, self-deprecating version that Bim had carefully crafted in his columns as if it were the whole truth. She clicked on "Suggest an improvement." "I see how the Bim Lanisell who was your father couldn't have killed anyone," she typed, and made Maxwell give it back to her.

"Do you know that I'm a little bit in love with you?" she asked. The foam had vanished from her beer, and the level of the liquid had gone down without her drinking it. The bartender refilled her glass with the exact motions he'd used to fill it, disappeared in exactly the same way. "There are places on the Web where we're having sex. Tender, healing sex." Of course Rima didn't know this about the sex. It could be kinky and abandoned. She was being polite. "Only you're younger and I'm named Rima."

"I won't talk about sex," Maxwell said.

"That's what you say now," Rima said. "Do you know why I love you? It's because I can leave you anytime. But always come back."

"Come back," he agreed. "We'll talk again, Irma."

"I'll come often," she told him. He needed her desperately. If it was left to Addison, he'd never be allowed to talk about anything at all.

(3)

Rima wrote a letter and then watched from her bedroom window in the hope that Kenny Sullivan would arrive. It was a bright day, and the ocean a glassy green. Rima had never seen *E. coli* looking more beautiful. There was a sailboat on the water with a yellow sail, many people on the sand.

Scorch and Cody came up the stairs with the dachshunds. They stopped halfway so the dogs could rest before the final push to the top. Scorch and Cody were holding hands, the sailboat floating like a cloud behind them, Scorch's red hair shining in the sun.

Overhead, Rima heard the Wit's End ghost walking. Maybe it was the woman from the Donner Party. Maybe it was the Santas, the whole booted army of them.

Luck was with her. She saw Kenny coming up the drive, and ran down the stairs and out the door to meet him at the mailbox. Berkeley and Stanford appeared, leaping about her in case her letter was something they could eat.

The letter was not for Kenny to take, which was the part she had to explain to him. It had no address and no stamp. The name on the envelope was Pamela Price. The letter was for Kenny to leave untouched in the box until it was picked up by someone, even if that took days.

"You have a pen pal," Kenny said. "Isn't that nice?" and maybe it was, but probably it wasn't.

Rima turned to go back inside. For a moment she saw Wit's End the way it would look when she was leaving. It shrank in the distance, the white and blue paint, the steep roofs, porches, bay windows, fish-scale shingles, and all four stories of it, long ago and far away and very small.

Dear Pamela," Rima had written.

> I enjoyed our talk the other night, but have decided to say nothing to Addison about it. I hope you'll agree it's best to leave the past in the past. I'm sorry you won't get to do your scene. I'm sure you would have nailed it.
>
> And please take care of Thomas Grand. Whatever may or may not have happened, he, at least, is surely innocent.
>
> I remain,
VTY,
Rima Lanisell

Acknowledgments

Thanks!

To Bogey's Books for the chair in the back where I wrote much of the book; to Doug Kauffman, Max Massey, and Mark Nemmers, who kept me on task (and baked me biscotti); to Stan Robinson, who sat in the chair next to me and wrote his own book as a model of how it's done.

To Tom Stanton, proprietor of Holy City Art Glass, for his tour of the Holy City grounds; his information, pictures, and articles about the cult; and his general delightfulness.

To my tech advisors: Susan Groppi, Jason Stoddard, and the impeccable Ted Chiang.

To Gavin Grant and Richard Butner, for random wit and inspiration, some of which you'll find right here in this book just as if it were my own.

To Susan Wiggs for the purloined letters.

To Jane Hamilton, Gail Tsukiyama, and Dorothy Allison, the wonder women, who provided early conceptual help, invaluable advice, and moral support, as did the very busy Sean Stewart, as did my daughter, Shannon; my son, Ryan; my daughter-in-law, Christy; and my husband, Hugh. Plus Berkeley.

To the usual suspects, my writing group, who helped doggedly through the middle bits and never got to see the end: especially Alan Elms, Debbie Smith, Sara Streich, Don Kochis, Clinton Lawrence, Ben Orlove, and Xander Cameron.

For helping with the book inside the book, the Rio Hondo regulars: Walter Jon Williams, Daniel Abraham, Eileen Gunn, Timmi Duchamp, Jay Lake, Geoff Landis, Mary Turzillo, Leslie What.

For helping with the not-as-final-as-I'd-hoped draft, the brilliant writers and readers Robb Forman Dew, Maureen McHugh, and Kelly Link. Each of you said something different to me, and all of it was stuff I needed to hear.

To the fabulous Marian Wood for help with absolutely everything, the wonderful Wendy Weil and the whole Weil Agency office, and the amazing Anna Jardine, who sweats the big and small stuff for me.

I am more grateful than I can ever say.